"Does that taste [...] father's other res[...]"

"It's fantastic," she answ[...] mouthful. "Where did th[...]"

He crossed his arms, his face expressionless. "I'm the chef."

Sloane nearly choked. Graham Cooper Jr., a chef?

"I trained at Le Cordon Bleu in Paris and worked in kitchens that made Gordon Ramsay's seem like Girl Scout camp."

Wow. His speech had the scratch of a broken record, as if he was used to giving it to naysayers. What did the heir to the Cooper dynasty have to prove anyway?

"It was all very good." Sloane squeezed a dollop of hand sanitizer into her hands. "You've obviously done a lot of work with these flavor profiles."

Cooper's mouth curved into a crooked smile. "No offense, but what does a food blogger know about flavor profiles?"

Sloane's pulse pounded in her ears as she stared at him.

His grin faded. "Wait. I'm sorry." He leaned his head in his hands, realized he was still wearing his work goggles and set them on the table. "I think that came out the wrong way."

"Whatever. It's fine. Can we get back to work now? I'm sure you also have better things you could be doing."

Two could play at this game.

Dear Reader,

I'm honored you've picked up this book! It was so fun bringing Cooper and Sloane to life and following their journey through food, healing and love. I hope their story reminds you that healing is always possible, even if you have to reclaim it one day at a time.

Warning: this book may cause hunger, so be sure to read with a warm chocolate chip cookie and a tall glass of milk.

PS: I love to hear from readers! You can find me at www.laurietomlinson.com, on Facebook at Author Laurie Tomlinson, or @LaurieTomlinson on Twitter and Instagram. Thanks again for reading!

HEARTWARMING

With No Reservations

——

Laurie Tomlinson

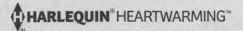

HARLEQUIN® HEARTWARMING™

Recycling programs
for this product may
not exist in your area.

ISBN-13: 978-0-373-36836-5

With No Reservations

Copyright © 2017 by Laurie Tomlinson

Printed in U.S.A.

Laurie Tomlinson is an award-winning contemporary romance author living in Tulsa, Oklahoma. Her stories are fueled by faith, steaming mugs of tea, and her belief that life should be celebrated with cupcakes and extra sprinkles. When she's not writing, she enjoys baking with her two little sous chefs and testing new recipes on her husband—especially if she doesn't have to do the dishes.

You can connect with Laurie on her website, Facebook page and Twitter.

To my husband, Jef, for being the ultimate hero inspiration with your strength, love and support. Thanks for being my Huckleberry!

Special thanks to:

My husband and two children for championing my dream and making space for me to write— and to the grandmas for all the babysitting!

Rachel Kent, my agent, for believing in my work; Dana Grimaldi, for discovering this story; my editor, Victoria Curran, for helping me strengthen it; and the rest of the team at Harlequin for their hard and superb work!

All the early readers who breathed life into this story in its early iterations. It wouldn't be the same without your input.

My ACFW community, writing friends, Alley Cats and my sisters Anne Love, Halee Matthews, Jaime Wright, Kara Isaac and Sarah Varland— they know all they have done.

Kathleen Y'Barbo Turner, Kristin Billerbeck, Carla Laureano and Jessica Patch—I wish that all writers could have author-mentors like you in their lives. Thanks for giving me courage and for making me believe in what I already possessed.

And most importantly, thanks to my Lord and Savior for being the true source of hope, healing and life to the fullest.

CHAPTER ONE

A STICK OF Irish butter, cubed into tiny uniform squares. Half-cup portions of white sugar, brown sugar, glittering in the light. And the star of the show, a mixture of chocolate chips and crumbled homemade toffee that was good enough to eat with a spoon. All showcased in sherbet-colored ceramic pinch pots and bowls from the flea market.

The *mise en place,* as the French said, was complete. Everything was in place.

Sloane Bradley found a calming satisfaction in the certainty that, when these proportions were mixed and baked, they'd turn out the most perfect toffee-chocolate chip cookies in existence. Gooey with just the right amount of crisp.

She was dialing up a crystal clear focus on the ingredients through her DSLR's viewfinder when her cell phone buzzed against the kitchen table.

Dana—VisibilityNet.

Her account supervisor was early by a full six minutes, which couldn't be a good thing. She was usually late.

"Dana. Hi." Any enthusiasm Sloane tried to muster fell flat.

"Sorry, Sloane." Dana didn't miss a beat. "I know we're ahead of schedule, but we had to move some things around today. Kathryn needs to start the meeting early."

"Kathryn?"

Dana sighed. "Yes. She asked to be on the call."

Okay, something was definitely up. Why else would the founder of VisibilityNet—the one who was usually just a signature on the checks—need to be in on this call? In the span of a breath, the parts of Sloane's job she treasured most shuttered through her mind. The subconscious rhythm of arranging ingredients and capturing the finished masterpieces. Her ability to conduct business calls from the comfort of yoga pants. Even the multitiered, color-coded spreadsheets.

Maybe *especially* the multitiered, color-coded spreadsheets.

Sloane nodded even though her supervisor couldn't see her and swallowed hard. "Okay. I'm ready."

Questions zipped through her mind as she smoothed her tailored blazer over her shoulders and sank into the cream-colored, leather dining room chair opposite her laptop. Could her job be in jeopardy?

Certainly not. Sloane was one of the ad network's most successful accounts. Her blog traffic was higher than ever. Brands paid a pretty penny to work with her. Clicks for third-party ads were on the rise. Email subscriptions were through the roof after her rustic herb pizza crust had gone viral on Pinterest earlier in the week. She liked it much better when VisibilityNet sent her kitchen gadgets to review and left her alone to do what she did best.

Blog.

But there was no time to figure things out now, no time to panic. Just the fizz in her midsection as her computer beeped to announce the incoming call. The video chat screen split in half as it connected. Two contrasting images swam into focus—barely postgrad Dana with her flawless milky skin, auburn topknot, and hipster glasses, and Kathryn with her signature silver-streaked black hair, pillowy lips, and catlike eyeliner tips.

"Good morning, Miss Bradley." Kathryn's puffy, plastic lips were slightly out of sync with the audio of her heavy New England accent. "Excuse me for skipping the formalities, but we really need to get to business quickly."

Sloane nodded, willing her clenched throat to relax. "Good morning."

"This is a very new deal, so please don't make this public yet." Kathryn filled her lungs for effect. "Is it correct that you volunteer for the City on a Hill Foundation?"

"I've been volunteering at their headquarters for a few years now." Sloane was intimately familiar with the organization and did everything she could to promote their efforts to educate low-income families about smart, sustainable cooking and grocery shopping.

"Then you know it's headed up by the Marian Cooper of J. Marian Restaurants. Well, it's her ex-husband's company now."

J. Marian Restaurants? With the sleazeball CEO who paraded around Dallas like he owned the place? He'd made a fortune selling fast-casual restaurant templates. Make-and-take pizza parlors. Noodle buffets. Cupcake and doughnut boutiques. He could feed a third-world country for a year by selling one of his custom suits—or denying one of his wife du jour's plastic surgery whims. Marian used to be married to that guy?

Relieved that this conference call was just a preemptive announcement, Sloane zoned out as Kathryn went on about "strategic partnerships" and "trend forecasts." All Sloane could focus on was her overwhelming urge to reach through the computer screen and adjust Dana's glasses, which were tilted a few degrees lower on her right eye.

When she heard the words *national network spokesperson*, however, Sloane's attention snapped to the nasal, authoritative voice of the VisibilityNet founder.

"Wait. What?" She registered her own deer-in-the-headlights expression on the screen.

"That's where you come in, naturally," Kathryn said. "Marian convinced them to hire you specifically. And it's perfect because you're local."

Panic gripped Sloane with razor-sharp claws as her fight-or-flight mechanism went from zero to sixty in a heartbeat. She nodded in the right places and scribbled notes on the pad of paper she'd placed on her makeshift desk for ceremony, never expecting to actually use it.

Son's restaurant opening this winter.

Recipe development.

Reviews.

Basically, VisibilityNet expected Sloane to shake hands with a lot of highbrow people.

In person. Wearing real pants.

This could not be happening.

Shaky words formed on the tip of her tongue. "And if I choose not to agree to this partnership?" Too late to take them back.

Dana paled, her eyes widening in shock.

"There is no choice in the matter." Kathryn let out a singsong little laugh.

Great. She thought the whole thing was a joke.

"Listen. We have a pretty good arrangement, Sloane. We increased your revenue percentage and gave you our top-tier accounts because people have been eating out of the palm of your hand with that whole organized food prep shtick."

"But—"

"Because of us, you get to work with some of the highest-grossing companies in the food industry. And all you have to do is put on a pretty face and post pretty little pictures of your food."

Sloane sighed. "I know, but I don't think you understand."

"I understand this." A muscle twitched in Kathryn's face. "You're contractually bound to do this and breaking your contract would mean severing ties with VisibilityNet. If you don't do this restaurant opening, then we don't get J. Marian Restaurants. A partnership with them on a national level."

"Just be the charming character who's won over hundreds of thousands of page views this quarter." Dana upped the pleasantries before Sloane could fight back. "It won't be a problem for you."

No problem? Right. They had no clue who they were sending to their front lines. No idea that, if her track record was any indication, their leader in ad revenue was about to be their undoing.

"Besides, the majority of your obligations surround the restaurant launch date. In a few months, it'll be like nothing ever happened."

A few months. Sloane could handle a few months, especially if the alternative meant losing her primary source of income. The noncompete agreement she'd signed ensured she would never receive so much as a coupon from those companies if she ever left.

VisibilityNet had a list of bloggers who would jump out of a moving train for those accounts. But losing VisibilityNet would change everything for her.

Sloane made nice for the rest of the conversation and ended the call, gulping in a deep breath to try to get the elephant on her chest to budge. No such luck. Her cell phone lit up immediately, and she snatched it before it could buzz.

"Dana, we're in trouble."

"What? Who's in trouble?" It wasn't Dana's chirpy voice on the other end.

It was her mother's.

"Hi, Mom." She forced a smile in an effort to hide the panic in her voice. "I thought you were someone else."

"*Who's* in trouble?"

Sloane let out a breath slowly. "It's nothing. Just a new contract they gave me today. Work stuff. It'll be fine." She winced at the last word. *Fine.* Everything was always *fine.* Only, it wasn't.

"Does that mean you can't come home for Thanksgiving? Or Christmas?"

Home. The little town in Indiana hadn't resembled home to her in ages.

She padded into her bedroom and folded the ironing board with a loud screech. "Yeah, no, Mom. I don't think I'll be able to make it this year. Maybe in the spring."

"That's what you said last year."

A stake of guilt punched through Sloane's heart as she paced to the kitchen. That's what she'd said for so many years.

"Would it be better if we came to you?"

"Well, with this new contract, life's going to be pretty busy." Sloane pulled a dustrag from a drawer and began scrubbing the dishes and props on the rolling wire pantry in her kitchen.

"As long as you're taking care of yourself, Sloanie. Spending time with your friends. Going to church. You've made friends, right?"

"Yes, ma'am." Probably not in the sense her mother meant, but she had friends.

By the time she hung up with her mother, two rows of pots and dishes gleamed, and every limb in her body was itching to medicate with a few miles of downtown Dallas pavement. To help her process this new work arrangement as something that was manageable—and now to take the edge off of the reminder of why her mother had called.

It was his birthday.

She bit her lip against the pressure of tears building between her temples and crouched to the immaculate tile floor. Bracing herself, yet again, for the crush of painful memories.

But in a way, Sloane saw a silver lining in

the conversation. Another one of her mother's semiregular attempts to reach out was over.

There was now one less time she had to remind her parents that the daughter they knew was gone. Things would never be the way they used to be.

CHAPTER TWO

IT WAS RAINING so hard that Sloane only caught glimpses of the buildings outside the car in between broad swipes of the windshield wipers. But according to her phone's GPS, the brick storefront barely visible from the rear window was the right location for J. Marian Restaurants' latest franchise venture, Simone.

She grabbed her compact umbrella. "Thanks," she told the driver, opened the door—and immediately stepped into a gargantuan puddle that soaked her black pants to midshin.

If this was seventy-five and sunny like the local news had forecasted, then Sloane was the queen of England.

Rainwater sloshed in her black flats as she scurried under the awning and through the heavy wooden door.

This couldn't be right. The inside of this café was nothing like J. Marian Restaurants' other prototypes—usually sunny and cheerful with modern decor, bright flowers and lots of clean lines. The best way to describe this place was a cozy, inviting cavern with a modern industrial edge to it. The walls were painted a dark gray framed by exposed galvanized piping. Reclaimed wooden tables were paired with mismatched chairs. A fireplace with crumbling brick occupied one of the corners, surrounded by squashy leather couches. Definitely European. And emptier than a ghost town, except for a contractor hammering at the leg of an overturned table in the back.

Sloane cleared her throat when the hammering paused and stretched to her tiptoes, watching for signs of life in the window of the door behind the counter. There was an impressive stainless steel espresso machine, a few large glass display cases and huge chalkboard panels spread across the serving counters waiting to be written on then hung behind the cash register.

So the restaurant mogul was up on the current trends. Good. It would make her job easier.

"Sloane Bradley?" The contractor walked in her direction, pulling off work gloves to reveal tan, muscled forearms.

"Yes, I'm here to meet with someone from J. Marian Restaurants."

They were supposed to be talking strategy about the restaurant's soft opening scheduled for Saturday. But at this rate, it would never be ready by then with only one worker on the job.

Though he certainly *looked* capable enough.

"You're from VisibilityNet, right?"

She commanded control of her wayward focus and nodded. This wasn't how the next few months were going to go. *On the clock, Sloane.*

"Is anybody back there?" She pointed to the door behind the counter then clamped her hands around the strap of her bag to make their shaking less obvious.

The man paused for a beat and pushed his protective glasses up to reveal appraising, gold-flecked brown eyes.

Sloane took a step back as her brain clicked into cognition.

No. It couldn't be.

"You're early."

It was. Dana had told her the Cooper family would send one of their PR suits, not their spoiled frat boy of a son. It was the face she'd seen on the magazines in the grocery checkout a few years ago, curled into a perpetual smirk. Accessorized by handcuffs, models and half-empty bottles. Only now, his pale, lanky angles had softened into serious lines.

Professional. Right. She must remain professional.

"I'm right on time, Mr. Cooper." Sloane zeroed in on the layer of dirt that speckled his hands. "May I call you Graham?"

Don't shake my hand. Please, don't shake my hand.

"I go by Cooper, actually. My father is Graham." He moved behind the counter to scrub his hands in the porcelain sink then disappeared through the door into what she assumed was the kitchen.

Sloane spun around—surely this was some kind of joke—and dropped into a chair at the table closest to the door. Better to make a quick getaway if she needed to.

Cooper reappeared right as she uncapped her trusty bottle of hand sanitizer and squeezed the gel into her palm. In his hands was a tray filled with stoneware dishes and a pair of mismatched mugs. Her stomach rumbled its appreciation for the smells coming from the tray.

Acting of its own accord, Sloane's gaze flickered over him with the new knowledge of who he was, just long enough to absorb the muscles filling his stained white T-shirt, the two or three days' worth of stubble lining his jaw and his brown hair mussed by the clear work glasses perched on the top of his head. Just long enough to register that he was even better looking in person as he wiped sauce from one of the plates with the edge of a cloth napkin.

But it was long enough for him to notice.

Heat spread across Sloane's cheeks as her stomach dipped in response to him. What? Did she think this was some kind of reality show or something? And why was her body choosing now of all times to behave this way? It had to be some kind of fight-or-flight misfire.

Cooper set the tray of food in front of her. "I thought I'd give you a preview of what we're going to serve at the soft opening in case you want to write about it in your little blog."

Sloane raised an eyebrow. *Little blog?* Apparently his good looks weren't all the gossip headlines were right about. But maybe his arrogance would serve her well. Anger and annoyance always had a way of making her less of an awkward disaster. They helped her maintain control.

She ignored his comment and reached for the crock of soup, focusing on the smell of hearty broth and some kind of caramelized white cheese.

Cooper gripped her forearm. "Careful. I just pulled that out of the oven."

She snatched her hand back as sparks of electricity scattered up her arm. Forget the hot ramekin. His touch might as well have been the lit end of a July Fourth sparkler.

Cooper unrolled a cloth napkin and placed a fork and a spoon on a saucer, reaching across the table to hand it to her. The silverware clattered against the porcelain in her shaky grip when she took it, as if the restaurant were positioned along an unsteady fault line.

He glanced from Sloane's hands to her eyes, a line creasing in his forehead as she reached into her bag and scrubbed the cutlery with a wipe before dipping her spoon in the soup.

"So, tell me a little about J. Marian Restaurants' vision for this place." She blew on the spoonful of broth, crouton and cheese, willing the soup to keep from dribbling back into the bowl since her hand still wasn't cooperating. "It's not like the corporation's other restaurants, is it?"

One bite of the soup threw Sloane back with an explosive blast of flavor.

Cooper smirked at her reaction. "Does that taste like it came from my father's other restaurants?"

"It's fantastic," she answered around another mouthful, already assembling her third bite. "Where did the chef come from?"

He sat up straighter in his seat and crossed his arms, his expressionless face the final brick in the wall he'd put up between them. "I'm the chef."

Sloane nearly choked on her soup. Certainly, her ears had failed her. Graham Cooper Jr., a chef?

"I trained at Le Cordon Bleu in Paris and worked in kitchens that made Gordon Ramsay's seem like Girl Scout camp."

Wow. His speech had the scratch of a broken record, as if he was used to giving it to naysayers. What did the heir to the Cooper dynasty have to prove anyway?

Sloane cleared her throat and pulled a pad of paper from her bag so she didn't have to respond, making notes as she sampled the rest of the food in silence. There was an apple and brie panini, a chocolate croissant, a hybrid between a French dip and a croque monsieur, a salted brown butter and berry tart. The food was divine—all of it. She had to stop herself from clearing the entire tray. If she was in business mode, this food was putting up an involuntary out-of-office reply for her. The only thing that kept her in check was the mental tally of calories she'd have to plug into the app on her phone later.

"It was all very good." Sloane squeezed another dollop of hand sanitizer into her hands as her own white flag of surrender to the food. "You've obviously done a lot of work with these flavor profiles."

The corner of Cooper's mouth curved into a crooked smile. "No offense, but what does a blogger know about flavor profiles?"

Sloane's pulse pounded in her ears as she stared at the amused individual across from her in shock.

His grin faded to wide-eyed panic. "Wait. I'm sorry." He leaned his head on his hands, realized he was still wearing his work goggles and set them on the table. "I think that came out the wrong way."

"Whatever. It's fine." Sloane stared at the goggles. What else could he have meant? He was surely trying to placate her because he didn't want to be inconvenienced by hurt feelings. She pulled her shoulder blades together. "Can we get back to work now? I'm sure you also have better things you could be doing right now."

Two could play at that game.

"Go ahead."

"So, Mr. Cooper. I asked you about the vision for this place. I take it you spearheaded the development yourself?"

Cooper laced his fingers behind his head, studying Sloane through heavy-lidded eyes. "Yes, ma'am. I wanted an answer to my father's way of doing things, which works for him, I guess, but in a different way."

Sloane scribbled the keywords that would help her remember their conversation later. "So you basically set out to create a restaurant that will cause a stir with how your father usually does things."

Cooper frowned and shifted in his seat, scanning her pad of paper. "I wanted to create an atmosphere that said *Stay awhile* and a cost-effective, sustainable menu that said *Savor*. You can read into that whatever you want."

"That's very European. And the name? Where does *Simone* come from?" Some bimbo he'd met while enjoying the Parisian nightlife?

Cooper's expression clouded. "Someone who was very special to me in France."

For how long? A week?

"She taught me how to appreciate food and enjoy cooking it. More important than anything I learned at Le Cordon Bleu." His words became more flavored with French as he spoke, as if saturated by the remnant of this woman in his mind.

"And, let me guess, she was a little reluctant to leave the motherland?"

Cooper looked up, his forehead creased. "No. She died right before I moved back."

Died. The word snapped against Sloane like a whip. "Oh. Wow. Well, she must have been… something…to, you know, name your restaurant after her and everything."

She focused so her breath didn't release in shredded gasps as Cooper launched into a story about Simone. Something about standing next to her over her stove top.

But Sloane's mind could only focus on one thing.

Aaron.

She'd unintentionally wandered into an area of Cooper's life she didn't have security clearance for. And the intrusion only served to land her square in the middle of the place she kept under lock and key in her own life. Every instinct told her to take cover from the impending explosion.

"Can I use your restroom?" She stood so abruptly that her chair clattered to the floor.

"The water's not connected—"

"That's okay. Just tell me where it is."

Cooper furrowed his eyebrows and pointed to a hallway on the far side of the kitchen.

The door to the restroom closed with a thunderous crash when Sloane heaved her hip against it. She pulled the jade-green sleeves of her cardigan over her hands and clutched the pedestal sink, leaning into it. *Deep breaths*.

She willed her racing heart to slow, trying to abate the pressure of backed-up tears.

Refold short stack of hand towels.

Angle off-center soap dispenser.

Normally she could handle talk of death just fine. It happened every day. But sometimes the jolting blow of emptiness sneaked up on her when she least expected it, even more than a decade after her best friend's death. The days and weeks surrounding his birthday were always terrible—agonizing at best and unmanageable at worst. Well, she'd have to learn how to manage it better if she wanted to keep her job. Even if it was clear Cooper wasn't a fan of the arrangement either.

With a few more deep breaths, the pressure softened a little, leaving a dull ache in its place.

Sloane straightened and watched in the mirror as the peach undertones returned to her pale skin. Her fingers worked with practiced precision to tame the stray strands in her blond braid. And then she was ready to face the world again. Ready to give Graham Cooper some lame excuse and retreat to the safest place she knew.

But she wasn't ready for the look on his face. For the way he stood and stepped in her direction when he saw her walking down the hall. For the trace of remorse in his confident facade that made her knees shake when he asked if she was okay.

"I'm fine," Sloane said. "But I need to be somewhere right now. Unless you have anything else to tell me, I think I've completed everything on the agenda for today." And, unfortunately, a bit more than she'd bargained for.

"No, of course. I think we're good." Cooper started gathering dishes as Sloane packed her bag. He disappeared into the kitchen then returned to walk her out.

Sloane paused in the doorway, a sputtering explanation forming in her mind. Maybe she could tell him she had a situation with her contact lenses. Or something to dispel the truth he'd certainly picked up on that she was a total wreck. But she fled with a flick of her hand the instant his eyes met hers. Before the tightness in her chest could escalate. Before the moisture in her eyes turned from annoying drip to full-fledged leak.

Once she'd made it to the end of the street and turned the corner, out of Graham Cooper Jr.'s sight, she leaned against a building and wafted air into her lungs with flailing hands. She called her car service and practiced her breathing exercises while she waited.

Inhale, two, three, four.

Exhale, two, three, four.

She'd try anything to keep her mind off Aaron.

Nine stoplights, sixty-seven trees and fifty-nine footsteps later, Sloane was in her apartment, hands scrubbed clean. Curled up in her bed where she finally emptied her lungs.

I can't take this forever.

CHAPTER THREE

GETTING THE RESTAURANT ready had spoiled Cooper, and now that he'd gotten used to the loose cotton of his work clothes, his go-to suits felt like wool straitjackets. But today he was leading a training seminar at the J. Marian corporate offices, so he had to be on his game and look the part for the group of franchise owners who'd flown in from across the country.

To mentally prepare, he'd taken his black Lab Maddie to their favorite park. The mechanics of throwing the ball and watching her bound after it had reset his focus from repairs and recipe testing. A long shower had washed the smells of the kitchen from his skin and gave him the chance to rehearse talking points for the training he'd led countless times.

But in the clean confines of the old Land Rover Defender he'd rebuilt, Cooper's mind veered from the gray Dallas streets to his sawdust-covered restaurant, alternating between his massive to-do list and scenes from the mind-boggling encounter he'd had with his new PR person.

He'd been too busy to do his research before the meeting. Totally unprepared for how stunning she'd be in her own unassuming way. She reminded him of those cartoons he used to watch with his sister, a fairy-tale princess who'd been forced to get a real job—milky skin, a healthy rose to her cheeks, immaculate braid in a warm, golden blond. Natural, he could tell, not bottled. But she'd traded in her ball gown for business garb. And judging by the revolving door of faces he'd seen on the woman, she'd traded in her happily-ever-after, too.

As he parked in his spot in the garage next to his brother's limited edition Audi R8, he shuffled the few facts he'd collected about Sloane Bradley. She was hesitant yet professional. Bold, yet there was something fragile about her that had nothing to do with the fact that she couldn't be much taller than five feet.

He moved on autopilot through the dim parking garage, remembering how Sloane had practically bolted when he told her about Simone. Cooper recognized the pain in her eyes like he was looking into a mirror. Yes, he was very familiar with the kind of grief that sneaks up on you. With the dark, smothering bag it throws over your head and the way it pushes you into the back of a moving van.

As he opened the sleek glass doors, he catalogued all thoughts of Sloane with the mental list of things left to do at the restaurant and stepped into the massive lobby—clean and white and futuristic with purple LED uplighting. The smell of new construction was acrid, more glue and fused metal than the round scent of aged wood he'd become accustomed to.

"Sandra said to tell you he's in a mood." The receptionist covered the mouthpiece on her headset and motioned Cooper to the elevator bank with a curt wave before continuing her phone conversation in a polite, robotic tone.

Perfect. He rode an empty elevator to the fifth floor, and when the doors opened, his father's assistant's desk was empty.

Graham Cooper Jr. His name in red marker on the top of a cream folder caught his eye.

Why was his file on Sandra's desk?

He reached for it, double-checked that he was alone and flipped it open.

"Are you looking for these?"

Cooper whirled around at the sound of his father's voice and pressed his back against the desk, closing his file with a nudge behind him.

His father brandished a trifold flier with the *Simone* logo and glossy images of Cooper's food that had been redone four times before he finally approved them. He didn't consider himself picky on principle, but this was *his* restaurant and it had to be just right. Only, the images still weren't quite there.

"Yeah, thanks." Cooper took the stack of proofs from his father and turned toward his office. "I'll send off these final revisions when they're—"

"I still don't know why you insisted on hiring some computer girl when you have a full staff of top MBAs at your disposal," his father muttered.

Cooper clenched his teeth around his knee-jerk instinct to mirror the acrid tone. Fighting back would accomplish absolutely nothing, he'd learned. "It's the twenty-first century, Dad. The internet is where the numbers are."

His father smoothed the lapels of a suit that probably cost more than the average Dallas corporate drone's monthly salary. "We lost Baker and Mayfield."

Cooper's mouth turned cottony. He'd thought the two oil millionaires were in the bag. The paperwork to open their first two restaurants, though coming along slowly, was mostly complete. He'd even broken a personal rule and played golf with them the other month, for Pete's sake.

"They're investing in real estate instead, and they won't be persuaded to change their minds. I tried."

He scrubbed his hands through his hair. "Yeah, well, they decide everything together." This was bad—worse because they weren't the only ones Cooper had lost since he'd gotten the restaurant off the ground.

"You're off your game."

The muscles in Cooper's neck tightened. "Dad—"

"You're late to work all the time." His father ticked off the items on his meaty fingers, pacing the plush carpeting. "You're never home, always flying from here to that restaurant." His voice rose. "It's not healthy—for you or the company!"

Cooper sighed, his shoulders almost shaking against the strong urge to slump.

"I mean, do you even sleep?"

He scoffed at his father as heat edged his face. "Of course I sleep." When he wasn't bolting out of bed to do *just one more thing*.

"I need to know that you're all in, Coop." The senior Cooper tented his hands.

"I'm here, aren't I?"

"Good." He clapped Cooper on the back, walking toward his office. "Then deal with that massive pile on your desk before anything else falls through. And take care of that training today."

Cooper watched his father leave, swallowing around the familiar itch in his throat that craved to be satisfied with a few cold Jack and Cokes. He cleared his thoughts and forced himself to relax, turning toward his own office.

It was a mess in there, half of his desk littered with coffee-ringed napkins and the other covered in tall stacks of file folders, at the top of which were the Baker and Mayfield accounts. Next on his list. Could they have been salvaged if he'd spent more time at his desk over the past few weeks? He snatched them up and let them fall in the metal wastebasket.

There. Two down, at least two days of follow-up calls to make and—he moved to check his watch, but it was sitting on his desk at the restaurant where he'd painted the interior walls early that morning. A glance at his laptop told Cooper he needed to be at the training auditorium in fifteen minutes, and he was meeting his restaurant manager after that.

He gathered a sizable pile of folders and locked his office. Even if it would be too late to call once his night at the restaurant was finished, at least he could take care of the clients who preferred to work by email. The company depended on him to recruit franchisees who would open their restaurants across the country—and to keep their business. It was a huge percentage of their annual revenue. So he'd work all night if he had to and possibly move some things around at the restaurant tomorrow.

Cooking had made him healthy again, a huge, necessary part of what had kept him away from the bottle for two years. But he owed it to his family not to let things go up in smoke. At least not again.

His father's words circled in his mind as if they'd forgotten something. If Cooper was going to get it together at the office, ready the restaurant and actually have customers when they opened the doors, he was going to need all the help from this "computer girl" that he could get.

THE PERFECT LIGHT spilled through the kitchen window of Sloane's condo, illuminating the crisp white plate, slate charger and teardrop vase she'd paired with a couple red-orange tulips. It shone like a spotlight on the star of the show, a juicy roasted lemon-rosemary chicken with the perfect golden-brown crust.

Not thrown together by the seat of her pants with the items in her pantry, as Cooper probably assumed. She'd scheduled the meal in her content calendar weeks ago, orchestrated so each ingredient was fresh from local farms when she cooked and photographed almost a month before each recipe's scheduled posting date.

Sloane wasn't even capable of operating on a whim. At least not anymore.

A tiny speck on the smooth white plate—invisible to most—caught her trained eye. She rubbed it gently with a napkin and climbed onto a chair for a look through her camera's viewfinder.

She adjusted the ISO speed.

Who does Graham Cooper Jr. think he is?

She dialed the aperture down a few notches. Who was she kidding? She'd almost lost it in front of him.

With one tiny movement of the shading screen a camera equipment company had sent her to review, she flicked all thoughts of Graham Cooper out of her mind and returned to her position on the chair, one foot in a clean sock perched on the table for optimum angling.

Her computer interrupted the moment of perfection, beckoning her to the kitchen counter with the rhythmic ring of an incoming video chat.

Sloane scowled as she hurried to the kitchen. There was only one person who could be calling right now. "This better be important, Grace." Sloane stuck her tongue out at her best friend to show she was joking when her freckled face appeared. Mostly joking. "I'm losing light."

"Good morning to you, too, Meezy!" Grace lived in San Diego, two hours behind Sloane. She was still in her pajamas even though it was past nine there. She'd nicknamed Sloane Meezy based on the name of her blog, *Mise en Place*.

"I wanted to make sure you got my gift." Her friend yawned, raking a hand through her fluffy red hair. "That's a pretty valuable piece to be floating around in the possession of the postal service."

The biggest kitchen catalog on the web, *Good Cooks*, had sent Grace a high-end enamel Dutch oven she already owned. So she'd taken pity on Sloane who had dropped her own brand-new one and shattered it during an unfortunate compound butter incident.

She shuddered at the memory of the slick beef short rib concoction that had covered every square foot of her kitchen. "I was going to text you after I finished my post for today. It's gorgeous. I think the purple looks better in my kitchen anyway."

"Good, good. Well let's get right down to it."

"What?"

"You and I both know I didn't call to chat about cookware."

Sloane sighed. Right. *That*. She should have known. "There's nothing to tell, Grace. I'm working with their son to open his new restaurant. End of story."

"Sloane, Sloane, Sloane. There's always more to the story. How did he act? Was he decent to you? Did he have an entourage?"

"Okay, Hoda." Sloane carried her laptop to the table and sank into the chair. She wanted to take a nap. "No, he didn't have an entourage. He was alone. Doing his own repairs, for goodness' sake."

"Did he say why he's been off the radar for so long?"

"He was in Paris. Going to culinary school."

"From America's party boy to chef who isn't afraid to get his hands dirty. Interesting." Grace typed something into her computer. "He doesn't sound like the monster Levi was thinking he'd be."

The web coding and design genius they'd befriended hadn't held back when voicing his opinions about Cooper's character, much less his stance on whether Sloane was fit enough to work with him in the first place.

"Well, we know Levi can be a little trigger-happy with his Google searching." Sloane laughed.

"Yes, my friend. You're absolutely right. So, was he as good-looking in person?"

Cooper's warm, caramel-colored eyes and his strong profile that could have been chiseled from granite appeared in hi-def in Sloane's mind.

Quick. Play dumb. "Who, Levi?"

Grace raised her eyebrows.

"I, uh—"

"I'll take that as a yes." Triumph played in Grace's eyes. Sloane was toast and she knew it. "Maybe I'll get to find out for myself in a few weeks."

Sloane sighed. "The conference."

"You have no excuse this year. It's practically in your backyard."

"I know, but—"

"*But* don't worry. I won't let them devour you."

This was why they got along so well. And why Sloane had finally agreed to attend their annual food blogging conference. It was true; she'd run out of excuses since the conference was in Dallas this year. But she couldn't deny it would be good to finally meet Grace in person, even if her throat closed up a little when she imagined being in a room with thousands of bloggers and readers that were much less intimidating from their 2-D cyber distance.

"Well, I won't keep you from your good light. Are we watching *MasterChef* tonight or what?" Grace was now typing furiously. Their conversation wasn't long for this world.

"Sure. Eight my time?"

"Yep. I'll tell Levi about it right now. And I'll tell him to back off. I think one grand inquisition about the Coopers is enough."

"Ha. Fat chance of that. Talk to you later."

Grace closed the screen, foregoing a good-bye now that she'd moved on to the next thing.

After Sloane picked a new pair of socks, she returned to the chicken, rearranged everything according to the slight difference in lighting and snapped several shots from a bird's-eye view.

Her meal might not be molecular gastronomy or whatever they taught at a fancy French culinary school. But she was going to teach some home cooks how to roast a chicken so bone-licking scrumptious that they'd never be satisfied with rotisserie from the deli ever again.

And she was going to buck up and prove she had a lot to bring to Graham Cooper's table—rattled first impressions or not.

COOPER SAT AT his desk in his favorite corner of his home—besides the kitchen—head in one hand, the proofs for *Simone's* promotional materials spread in front of him. They were clean, bright, cheerful—all the trappings of the J. Marian corporate signature. But all wrong for *Simone*.

He'd been staring at them for what felt like hours, absently rubbing circles into Maddie's fur with his foot. He couldn't put his finger on it or name exactly what changes he needed to make. Design had never been his forte. Not like sales and customer service were. But he knew the tone didn't work at all. It fit what he was going for about as well as Maddie crammed into the nook under his desk, knobby legs sticking out in every direction. He sipped cold coffee, its acrid taste a far cry from what he would have been drinking a few years ago. It sure would make these proofs easier to swallow.

He sighed. Something had to give or history would repeat itself. He'd lose everything he owned if it meant he could stand the person he saw in the mirror each morning.

Cooper swallowed hard. Even the restaurant.

No. He sat up and turned the proofs over so all that was visible was the back of the page, frustration gnawing at his foundation like a termite. He'd been through too much to let his restaurant slip through his fingers.

And then he saw it. The scrap of J. Marian letterhead had slipped through a pile of papers. *Sloane Bradley*, it read in his father's assistant's slanted script. No email address or phone number. Not even the address for her website. Simply a name that opened the starting gate for a fresh round of loping thoughts.

He swiped a finger across the trackpad of his laptop and opened the browser. *Sloane Bradley food blog,* he typed into the search engine. The first result had a thumbnail of Sloane along with a short introduction to her website. Cooper cracked a half smile when he saw the title was French. *Mise en Place*.

"Dude, maybe you should get some glasses."

Cooper shot up, and Maddie scrambled from beneath the desk, scattering a stack of papers with her tail in her excitement. "How about you warn a guy before you creep up on him like that?" He grinned to show he was joking. And to downplay the fact that his face had been inches from Sloane's picture on his computer screen. "How long have you been here, man?"

"Just got home a few hours ago." Jake Neighbors traveled all across America, helping surgeons install pacemakers and defibrillators all hours of the night in hospitals that didn't have the technology. Cooper saw his roommate one or two nights a week—if he was lucky. Most of the time, Jake was catching up on sleep.

Judging by the rumpled T-shirt and sweatpants, that's exactly what he'd been doing. "Well, don't let me intrude on your beauty sleep, Neighbors. Because you need a lot of it."

Maddie snatched her ball and pushed it against Jake's leg. She'd given up on Cooper ages ago.

"Who's the girl?" Jake bent and scratched Maddie's ears.

Cooper shrugged. "Someone my mom recommended to help promote the restaurant."

"Yeah?" Jake leaned forward on the desk for a closer look. "How's that been going?"

Cooper sighed and picked up one of the proofs, extending it toward his roommate. "It's going, I guess."

His roommate's face was unreadable as he scanned the brochure. But Cooper was pretty sure he saw him wince. "Why don't you see if this woman…" He waved a finger at the computer screen.

"Sloane."

"Sloane. Why don't you see if she can help? I mean, these are good and everything, but her style seems more up your alley, you know?"

Cooper nodded, trying to reconcile the hot mess of a girl he'd met at the restaurant—she'd wiped her silverware, for crying out loud!—with the spirited image she conveyed on her website.

Once Jake had left to run some errands, Cooper opened his browser and dug deeper.

So, her thing was *mise en place*. The recipe prep. Neat piles of ingredients staged so they were appealing to the eye. He got that about Sloane, in the way she'd rearranged things and seemed to have a particular order as she sampled his food at the restaurant.

She was an interesting girl—feisty, even. And she certainly wasn't lacking in the looks department. The head shot on the website header affirmed that. Her shiny blond hair was pulled to one side, full lips parted like she was about to say something to the person taking the picture. The light pink of her sweater highlighted something younger, an almost playful vibe. Totally different than the guarded professional he'd met. A black apron with her *Mise en Place* logo accentuated her figure, petite and curvy. Trim, but healthy enough to show she wasn't the kind of woman who only ate birdseed and water. He could appreciate a woman who didn't refuse a fluffy, buttery roll or two when the bread basket was passed around. Life was too short for that.

Cooper rested his chin in his hand and scrolled to her most recent post, a recipe for pumpkin spice cake doughnuts prepared two ways. Some were sprinkled with a spiced sugar concoction and the others were drizzled with a multilayered vanilla bean glaze.

He did a double take and leaned close to the computer to make sure his eyes weren't playing tricks when he saw that her post had over two hundred comments. And he could see why.

Sloane's images were gorgeous. From the assembled ingredients to the close-up of the baked, spongy center. And the final product arranged in a doughnut pyramid, shot on a vintage sherbet-colored cake stand against a wood pallet backdrop.

Jake was right. This was what he wanted for *Simone*. Charming, rustic, cozy, mouthwatering. Just like he promised the real Simone it would be.

Maybe his mother's instincts were spot-on and Sloane could do his restaurant promo justice.

There it was. A glimmer of hope where he'd had nothing a minute before. He had to talk to her. He scrolled through his inbox, scanning the names for one that might have her contact information. "There you are." Finally. He tapped the numbers into his phone.

It wasn't until it rang that something twinged in the pit of his stomach. The warning sign that perhaps he should have thought this through a little better.

She answered as he was clearing his throat.

"Sloane, it's Cooper." Silence. "From *Simone*?" It felt good to say that out loud.

"Right, right." Her tone remained flat, all business. "What can I do for you?"

He cleared his throat again, replaying their last meeting. Did he do something to offend her? He couldn't remember. But that didn't matter. Even if she never wanted to work with him again, it was time to lay it all on the line.

"I need you."

"THANK YOU SO much for coming on such short notice." It was the third time Cooper had said it, but he didn't care.

He picked up the last box from the trunk of the black Lincoln Town Car that had brought Sloane to the restaurant.

"Careful with that one," she warned him, looping one forearm through the handle of a reusable bag and bunching the brown cotton of her skirt in the other to protect it from the wild winds. "Thanks, Henry," she called to the uniformed driver.

What was up with the car service? Maybe hers was in the shop or something. But that wasn't important right now. The fact that she was there to save his bacon was all that mattered.

Cooper set the last box on the stainless steel prep area of the kitchen with the rest of Sloane's impressive assortment as she began opening containers and lifting a menagerie of items from them—plates, stands, serving dishes, ceramic spoons of inviting colors and textures.

"Where do you find all of this stuff?"

At first, Sloane ignored him, her eyes sweeping back and forth between the props. She shook her head, and the focus returned to her eyes. "eBay, mostly. Online shops. May I see the food you prepared for this shoot?" Quick. Impersonal. Proper.

"Um, yeah." He ran a hand through his short curls. "It's right over here."

Cooper watched as Sloane inspected the dishes he'd made for her to photograph. Her expression didn't look promising—somewhere between fierce concentration and measured grimace.

"Okay. I can work with this," she finally pronounced. Without a word of explanation, she picked up three of the plates and whisked them from the kitchen to the café.

Cooper followed suit with the rest of the plates but stopped when he saw Sloane moving from table to table, inspecting each surface. What was she looking for? Crumbs or something?

"The lighting is best right here." Sloane framed a patch of light on one of the front tables with cupped hands. "But we don't have much time."

"Just tell me what you need me to do."

Sloane looked up at him. For a moment, he saw a flicker of warmth in her blue-gray eyes that jolted him enough to raise the hair on his arms. And then it was gone.

He stood at a distance, nibbling the thumbnail of one hand. Watching as Sloane moved in silence, transferring food to her dishes, expertly molding and reshaping with silverware, dabbing crumbs and smudges from immaculate surfaces. Adjusting her camera and snapping photographs from every angle imaginable.

Food styling had never been Cooper's thing in culinary school. But this took it to a whole new level. Precise. Methodical. What Sloane was doing was an exact science she could write the book on.

She didn't acknowledge him again until the very last shot when she looked up and, after a fleeting blink of confusion, seemed to remember that he was there.

"You don't happen to have milk here, do you? Or cream? And a tall glass?"

Cooper saw where she was going with this and jogged to the kitchen. The milk may have been a day or two expired, but its only purpose in life was to look good next to a molten chocolate cake.

That, it could do.

Right as Sloane had the shot lined up, something occurred to Cooper. "Wait. Just a minute."

He hurried into the kitchen, opening drawers and slamming them, upending packing materials and dishes until he found a plastic bag and tore it apart with his teeth on his way back into the dining room. He placed the teal-striped straw he'd gotten from a vendor in the glass of milk and stood behind Sloane to survey it from her vantage point.

She whipped around, a glimmer of life in the wide blue-gray eyes he now noticed were rimmed with brown. "You're a genius!"

"I'm glad my sole contribution pleases you."

After snapping the last photo of the molten chocolate cake, Sloane heaved a sigh and plopped into the chair. "You don't mind if I eat this, do you?"

Cooper shook his head, mind blown. "Go ahead." He laughed. "But the milk is at your own risk."

She rubbed on hand sanitizer and polished her spoon with a wipe before digging into the cake. "Mmm. This is so good." The cake's liquid chocolate center pooled at the corners of her mouth, and Cooper tore his eyes away.

"They're going to be lining up for this cake alone—mark my words."

"We'll see about that. It's about the only thing I like to bake. I'll take a knife and a skillet any day."

Sloane's head snapped up from the cake. "What's so bad about baking? It's pretty much the best thing ever."

"There's no...improvisation in it." Cooper pulled out a chair from Sloane's table and sat on it backward. "It was my least favorite thing about culinary school. Everything has to be so measured and set in stone or else it turns out awful."

She took another bite and chewed it delicately, staring at the rich, gooey cake in front of her. "Set in stone isn't always awful. Here." She handed him the camera, her white-collared shirt draping open at her smooth, pale neck. Her thumb rotated the dial, demonstrating how to scroll through the pictures.

They were exactly how he wanted to represent the bistro. The lighting, the angles, the food...it was all amazing. She'd really done it.

"Not bad for a measly *blogger*, is it?" Sloane narrowed her eyes, a half-smile curving her lips.

"These are perfect, Sloane. Seriously."

She scraped her spoon against the bottom of the ramekin, avoiding his eyes. "You didn't seem to think I had much to offer when we met the other day."

"Sloane, that didn't come out the right way at all." Cooper dropped his head in surrender. "I'm sorry I said it like that. Clearly, I need you to make this happen."

"I know." Sloane's voice was even. Not arrogant, just stating the obvious. "That's why I'm here. It really was a logical move to put your focus on online marketing for this project. You're attracting a different crowd, Cooper. J. Marian has the soccer mom and older crowd down, but this—" she indicated the room "—your people are different. They're waiting to find you online."

She was right. And the confidence in her voice told him she knew how to make that happen.

Memory card clutched tightly in his palm, Cooper walked around the back of the Town Car to thank Sloane after the last of her serving props had been loaded in the trunk.

To his disappointment, the distant, professional version of her had returned the minute their conversation reached a lull. Maybe feeding her chocolate cake was the magical key to unlock her. To give her permission to relax a little.

Before he could reach her window, she was gone with a swift wave and a tight smile, leaving a deluge of questions in her elusive wake.

CHAPTER FOUR

TRAFFIC WAS SO backed up with cars arriving for the soft opening that Sloane's driver could go no farther. She had to walk two blocks to *Simone*, camera bag bouncing against her hip. This was one of the reasons she never wore heels, even for nice occasions. No amount of beauty was worth the blisters.

But fortunately, there were no torrential downpours or hurricane-grade winds. The sky was clear, a pleasant breeze wafting through her filmy aubergine dress. Just cool enough that she knew the warm flavors and comforting atmosphere would be spot-on.

Now she knew exactly how to begin her article.

With one gloved hand on the polished copper door handle, she paused to take a deep breath and tried to drown out the sounds of the crowd inside.

One. Two. Th—

The door flung open, careening her into the

restaurant. Her camera bag slid down her arm, and she was mere inches away from eating some serious floor when two solid arms caught her around the waist and shoulders and lowered her to the floor at a much safer velocity.

"I'm really sorry about that," a booming voice said. "Sometimes I don't know my own strength."

Sloane looked up to see perfect white teeth surrounded by a charming smile. And a face that looked oddly like Cooper's.

"Hello." He drew out the last syllable suggestively as his gaze moved from her face to her peep-toe flats and back. Holding on to her hand just a little too long. "Have I met you before?"

Sloane felt a gentle tug on her elbow. The real Cooper appeared at her other side, syrupy eyes filled with irritation for the man he'd just pulled her away from.

His look turned to concern as he faced her. "Are you all right?"

"I—" She darted her gaze between him and the person who'd spared her from certain humiliation. Same height, same muscular build, same chiseled facial structure and cleft chin. The other man had reddish-brown hair to Cooper's mocha color and eyes so dark they were almost black in place of Cooper's honey-flecked ones. "You're…?"

"Brothers." Cooper sighed. "Sloane Bradley, meet Owen Cooper. Director of marketing at J. Marian Restaurants."

"*Twin* brothers." Owen's million-dollar grin was a stark contrast to Cooper's flat reluctance. "Pleased to make your acquaintance."

Cooper rolled his eyes. "Sloane is the food writer helping with the launch."

"Nice to meet you, as well." Sloane's voice came out shaky, no doubt compounded by her heartbeat's seismic proportions. Was it her almost-fall and rescue that was whipping her into a tachycardia? The two very good-looking men on either side of her? The warmth of Cooper's hand still holding her elbow?

And, goodness, did he clean up nicely. Cooper's eyes practically glowed in the low lighting. His now stubble-free jawline could cut glass.

Sloane's stomach dipped as she recognized the Cooper patriarch approaching, motioning his sons to him with a commanding expression. Cooper gave her an apologetic look before following his brother.

With their backs turned, she took the opportunity to smooth the hem of her dress and rearrange her Spanx in one stealthy movement.

She took in the room. So. Many. People. *Just breathe.* She only had to do this for a few months. Then things would return to normal.

When Sloane turned, Mr. Cooper was still speaking to his sons in a hushed tone. He was dressed in a dark, textured dinner jacket that looked fresh from the tailor. The woman at his side—gorgeous, with a sparkling planet on her ring finger, long white teeth that seemed to go on for miles and half his age—said nothing.

Unsure where to go or what to do, Sloane scoped out the restaurant decor. Cooper had pulled everything together in time. And he'd added a touch of elegance with low lighting and rustic burnished candlesticks on every table.

But the best part? Massive canvases of the photos she'd taken had been hung on each wall, flanking a huge black-and-white portrait of an older woman—probably seventy or so. The contrast and lighting of the photo highlighted her lined face, wide cheekbones, and deep set of her eyes in a way that showcased her strength and dignity. Though her mouth was set in a firm, thin line, there was a sparkle in her clear eyes that spoke volumes about her and also made her very French. Made Sloane want to know her.

She tore her gaze from the portrait and turned to the Coopers. Owen was deep in conversation with a woman she recognized as a network news anchor while Mr. Cooper and his wife moved on to more schmoozeworthy pastures.

"Come with me." Cooper's low whisper startled Sloane and sent shivers down her spine. "I know just the spot for you."

He led her to a table with a small chalkboard sign marked Reserved. Seated there were a blonde who looked fresh from the beach and a woman with the regal elegance of a politician's wife—Marian Cooper.

Sloane sucked in a trembling breath. If she could have any superpower right now, it would definitely be invisibility. Cooper destroyed any possibility of that when he interrupted their conversation. "Ladies, excuse me."

They turned toward him, mirroring his charming smile. Sloane flinched as his fingers brushed her bra strap and came to a rest on her lower back.

"I'd like you to meet Sloane Bradley, freelance writer and ambassador for VisibilityNet.

She'll be working to expand our presence on the web."

Sloane listened closely for a dismissive air in his tone, still a little stung by his words a few days before. But if he still thought her job was ridiculous despite all of the help she'd given him, he hid it really well.

"Oh." The blonde straightened to her full, runway model posture. "You're a blogger, right? I think I've seen some of your recipes on Pinterest."

Sloane swallowed a lump in her throat, wishing more than anything that Grace or one of her faithful blog commenters was here to do the talking.

"Yes, her recipes have built quite the following," Cooper answered for her. "This is Trina Taylor, local reporter for the *Dallas Morning News*."

"Oh, I've heard of you, too," Sloane said. "You have quite the reputation around here."

"Persistent?" Trina raised a shaped eyebrow.

Sloane nodded. "Yeah, something like that." Though she'd never met the reporter in person, *ruthless* was the word people most often used to describe Trina. It was an excellent quality for a young journalist, but Sloane preferred to stay away from them in general. Maybe it was all the questions.

Cooper moved behind his mother's chair. "And this stunning creature, as you know, is my mother, Marian Cooper."

"Hello again." A nervous laugh escaped Sloane, followed by an even more awkward wave, if such a thing was possible.

The older woman smiled, her familiar golden-brown eyes glowing. "Hi, Sloane. You're welcome to sit at our table."

Calmed by Marian's drawl, Sloane pulled out the chair next to her. "That's very kind of you."

Cooper stepped aside as a server arrived with a tray of appetizers. His head swiveled toward the door, where people dressed in expensive suits and glittering jewels filed inside. "I need to say hello to a few other guests," he said over his shoulder. "So I'll leave you ladies to enjoy the evening. Let me know if you need anything."

Trina dove right in when he was out of earshot. "So, Ms. Cooper, what is your role at the company these days? Are you here on official business?" She tore a leaf from the roasted artichoke and sucked it delicately. "Mmm. This is delicious."

Part of Sloane was glad Trina wasn't the type to pull her punches. Maybe Sloane would get some answers about this family that she didn't have the clearance to ask.

"You want to know how they handle the jilted matriarch at these kinds of things?" Marian's expression didn't waver.

"That's not what I was asking, but if you're answering…"

Please be careful what you say! One wrong step and Marian could find herself snapped up in a proverbial bear trap, if the amusement twinkling in Trina's eyes was any indication.

"Though I elected to focus on the City on a Hill Foundation, I'm still very interested in the company that has my name on it, even if I'm not involved with the day-to-day operations."

"Of course." Trina gave a little nod.

"But beyond keeping an eye on my investments, this is one of the biggest nights in my son's life. Anything else is a nonissue."

Good for her. Kind, but still firm. Jilted or not, the woman could hold her own.

Sloane glanced at Trina, measuring whether the reporter was daring enough to dig deeper. Not now, her firmly pressed lips told Sloane. But her calculating eyes said there would definitely be a later.

A silence settled over the table as they sampled the French onion soup. Sloane focused on picking out each ingredient in the broth as the hum of chatter in the room and the soft, dulcet French music whitewashed her senses into a warm calm.

Once she was thoroughly relaxed, she excused herself and pulled out her camera to take some action shots for her recap article. The hoity-toities were too focused on their food to notice her, which was exactly how she liked to keep it. She even captured one of the Dallas-Fort Worth area's district attorneys midbite, staring at his croque monsieur as if it had been laced with some kind of love potion.

Trina's chair was empty when Sloane returned, traded for a spot next to Cooper and Owen. Judging by the look in Trina's eyes and the way she was half hanging on Owen, it seemed she was about to lap the Cooper brothers up with a spoon.

Nope. That was none of Sloane's concern.

"Your son is an excellent chef, Marian." She put her fork down after finishing her chocolate lava cake and leaned back in her chair. "I'm pretty sure I'm going to have to cut my Spanx off when I get home."

Marian chuckled. "Yes, Graham's always

had a special talent when it comes to cooking. He and his sister were making us dinner when he was practically still in diapers."

Sloane smiled at the image of a toddler standing on a chair and stirring something over a stove.

"We put him to work in our first restaurant when he was fourteen." The smile vanished from Marian's eyes. "There was a time when I didn't think he'd ever cook again." She blinked several times, and the twinkle was back. "He's come a long way here."

Sloane nodded dumbly as Marian's words echoed against the corners of her mind. She'd practically lived under a rock for the past several years and even she knew enough of the story to see he wasn't the same person. Though Sloane was beginning to get the feeling all she saw was the tip of a very jagged iceberg.

She scanned the room for Cooper and started when she found him looking directly at her.

Whoa. She felt like a dunk-tank seat had plunged her into water.

He smiled and gave her a little nod before returning his attention to the white-haired lady making animated gestures in front of him.

Distraction. Sloane needed a distraction from Cooper and locked her gaze on the black-

and-white portrait of the older woman. If that was a stock photo, it was spot-on for the restaurant. "Do—do you know who that is in the picture?"

Marian turned in her chair for a look. "Did Graham not tell you?"

Sloane shook her head.

"That's Simone. The woman this restaurant was named for."

"Simone?" That couldn't be her. The moisture evaporated in Sloane's mouth and throat.

"My son rented her upstairs apartment when he moved to Paris, and she really got through to him when he needed it the most. If it weren't for Simone…" Marian swallowed hard. "Well, I don't know that I'd have two sons right now."

Sloane nodded, transfixed on the photo as Marian's words sunk in. With the record straight about her horribly false assumption of Simone, it was clear every interaction she'd had with Cooper needed a fresh interpretation.

"So, are you from this area?" Marian leaned her elbows on the table, the gold in her bracelet catching the candlelight. "What's your story?"

I moved here because I couldn't handle my hometown—and my hometown couldn't handle me.

"No. When I graduated from college I basically took out a map, closed my eyes and pointed to a random spot." Sloane sipped her water. "There are lots of good things happening in Dallas."

Marian pressed her lips together. "Do you get to see your family often?"

What? Was this woman in league with her mother?

"We, uh, keep in touch." Sloane crossed her legs and smoothed her dress.

Marian nodded, her eyes narrowed with understanding. She knew there was more to it, but unlike Trina, she was polite enough not to pry.

Sloane had been back to the place she grew up, that one-stoplight Indiana town, once since her high-school graduation. And that was only to pack a few things and ship them here.

"Well, you've done quite well for yourself with your website," Marian said. "I appreciate everything you do for the foundation, and when I found out your line of work, I had to check out VisibilityNet. I'm looking forward to seeing where this partnership goes. Depending how this launch fares, I think it could lead to a bigger deal with this company."

"Wow," Sloane injected enthusiasm into her tone. "I think my bosses would give me their jobs if that happened. They would *love* the opportunity for a contract with J. Marian Restaurants."

She, on the other hand, would love to go back in time and tell Blissfully Ignorant Sloane to never take her comfy job for granted. She looked up as a figure stopped next to their table, and Cooper Sr. aimed a searing glare at her before moving on.

Yes, if she could do it over again, she'd definitely reread her contract and negotiate the whole human interaction thing before she signed on the dotted line. She glanced at Marian to see if her ex-husband looked at all total strangers like that. But the woman was distracted, stifling laughter into her napkin. The source of her amusement? Cooper angling farther and farther away from Trina's less-than-subtle advances.

"He's a totally different person," Marian said, sipping her water. "Owen, on the other hand—"

An earsplitting whistle commanded the silence of the entire room.

Cooper had moved to the front of the restaurant and was seated on the counter. "Thanks for breaking bread at *Simone* tonight," he said, earning the applause of his patrons. "It means the world that you're willing to share this moment with me."

His cell phone buzzed loudly against the counter's surface, but he didn't flinch.

"I want to thank my dad for supporting my vision even when we didn't see eye to eye."

The older Graham Cooper uncrossed his arms, the smug line of his mouth curving into a beaming grin before snuffing out.

"And my mom, Marian, for being brave enough to put all her eggs in one basket and taking a chance on that first restaurant years ago." Cooper slid off the counter and crossed to their table. "Our family's been through a lot, and I can't imagine that J. Marian Restaurants would have survived without a person like you at the helm."

While Cooper's father was the great and powerful Oz of J. Marian Restaurants, Marian had been the mastermind calling the shots behind the curtain. And that made sense, given that it was her money that had funded the company in the first place.

Cooper bent to kiss his mother on the cheek.

"Jordan would have been so proud of you," Marian whispered, squeezing both of her son's hands before he returned to the center of the floor.

Jordan? Who was Jordan? Judging by the sheen in Cooper's eyes and the way he kept glancing at his mother while he thanked his staff and did the obligatory name-dropping, he was someone special.

"Thank you for sitting with me and keeping me entertained this evening." Marian stood as Sloane gathered her things to leave after Cooper closed out the evening. "I look forward to getting to know you better."

"You, too, Marian." Sloane put her hand in Marian's outstretched one and returned her gentle, maternal squeeze.

She waved to Cooper as she joined the herd leaving the restaurant and mouthed "Thanks." He started toward her before he appeared to remember he was in the middle of a conversation with an older gentleman. Cooper smiled apologetically and returned his attention to his guest.

As she stepped into the street where her car was waiting, for some reason Sloane dabbed at tears in her eyes. She couldn't stop thinking about the way Cooper's mom had squeezed her hand. A weird mixture of sadness and relief pulled in her chest as she replayed the events of the evening in the back of the car, then later as she showered and dressed for bed. As she brushed her teeth, words ran through her mind like a scrolling marquee, the restaurant review she knew she had to write now or else she'd never sleep.

Once it was finished, when she was finally snuggled into her covers in the dark familiarity of her apartment, she allowed her muscles to relax and closed her eyes—only to snap them wide-open. How could she have forgotten to schedule her social media posts for tomorrow? It was something she did every night without fail.

Maybe I can skip it. Just this once.

But visions of the chaos it would spin into her morning schedule unsettled Sloane enough that she shoved her feet into her slippers and wrapped a cozy throw around her shoulders.

After the posts were lined up, she crawled into bed with the quiet reassurance that everything was in order. Everything except for the niggling confirmation that the suspicions she'd had from the beginning of this assignment were one-hundred-percent founded.

The Cooper family was about to unravel her, bit by precise bit.

IT WAS MIDNIGHT, and Cooper sat on the leather couch in the corner of his restaurant, bathed in the flickering light from the fireplace. Still in disbelief that it was *his restaurant*.

His guests were long gone. The overhead lights were turned off. He'd switched the French jazz to a playlist that always helped him wind down. He'd just said goodbye to his manager, Janet—the early-fifties woman who reminded him of Simone. She was brusque and hardworking but the pinnacle of kindness when the people around her needed it the most.

The staff had swept the place clean, chairs overturned on the tables, stacks of clean dishes piled here and there. He was left with a to-do list that could probably reach Austin, including adjusting some of the ingredients on his house salad that didn't quite suit the less adventurous palates in attendance.

But all of that could wait. For now, he would sit. He would relish the fact that he wasn't the one bored at one of his parents' events anymore. This was *his* restaurant. His pièce de résistance. Those people had all been here for him, perhaps like rubberneckers driving past the scene of a three-car pileup to witness Graham Cooper Jr.'s potential crash and burn. But they had been his to take care of nonetheless.

And, with the exception of a few people who couldn't appreciate a good Blue Stilton in all of its pure and pungent glory, he'd had them right where he wanted them.

Cooper unpeeled the wrapper from a straw and chewed on the tip of it. He closed his eyes and blew the air from his lungs slowly, drawing up an image of the people who'd filled these seats, familiar faces he'd seen dozens of times in the news, at important events, in meetings with his father. But he'd never seen those faces flushed with satisfaction, lined with laughter, relaxed and rumpled. Lingering over his empty plates. His vision for *Simone* was circling the corner, close enough to reach if he leaned a little.

But he'd had to avoid his father, who'd worn a scowl most of the night and had actually pulled him and Owen aside to ask about a work issue.

"This doesn't concern me," he could picture Simone saying in her tiny kitchen as she cut a pat of butter into a frying pan. "The only thing that matters is what you decide to do."

His phone buzzed on the couch next to him. A text from Owen.

Might not make it tomorrow. It's going to be a late night :)

Cooper rolled his eyes. Different night but same song and dance from his brother.

Owen had left without a word, laughing and flirting shamelessly with a giggling trio of girls. Daughters of politicians or lawyers, probably. Of course Owen was going to flake on their standing basketball game.

At least Owen hadn't gone near Sloane for the rest of the night. Cooper had made it clear to his brother that Sloane was different. Off-limits. Not another one of Owen's conquests to wring dry and leave hanging on the laundry line next to the others. Not that Sloane would let that happen anyway.

When he dismissed Owen's text, the red bubble of his unopened emails seemed to magnify on his screen. Forty-six issues that needed his attention. Forty-six fires he needed to douse. Forty-six people he was potentially failing in the pursuit of this restaurant.

As Cooper watched the fire cast swaying swaths of light across the dark café, he felt a dry pull in the back of his throat. The tip of panic crept into his consciousness before he shoved it away and allowed his focus to float free. He could almost taste the smooth, rich Jack Daniels and feel its tang burning across his tongue, through the back of his mouth.

He swiveled on the couch, the necks of the oil and vinegar bottles on the expo counter glinting in the light of the flames, taunting him.

For over two years, he'd been sober. Surely he had it under control enough to manage one sip. He'd intentionally avoided stocking alcohol in the restaurant for this very reason despite the revenue it would bring. But there was a liquor store half a block away, a gas station on the corner.

One drink wouldn't hurt anything, right? Only one glass of the easy stuff.

Cooper growled and snatched up his things. Yes, in his experience, one drink could ruin everything. Because it never ended up being just one. When he was drinking, he was a human tornado that destroyed everything in its path. There was too much at stake, too much life in this restaurant to risk it.

He put out the fire and locked the restaurant behind him, leaning against the door and allowing the cool autumn air to calm him. Willing himself to fight the craving that was so strong he could taste it.

Jake. If he texted his roommate, maybe he wouldn't do something stupid. As he pulled his phone from his pocket, an alert lit the screen. New email from Sloane.

Mr. Cooper,
I just scheduled the article to post in the morning. Here is a copy in case you're awake and want to preview it before it goes out. If you have any questions, please let me know.
Cordially,
Sloane Bradley

He chuckled and clicked the link to the document, leaning against the heavy wooden door as he waited for the text to load. Something flickered in his chest. Was he *nervous* about what Sloane had to say? Or had he simply stolen too many bites from the pastry tray?

The article popped up on the screen, and he read it in Sloane's distinct silky voice.

Influenced by head chef and developer Graham Cooper Jr.'s time in Paris, Simone is a groundbreaking addition to the J. Marian Restaurants family. The cozy atmosphere offers patrons a respite from the bustle of downtown Dallas, and the commitment to quality in its diverse menu proves that a fast, casual concept doesn't have to be synonymous with hurried and uninventive.

He scrolled through Sloane's reviews of the dishes she had photographed—crisp, inviting images of hearty breads and fresh vegetables and bubbling cheeses with vivid descriptions of each taste and smell.

And to think he'd ever questioned what use she would be for him. For his restaurant. He'd never second-guess one of his mother's recommendations again.

With the last sentence of the article, his fate was sealed. The emotions of the night all whisked together from the corners of his brain to form a lump in his throat.

Simone represents a thoughtfulness, precision and execution poised to revolutionize the fast-casual restaurant experience—a can't-miss if you're in the Dallas area.

Cooper stared at the screen, sinking down the outside wall of his restaurant to a crouch. For the first time since he said goodbye to Simone, he had an ally. Someone who believed in him and not just because they shared his blood. Who cared that Sloane was paid to write these things? Whoever she was, guarded and talented and fiercely protective of her camera, with her words, Sloane Bradley made him feel like he could do anything.

"À la bonne heure." Cooper could almost

hear the words Simone often told him as she poured tea into his mug. "In good time."

Had his time finally arrived?

CHAPTER FIVE

"Juan David, maybe you should wash your hands before you eat that."

It was Thursday, the highlight of Sloane's week. She got to spend a few hours in the kitchen with the kids in the City on a Hill after-school program.

It had started out as a guilt thing. Voice mails from one of the administrators, which she'd ignored twice. A sloppy demo of grilled chicken salad that the kids ate only because they were trying to be nice. But they'd warmed up to her, just as she was. No questions asked. No pretenses. Her heart had opened quickly to them in ways she didn't think she was capable of after the accident. Now on Thursday afternoons, those kids were her safe place—a reminder of who the old Sloane was. A glimmer of hope for who she someday could be.

Juan David wiped his nose again with the back of his wrist and looked at Sloane, his grin as cheesy as the pot his right hand hovered inches above. "Yes, Miss Sloane." He stepped off the stool and jogged in the direction of the hand-washing station. His place on the stool was stolen by his little sister Samira, who wasted no time dipping her spatula into the roux for a stir. This beautiful six-year-old with uneven dark bangs and a gap-toothed smile had great instincts in the kitchen.

A group of three older kids returned, balancing a cutting board of turkey kielbasa sausage and scallions they'd chopped under the careful supervision of their teacher, Miss Jaime.

"Look at those perfect knife cuts!" Sloane took the board and carefully set it on an empty stretch of counter. "Are you sure you guys even need me here?"

Three pairs of eyes rolled in response to her hyperbolic enthusiasm.

"Duh, Miss Sloane," said Chloe, the only girl of the trio, a spitfire who was eight-going-on-eighteen. "What do you think?"

Sloane knew she wasn't supposed to have favorites and really did love all of the kids. But those three—Miles, Chloe and Davon— were the ones she'd been with the longest and the ones she most looked forward to seeing every week.

Especially Davon. He had a soft spot in her

heart because he reminded her of an eight-year-old Aaron, only with a much louder personality.

"I think you guys had better start helping Emma grate some cheese because this sauce is almost ready." Sloane nudged the side of Davon's grainy oversize polo shirt with her elbow. No response. Something was bothering him.

"Miss Sloane, I—" As if in slow motion, Samira's little cobalt-colored eyes screwed up and she turned and sneezed before Sloane could react, covering her arm and the hip of her jeans in germ-infested bodily fluids. Immediately, she could almost feel a crawling sensation. *Keep it together, Sloane. It's not that bad.*

"It's okay, Samira." Sloane gingerly placed a clean, gloved hand on the girl's shoulder. "Bonus points for not sneezing in the food. I guess you and Juan David caught the same cold, huh?" She motioned to Jaime to take over the roux and then guided Samira to the hand-washing station. Armed with a hefty stack of paper towels and Sloane's hand sanitizer, they cleaned themselves off as best as they could.

But as Sloane supervised the methodical Chloe stirring in three different cheeses, she checked the clock on the wall every few minutes, trying not to let any part of her skin come in contact with her jeans. Only a few minutes stood between her, a hot shower and a fresh change of clothes.

The timer on the stove went off.

"The pasta is ready!" a chorus of voices proclaimed.

"Okay, everyone," Sloane said in her most obnoxious, booming voice, "stand back." She slipped a pair of oven mitts over her fresh plastic food service gloves. "Davon, colander?"

He shook his head and took a step back, an uncharacteristic darkness etched into his long-lashed green eyes.

"Okay. Miles, colander?"

"Ready, Miss Sloane." Miles steadied it in the sink and backed away quickly.

"Hot water coming through!" Sloane sang in a high-pitched voice that made the kids erupt into laughter. She emptied the pot into the sink and turned her face so the steam didn't burn. "Shoom! Shoom! Shoom!" She threw her hands up and down, mimicking the billowing steam to the kids' laughter. Shaking the remaining water from the colander, she whisked it to the stove again and poured it in the pot with the finished roux. "Miles, Chloe, Davon. Do you have the rest of the cheese?"

"It's ready," Chloe said.

"Yes, Miss Sloane."

Silence from Davon.

Miles sprinkled it into the pot—with clean hands, Sloane checked—as Chloe stirred. Davon stood back, watching with his arms crossed.

Sloane's chest hitched as he swiped at a tear in the corner of his eye. Her little friend was usually so enthusiastic. And ornery. The others had to fight to share the energy and attention of the room with him.

"And the grand finale. Drumroll, please." As the kids rapped their hands against the counter, their stomachs, thighs—whatever they could find—Sloane scraped in the turkey kielbasa and scallions and evenly distributed them in the cheesy mixture. "All done. Look what you guys made!"

Six small heads crowded around for a glimpse of the pot's contents, and Sloane had to admit it looked amazing.

"Wow," Samira said. "And we can make this at home?"

Sloane nodded and banged the spatula against the pot to free a clump of excess cheese. "It's a lot better for you than the stuff in the box, too."

"I bet it doesn't taste as good." Miles jutted his round chin.

"Okay, then." Sloane raised her eyebrows. "You don't have to try it. More for everyone else."

Even though he was grinning and clearly knew she was joking, the fleeting look of panic in Miles's blue eyes made her laugh.

"Oh, I'm going to try it." He grinned.

Sloane sent everyone to wash their hands and scooped portions of healthier macaroni and cheese into disposable bowls.

Juan David was the first kid to return. Sounds of contentment escaped around his first mouthful of pasta.

"I agree." It may not have been quite as cost-effective as boxed mac and cheese, but it was close. And it was tastier, judging by the satisfied looks on everyone's faces as they devoured the meal. The flavors stood on their own—the whole wheat penne, chunks of hearty turkey kielbasa and crunchy little flecks of green onion.

When the last bowl had been scraped clean, Sloane said goodbye to the kids, making sure they all had their recipe cards and grocery lists in tow. And then as she was elbow-deep in suds and dirty pots and pans she felt a pair of thin arms wrap around her aproned waist.

"How you doing, Davon? Everything okay?" Sloane dreaded asking that question with these kids. Their lives were so unstable that she never knew what answer she was going to get.

Her suspicions were confirmed when he shook his head. "My mom's been really busy with school and work. And my Big Brother Carl's moving away, so he won't get to pick me up from school anymore."

Davon had a brother? What bad timing for a move with their mom in the thick of third-year law school. "But you'll still get to see Carl at holidays and stuff, right?"

"Naw, Carl's not my real brother. He's just a guy from an agency. He has a kid my age and everything. But he was real cool."

"It'll be okay, Davon." Sloane stifled a wince. "Your mom's almost finished with school, and I know you're going to get a new Big Brother soon." She hated how lame those words sounded, too aware of the emptiness behind the platitude.

For a moment, Sloane could picture the faces of the people she'd known her whole life looking at her like she was a stranger after the accident, some with pity, but most fidgety and uncomfortable. *Everything's going to be okay*, they'd placated her, probably to make sure she stayed quiet. *We're here for you.* And then they'd avoided her.

His eyes widened as his aunt appeared in the doorway. "Don't tell anyone I said anything, okay?"

"Okay." Sloane waved at Davon's aunt, who picked him up most days while his mom was in class.

"See you next time, Miss Sloane. And, uh, thanks."

Her heart broke for Davon as she watched his aunt hurry him along. He was such a good kid. His mom had done a great job with him as she worked hard to build a better life for them after her husband's death.

As Sloane's hands worked to finish the dishes, she made a mental note to ask around about Davon getting a new City on a Hill Big Brother. Because if things weren't okay in her little friend's world, things weren't okay in hers.

"What kind of *salad* could possibly be so good that you've disturbed my reading?" Sloane's neighbor stomped across the hall to her apartment that evening.

"Trust me, Mrs. Melone." Sloane let the older woman in. "It's life changing."

This was their thing. Mrs. Melone pretended

to be a crotchety old woman. Sloane played the sort of neighbor with lots of excuses that required the older woman's presence. But in reality, they were doing each other a favor.

They both needed someone, anyone, to check in every once in a while.

Mrs. Melone was the wife of some sort of Old Hollywood producer who was always in LA. She was way too stylish to be crotchety. And if she were half as grumpy as she made herself out to be, she never would have agreed to try the salad that spun Sloane into a dancing fit that could rival the cheesiest of touchdown celebrations.

Never mind that it took Sloane three tries and ten minutes of coercing to get Mrs. Melone here. When she finally said the word *bacon*, Mrs. Melone was sold and grabbed her purse faster than Sloane had ever seen the woman move. Way faster than a woman working on her second hip replacement should ever move.

Sloane took her laptop from its usual spot on the dining room table and guided Mrs. Melone to the chair where the salad was still perfectly posed from its earlier photo shoot, complete with a bud vase of gerbera daisies that made the fresh greens pop.

The older woman made a big ceremony of

shaking her head, dangle earrings clinking as she assembled a bite with the best proportion of romaine lettuce, bacon, bleu cheese, lemon-herb chicken and the creamy date and Dijon vinaigrette, then stuffed it in her mouth. Her eyes lit up.

Case. In. Point.

"Good, isn't it?"

"This is…so flavorful." Mrs. Melone shoveled in another bite.

Sloane grinned and leaned her elbows on the table beside her neighbor. "See, aren't you glad I made you come over to try it?"

Mrs. Melone's stylish silver bob snapped in Sloane's direction, the scowl on her lined face churning as she chewed her salad. Then her lips curved in the slightest hint of a smile and she took another bite.

Victory!

"Did you get this recipe from the Cooper boy?"

The triumphant sound track came to a screeching halt. "What?" How did she know?

"Graham Cooper. The restaurant you're working with." Mrs. Melone made a clicking sound. "Oh, don't act surprised. You've advertised it to the world on your website."

"I didn't know you read my website." Sloane

crossed her arms, pulling the ends of her cardigan tighter around her waist. As if *that* was going to help her feel any less exposed.

"Yes. Ever since Mitzi Mason from the country club told us about a feature they did on you in the Sunday paper. So about—" Mrs. Melone's eyes shifted in thought "—two years or more."

"And you're just now saying something to me?"

"It never came up!" Her expression went from stubborn to sly. "Are all the stories about him true?"

"No." This had to stop right there. "And to be honest, I don't want to hear the stories about him." Grace and Levi had told her enough. At every opportunity.

Mrs. Melone nodded and took another bite as if it was no big thing. "This is divine. You'll have to make this for my Bunco club. You're all they talk about, you know."

Mise en Place had page views from countries all over the world. But somehow knowing her neighbor's inner circle of socialites were among those readers pried open the tight disparity Sloane had created between her real life and her website.

"Do you want to take a picture of me for

your website?" Mrs. Melone had already put down her fork and was applying a raspberry lipstick that only she could have pulled off. "You know, so your mother won't worry?"

"I…" She stood and busied herself with packing up the salad leftovers to mask her shock. What, was the woman combing through her website comments or something? "What do you mean?"

"I may not have children, but I had a mother once. It's weird what they turn into with a daughter living in a strange city by herself."

"You've got me on that one," was Sloane's weak offering as her mind pictured a younger Mrs. Melone with curls tied in a handkerchief and hat boxes stacked in the back of a classic convertible moving to Hollywood by herself. "But I'm afraid the lighting's all wrong for a photo now."

Mrs. Melone's nose turned up. "Well, I wouldn't want my internet debut to take place in bad lighting. I'd never hear the end of it from the girls."

Without ceremony, the older woman stood and took the container of salad leftovers, quicker and more agile than Sloane had ever seen her. Maybe it wasn't just the bacon putting a fresh spring in her step as she walked down the hallway. "I think even my husband will enjoy this when he gets in tonight. And he doesn't do salads, no matter how I spin 'em."

"You'll have to let me know." Sloane watched her neighbor walk toward her apartment. Mrs. Melone usually moved at a much more snail-like pace, leaning against her signature silver-adorned cane. Now she didn't even have a limp. "Hey, Mrs. Melone."

Mrs. Melone turned around, fists framing her waist.

"I noticed you're not using your cane anymore."

She cracked a genuine smile. "Yeah, I've been doing yoga for the past few months, and I'm a new woman." She whirled around in a little circle. "I've been sleeping through the night for the first time in years. I guess I must have done *something* right when I was younger to deserve this."

Sloane's laugh sounded counterfeit. "You don't really think it was something you did right that took the pain away, do you? Besides the yoga, I mean."

Mrs. Melone shrugged, one cheek dimpling. "All that matters is that I'm pain-free."

"I'm glad." Sloane stifled her unspoken questions with a smile. She wasn't going to even begin to go there with Mrs. Melone.

Sloane's mind had been swirling with theories on healing for over twelve years. The silent bleed in Aaron's brain that killed him. Her own guilt and broken thought processes and everything else that had all but imprisoned her. If some quota of right was what it took, Sloane would be a prisoner forever.

But maybe Mrs. Melone was onto something. Maybe life could trend upward when it was least expected, in a way that was unexpected—no flashes of lightning or spectacular deeds required.

"Cooking for your bridge friends—I'm sure we can work something out." The words that tumbled from Sloane's mouth were certainly unexpected.

"It's Bunco." Mrs. Melone bore an ornery grin. "Bridge is for old people."

Sloane shook her head and watched Mrs. Melone, looking all Hollywood-on-the-down-low in her flowing gray pantsuit, unlock her apartment door. The whole exchange was still mind-blowing. Blog readers this close to home—literally. The puzzle pieces of healing that had no logical fit.

So she tried to process it, one sparkling pot and plate at a time.

CHAPTER SIX

BEATING OWEN NEVER felt as sweet as it should because, most of the time, he was a sore loser. But sometimes it was downright satisfying.

Their father's basketball gym—borderline ridiculous with its floor-to-ceiling glass-paneled walls, mounted flat-screen TVs and built-in overhead speaker system—was warm and humid despite the morning air filtering through the retractable window they'd opened. Out of the corner of his eye, Cooper watched his brother on the opposite end of the bleachers, silent for once. But he communicated volumes in his jerky, furious movements as he unlaced the blue-and-green custom Nikes he'd been given by the leading scorer on the Dallas Mavericks.

Owen lived in downtown's swanky Victory Park neighborhood by the arena and went to almost every basketball game. He was practically part owner of the franchise, pouring in money and enjoying the perks without the responsibility of decision-making.

But his expensive shoes hadn't saved him this time.

"Maybe you should ask your NBA friends for some better shoes. Something with a little more…traction." On his game-winning possession, Cooper had faked Owen so hard that his brother had eaten some serious wood floor.

Owen heaved a grumbling sigh that made Maddie's ears perk up from her lazy position on the floor. But the half grin on his face when he looked up gave Cooper a warning twinge. "No, for once, you were better than me out there, big brother. And you know what? I got you a little something for your win. I almost forgot."

Cooper definitely didn't like where this was going. "The funding for a print ad campaign for *Simone*?"

"Oh, no." Owen gave a creepy laugh. "Something that will last you much longer. Much more rewarding."

"Lay it on me, Owen."

Owen pulled his cell phone from his gym bag. "I got you a new little brother."

"What's that supposed to mean?" Cooper rolled his eyes.

A glimpse at Owen's cell phone answered Cooper's question. There was a photo of a little boy wearing a wrinkled suit and an uncertain smile. "You'll be spending some quality time with this guy."

"Owen…"

"Hey, don't complain to me. Dad's the one who volunteered you, probably so he could boost your image in the annual report."

The pieces clicked together in Cooper's mind. A press release his mother had sent about an event for the City on a Hill Foundation. "No, no, no, no."

"It's a done deal, Coop. Mom matched you up with him herself." The teasing demeanor slipped. "Look, this is the first thing Mom and Dad have agreed on in who knows how long." Owen slid the phone into his pocket. "It's not that big of a deal."

Cooper clenched his back teeth together. He couldn't argue with that.

"And you know what? I wasn't going to bring it up because I know you've been dealing with a lot, but does the name Martin Cadell mean anything to you?"

Panic twisted in Cooper's chest.

"Lunch and golf at the club?"

He couldn't have.

"He showed up to the office at our designated meeting time, and when you were nowhere to be found, I told him you had an emergency and took him out myself. Gave him the whole spiel."

Cooper threw his head back and grabbed fistfuls of hair. How could he have forgotten?

"Luckily his file was on the very top of the *mountain* that's been living on your desk."

"Oh, my gosh." Cooper had no words, no way to possibly weed intelligence from the tension knotting his brain and body.

Owen grabbed the strap of his bag and pulled it over his head, walking backward to the door. "Yeah, well, Dad doesn't know about it, and I think Cadell's in, no thanks to you. But you need to get it together. Maybe this kid will help."

Cooper nodded, mumbling thanks as his brother left. Never in his professional life had he bailed on a potential client pitch like that. He was lucky his father hadn't intercepted the man—and unlucky that Owen now had the upper hand on him. Who knew when this would come up again? Who knew what else Cooper would space out on if he could forget something this important?

The second the doors closed, he picked up

the basketball on the bleacher next to him and hurled it across the gym. But the sound of rubber slamming against the wall wasn't as satisfying as he'd hoped.

No sound or gesture or act of destruction could make a dent in the hollow feeling that could only be filled by one thing.

COOPER PRACTICALLY JOGGED from the gym to his car, chilly morning air wicking the sweat from his bare chest and stomach. All logic and reason were still muted after the infuriating reminder from his brother. And he wanted to keep it that way before he could change his mind.

No one would ever have to know. It would just be a one-time thing.

The phantom memory of a chilled bottle in his hand took him past his father's security gate. The smooth amber pouring into a bar glass sped him well over the speed limit down the highway, to a store where he knew nobody, winding through the streets of downtown Dallas with fifty dollars of liquid fire seemingly burning a hole through glass and paper from the passenger seat to get to him.

His hands were shaking by the time he

parked his car. And he almost didn't see her as he fumbled the key to his restaurant.

It was Sloane, peering into the café through the front window, one hand clutching a ribbed gray cardigan in front of her and the other cupped over her eyes to shield out the morning sunlight. Smooth black yoga pants clung to slender, elegant legs and hugged her sleek silhouette.

With the rigid lines of her buttoned-up professionalism dissolved and her hair let down, Sloane was actually kind of…

No.

He ripped his gaze away from her as she turned to face him.

Hands off. Eyes, too. He switched the bag from his right hand to his left behind his back, the bottle suddenly weighing much more.

"Oh, Cooper. You scared me." Her gaze darted up and down his frame. In his hurry, he'd forgotten to put on a shirt. "I'd apologize for showing up in my workout clothes, but…"

A rosy blush spread across Sloane's cheeks— from the autumn morning air or embarrassment, Cooper didn't know. But her smile warmed him to the bone. "I was hoping you'd be here. I mean, I thought you might be. You're pretty much *always* here or at the office, right?"

"Close enough." He unlocked the front door and let her in. "To what do I, uh, owe the pleasure?"

Sloane paused, rocking on clean white tennis shoes as he closed the door. Keeping her narrowed gaze on anything but his unclothed upper body. "I have that presentation this week and wanted to borrow your memory card with the images we took."

Memory card. Memory card. "I think it's in the back. Wait here a sec." As he turned, the bag in his hand bumped the door, almost falling from his grasp. But gone was the itch of old, memorized habits, replaced by the pit of guilt.

Sure, he'd almost cost the company a massive amount of money, but was it worth it? Was he still this out of control?

He pushed through the swinging door to the kitchen and threw the bag in the trash before retrieving it, smashing the nose from it, and pouring the contents down the sink. Rinsing every last drop of temptation down the drain as he breathed through his mouth.

With the bottle no longer a threat, he pulled the black sweatshirt he kept at the restaurant over his head and began rifling through a pile of forms and instruction manuals until he found the envelope with the tiny memory card.

Saved by the memory card. If Sloane hadn't shown up, he'd probably be sweating and sloppy, halfway through the bottle by now.

"Here are the pictures."

Sloane's fingers, sliding some rusty nuts and bolts he'd left on one of the tables into neat piles, caught Cooper's attention. For some reason, he couldn't meet her eyes. Something about her made him feel raw. Like he should be so much better—that he *could* be so much better. Maybe it was her review, full of a hope that he'd been starting to lose. But that wasn't all that long hours and stress had chipped away.

With his dreams in the balance, Cooper's guard had slipped. He needed to get things under control. To carve himself away from work and the restaurant to make sure he could stay healthy.

"Hey, is everything okay?"

Cooper pushed through the fog of his thoughts to the high-definition clarity of Sloane's eyes. His gaze slipped down to the thin black strap separating the ivory curve of her neck and her bare shoulder where the sweater had slouched off. He blinked slowly and shrugged.

"Did you hear anything I just said?" She pulled up the collar of her sweater, a crease forming between her eyebrows.

He sighed. "Sorry. Just dealing with some work issues. Nothing to write home about."

Sloane shifted uncomfortably. First she'd caught his wandering eyes, and now he was alluding to problems she didn't want to hear about. Time for a subject change.

"Why don't you let me make you some brunch?"

She shook her head. "No, that's really not necessary. I'm sure you have as much to do as I do."

"C'mon. We can talk about your presentation to corporate. That's coming up quick, isn't it?"

Her posture softened. A drop of panic bloomed behind her pupils before it disappeared again. "Okay."

She explained her plan as he lined a muffin tin with flattened slices of bread and whisked together an egg mixture to fill them. By the time his toasts were out of the oven and plated, he was practically floored by her preparedness. She seemed to know more about the inner workings of his restaurant, its niche demographics and return on investment figures than he did.

"Any tips on winning your dad's approval?" She pressed the pad of her finger to the buttery bread crumbs on her empty plate, searching his eyes with an almost childlike glimmer of hope.

Cooper turned toward the window and squinted against the slicing sunlight. "You're asking me?" He forced his tone to be light, unable to crush her optimism with the cruel reality she'd see in his face. But it was true. After thirty-one years, he hadn't exactly cornered the market on pleasing his father.

He'd sat in on countless meetings in which even seasoned executives stumbled over their words, intimidated by his father's innate and often frigid defense of the family, the company and their assets. That facade tended to thaw once someone proved their worth. If he got a hold of Sloane and decided she couldn't be trusted according to his arbitrary standards, she'd be out the door in less time than it took to crack an egg. With her impressive show of knowledge still fresh on his mind, Cooper couldn't lose her now.

But as he improvised advice that might help Sloane stay off of his father's radar and watched her fingertips push the last remnant of the meal he'd made between her lips, Cooper made a promise to them both.

After she left, he picked up his phone and made a call.

As much as Sloane had already done for him, there was no way on earth he was going to let her experience his father's bad side.

CHAPTER SEVEN

"YOU'VE GOT THIS. This isn't even close to the hardest thing you've had to do."

Sloane paced the immaculate Persian rug in her apartment building's entryway, repeating every affirmation she could think of and practicing breathing techniques.

Any minute now, her car service would arrive to take her to Cooper's restaurant to talk about her promotional strategies in front of who knows how many people.

She'd lobbied for an online presentation, using every excuse in the book. But the Coopers weren't dissuaded. The very last second to change her mind came with the appearance of a shiny black sedan. It was now or never.

"Do you think you could play something classical?" Sloane asked the driver the second the door was open. She placed a box in the seat and hauled her heavier-than-usual bag to the floorboard. "Oh, sorry. Hello." Thank goodness it was Mr. Harrison, who knew her idiosyncrasies as he'd taxied her several times before.

The older man's eyes squinted as he smiled. "Sure thing, Miss Bradley."

She sank into the seat and willed the muscles in her face to relax, ignoring the hair she felt escaping from the low bun she'd spent thirty minutes getting just right. Trying to pay no mind to the fresh wrinkles forming under her sweater vest. She allowed the woodwinds of a Debussy intro to wash over her, resisting the urge to rehearse her talking points again. The basil-and-berry scones she'd baked for the meeting had gotten to hear all about those talking points as she measured and mixed them into fluffy, golden-brown existence.

Sloane had arranged her pickup early enough that the streets of downtown Dallas were eerily clear. Or at least not slammed with the bumper-to-bumper traffic the city was known for.

"Big day today?"

She met her driver's dark brown gaze in the rearview mirror. "Yes, sir."

"You'll do great. I know it."

Since *Simone* wasn't officially open yet, Cooper had asked to meet there. So at least she didn't have to worry about navigating an unfamiliar high-rise. Mr. Harrison barely had the chance to pull up to the front of the building before Sloanc opened her car door. She gathered the decorated box of scones then smoothed down her pencil skirt with her free hand before grabbing her bag.

"Thanks, Mr. Harrison," she said, closing the door with a bump of her hip. "I'll try to save you a scone."

She stopped in front of the door and took a deep breath. If her history with this entryway repeated itself right now, she'd just call it a day. Maybe it was time for a new job anyway.

But before she could reach for the handle, the door opened—with plenty of space—revealing Cooper's easy grin on the other side.

"Morning, Sloane." He took the box from her and touched a hand to her back as she crossed the threshold of the restaurant. *Yeah, I remember what happened before*, his sly smile said.

While Sloane had been bracing herself for a room full of men and women in suits—Cooper had said shc'd be presenting to their executive staff—the restaurant was empty except for Marian.

Oh great. Had she misread the time in the email? Or did the rest of the staff not care about Cooper's restaurant that much?

She swallowed hard. Suddenly a room of corporate drones sounded more appealing. The fact that Sloane was about to have Marian's undivided attention intimidated her. Especially because the matronly figure who'd sat next to her at the soft opening had transformed to a crisp, no-nonsense chairperson of the board. She was surrounded by coffee. Two insulated cups with coffee collars. A gargantuan thermos. One of Cooper's rustic, mismatched cup-and-saucer sets. She was plugged into her Bluetooth, having an animated conversation, typing on her cell phone with both thumbs.

"So what did you bring?" Cooper tugged at the twine on top of the box.

"Oh, it's just a little..." Sloane clamped down on her trembling lip as he opened the lid. "When you said I'd be presenting to the executive staff, I thought it would be..."

"Everyone who matters? Right here." He swept his finger in an arc from his chest to the table where his mom was sitting and took a big bite. His face lit up. "Oh, these are good, Sloane. What is that? Basil?"

She nodded. "I've done a berry-and-basil ice cream on the blog before, too." Her teeth chattered, though the room was warm.

It's just two of them, Sloane. You can do this. Only, one of them was the woman who had launched two powerful organizations, who possessed a force Sloane didn't want to be on the bad end of.

And the other, well…

She stole a glance at his broad shoulders. A shudder rippled through her as he placed a scone on a napkin in front of his mother and gathered her empty coffee cups.

"Foundation stuff," he said. "She'll just be a few more minutes. Can I make you a fine espresso beverage in the meantime?"

"No. I'm okay." Or at least Sloane would be when his mom got off the phone and she could put this presentation behind her.

Marian ended her call a few moments later, setting her phone on the table with a huge sigh. She picked up a scone almost as an afterthought and took a bite. With one swipe of a hand across her face, her smile was back. Her warmth. "These are delicious, Sloane," she said. "Graham, you really need to see about putting these in your restaurant. They'd get gobbled up."

"I'll take it into consideration." He raised his eyebrows at Sloane, who felt her lips twitch in triumph. "Now let's get this thing started. Are you ready?"

Marian's gaze darted to the window. "Where's your father? Owen?"

Cooper's smile faded. "Fifteen minutes late?" He shrugged.

No sputter. No roll of the eyes. Marian just nodded serenely. "They must have gotten caught up at the office, but I don't have very much longer. Let's get started without them."

Sloane took a deep breath. "Okay—"

"Wait." Marian stretched her arms above her head. "Would you mind terribly if we moved this meeting to the little green at the end of the street? Some vitamin D would feel good on these old bones." The half smile that came with her question wasn't high-maintenance or demanding. But meeting outside would throw off Sloane's entire presentation without access to the slides she'd sacrificed her morning run to finish.

Cooper looked at her expectantly.

Like she would ever say no to Marian Cooper. "Uh, I think I could work with that." Sloane raised her eyebrows to inject some optimism into her tone, the way her high-school drama teacher had taught her.

As they walked the short distance to the

little park, she tried to rehearse her talking points. But her mind drew a big, fat blank.

By the time Cooper and Marian were seated on the gray stone bench squinting at her in the laser rays of morning sun, Sloane had lapsed into full-fledged panic. She was back in that high-school theater again, clamming up when she had to rehearse in front of a few people, yet totally fine playing Juliet with the entire school in the audience. "Let me just get my tablet." She turned away from them and balanced her bag on the ledge of the chiseled stone water feature, sliding out her tablet.

Weird. It had somehow powered off since she left her apartment.

Sloane pressed the power button, and the battery icon blinked at her, mocking her with its directive. *Plug into power source.*

No. This couldn't be happening. She'd triple-checked before she went to sleep last night that it was plugged in. It'd been in her bag since she unplugged it from the wall. Off to preserve every ounce of energy, she'd thought.

"Everything okay?" Cooper appeared at her side, his eyebrows knitted together.

Sloane brought a clammy hand to her forehead and mopped at the sheen of perspiration. "Not exactly." She bit her lip and squeezed her free hand at her side. "My technology is failing me, and I don't know what to do. I had an outline, a slideshow presentation, and now I have nothing to show you."

"Okay. It's no problem, Sloane." He lowered his voice so his mom wouldn't hear him.

"Is something wrong?" Marian asked.

"Not at all." Cooper winked. "Can you sit tight here for a minute, Mom?"

The older woman shaded her eyes and smiled at them. "You bet. No worries. This sun feels amazing."

The hair on Sloane's arms prickled as Cooper gripped her forearm and nudged her toward the restaurant.

"Do you have your presentation saved somewhere? Email, maybe?"

"I emailed it to myself. Why?" Sloane had to practically jog to keep up with him.

He opened the restaurant door. "I was going to wait to show this to you until after the presentation, but I got you a little something."

Wait a minute. He was choosing now of all times to give her something? With Marian waiting?

They crossed the kitchen to a door Sloane had always assumed led to the alley. But it was an office of sorts, with a desk, computer and chairs.

Cooper motioned to a square wooden table assembled in the corner opposite from the desk. "This is for you if you ever need a workspace. I had no idea it would come in handy this soon."

He'd arranged a bouquet of colored pens in a chunky ceramic mug printed with the *Simone* logo. Paper clips, Post-it notes and bigger notepads were lined neatly in one corner, arranged by color. A flutter of picture-perfect giddiness set loose in Sloane's stomach. Bottles of hand sanitizer and antibacterial wipes occupied the other corner.

"It's not much, but—"

"It's perfect."

His lips twitched into a tiny smile. "You like it?"

"*Oui*, chef. Thanks." Their eyes held for less than a second, charged with a rushing revelation for Sloane.

Cooper had been paying attention. And, despite all the weirdness, he *got* her.

She used his computer to print the presentation straight from her email. They were back in business.

Marian was typing on her phone when they returned, lips moving along with her thumbs.

Cooper gave Sloane's shoulders a reassuring squeeze and motioned for her to sit next to Marian. Then he slid to her other side with a waft of freshly baked dough and espresso.

Somehow her presentation had turned into a discussion that was much less intimidating. Her preshow jitters had dissolved, thanks to Cooper. Sloane showed them her edited images and rough sketches of posts, answering their questions along the way. She gave them profiles of the online magazines and high-traffic websites where her articles and reviews were scheduled to appear and the rough projected statistics she could remember. They complemented her ideas with kind, helpful input she jotted into the margins.

And somehow Sloane formed coherent sentences despite her constant awareness of the arm crossed behind her back so they could all fit on the bench. The biceps brushed against her shoulder blade. The hand gripping the bench just inches away from her hip.

He'd turned this big, scary presentation into something personal. Something fun.

Something safe.

"It's obvious you were the right person for

the job." Marian squeezed Sloane's arm when it was over, her lined lips curved into a warm, genuine smile. "With those kinds of numbers, *Simone* might be on track for the biggest opening in company history."

"Thank you, Marian." Sloane returned Cooper's sidelong grin. "I sure hope so."

Marian pressed a button on her phone, frowning at the screen. "I hate to run, but I have an appointment I can't be late for. Do you two have everything you need?"

Sloane looked at Cooper and shrugged.

"Yes, ma'am. We'll keep you updated about the impression figures."

Marian nodded, hugged Sloane and kissed her son on the cheek before striding in the direction of the restaurant.

"Is she always like that?" Sloane watched her disappear down the street.

"Like what?"

She smeared some lip balm onto her lips and spent extra time rubbing it in to find the right word. "Driven?"

Cooper's smile faded. "She didn't used to be, but she's been through a lot. That's just how she deals with things."

Sloane's throat dried at the thought of someone as nice as Marian going through a divorce and then watching her ex-husband rebound with women half his age. She couldn't even imagine. "I'm glad your father wasn't here—for her sake, I mean."

"No, they're good. They're civil." He scrubbed a hand over his face. "They've gotten used to being in meetings together, I guess, and as long as it's all business, they're okay." Cooper took a step toward the restaurant and waited for Sloane to follow. "She was really impressed with you—and she should be. You really know what you're doing."

Sloane looked up from counting the inlaid bricks on the sidewalk and crossed her arms. "Admit it."

He turned to walk backward. "Admit what? That you're brilliant?"

Her feigned indignation halted like a scratched record, insides plunging at the look in his eyes. "I was just going to say that food writers are more competent than you think."

"I'm never going to live that down, am I?"

Sloane shook her head, grinning at the sidewalk.

They walked the rest of the way in silence.

"After you." Cooper held open the restaurant door.

"Thanks." Sloane felt the toe of her boot

catch on the corner of the stiff rubber mat and sucked in a sharp breath before she stumbled into somebody.

And once again, it was Owen's strong hands wrapped around her arms that rescued her.

"Are you going for frequent flier miles, Miss Bradley?" he drawled, his dark eyes twinkling in amusement as his fingers traced from her elbow to her shoulder.

Sloane felt warmth spread across her cheeks and pulled her arms away. Any reply lunged down her throat when she saw his father standing next to him, face the color of beets and cheeks puffing with the failed attempt to form words.

Cooper took a step forward, wedging himself between her and Owen.

"Where have you been?" his father asked. "We've been waiting here for over half an hour."

"What? I thought it started at ten." Sloane's pulse galloped as she dug through her bag for the paper-clipped stack of paper. The one she knew had the meeting time written on her official J. Marian Restaurants docket.

"She was right on time, Dad."

"See?" She tilted the paper in Mr. Cooper's direction. "Executive staff presentation. Ten o'clock." Though she was sure the fact that the time and place were written in green pencil lent loads of credence to her claim.

Mr. Cooper turned to his older son. "When I called her, Sandra swore up and down that *you* told her ten-thirty."

Cooper squared up to his father, his features lit with blazing intensity. "Then there clearly must have been a miscommunication somewhere. Sloane can email you a summary if you want, but I'm the one who hired her, and I'm confident she's on the right track."

Mr. Cooper's eyes darted between Sloane and Cooper. "You know what? I think I'll have Sandra reschedule with the two of you."

"Here we go again," Owen said under his breath, turning away from them.

"I think I deserve assurance, son, that you won't miss any more important commitments because of this restaurant."

Sloane's jaw dropped along with her eyes at the bitterness in the last word. Even Owen seemed to choke in surprise. Awkward was an understatement for the charged silence between the father and sons, Cooper glaring at Owen. And then, with a disapproving shake of his head, Mr. Cooper snatched his jacket and briefcase with one hand and dialed his phone with the other.

"Sandra? Check my schedule and see if I have any availability for a meeting this week with that blogger who's working with my son. Thursday isn't an option." Based on the unflattering emphasis Mr. Cooper placed on the word *blogger*, it was clear where his son's preconceived notions about her career had come from. He ended the call without a *goodbye* and paused in the doorway. "Next time, give my girl the right time." The door slammed behind him so violently that the glass shuddered.

Owen traced his father's steps, planting his oiled leather Oxfords where Mr. Cooper had been standing seconds before. The locked-eye, twin-ESP thing the brothers had going between them communicated Owen's misery. But he took a hesitant step toward the door. Whether he wanted to side with Cooper or not in whatever was going on, it was clear his duty rested with their father. He dipped his head in Sloane's direction, his trademark schmooze absent. "Always a pleasure, Miss Bradley."

And then he was gone.

Just like that, the quaint memory of Sloane's neat new desk was tarnished. The victory of getting through her presentation with re-claimed confidence didn't matter.

Cooper turned to her, clearly struggling for words.

"I'll get that entry mat replaced," he said, his voice zapped of its usual strength.

CHAPTER EIGHT

"CAN ANYONE GUESS the secret ingredient in these popsicles?" Sloane asked the eight wide-eyed children with tomato sauce stains on their faces.

"Blueberries?"

"Yogurt?"

She nodded. "Those are in there, all right. But they're not very much a secret, are they?" The kids laughed at Sloane's wrinkled nose. "Okay, you guys have waited long enough. You can go ahead and dig in, and I'll tell you later."

Eager hands plunged to the middle of the table, colliding, tangling and grasping the ends of the sticks.

"Make sure to pull the popsicles out slowly and carefully." But Sloane was a few seconds too late. Miles and Samira both held bare sticks in their hands, staring in shock at the silicon molds still filled with frozen berry-blended yogurt. "That's okay, guys." Sloane braced herself against the desk and wrestled to free the popsicles from their captivity. After streaming some water over the molds, the popsicles broke free, looking a little worse for wear. But the kids still gobbled them up.

For a moment, she watched them like a proud mama bear. Their excitement—their innocence despite all they'd been through—had this way of washing her with serenity like nothing else could. When Sloane was with the kids, she was not that bumbling klutz who was all over the place because of some lame presentation.

When the last stick had been licked clean and the kids were taking turns washing their hands—Sloane would make germ-conscious citizens out of them yet!—she told them the secret ingredient.

"Spinach?" Davon clawed at his tongue. "That's nasty!"

She crossed her arms, pretending to be offended. "You sure didn't act like it was nasty." She picked up the empty molds to prove her point.

"I guess it tasted pretty good," he admitted.

"Do you think you guys would eat more spinach if it tasted that good all the time?"

Yeses and *Yeahs* and *Mmm-hmms* were their responses. Except for Davon, who shook his head.

It seemed Sloane had a little project on her hands.

The supervisor saw the kids off to their respective destinations, and Sloane set to cleaning their huge mess.

Note to self: never take on homemade marinara, salad and popsicles in the same morning—in a makeshift kitchen, no less.

Davon's ride still hadn't arrived by the time the last pot was sparkling clean.

"My new Big Brother is supposed to pick me up today." It was probably the fifth time he'd told her that morning, though most of the brightness had waned from his voice. She'd heard all about how much fun they'd had at the batting cages two days before. For Davon's sake, Sloane really hoped this guy didn't flake on him.

"Do you have a phone number for him?" She dried her hands on a towel and pulled her cell phone from her purse. When she saw the person who appeared in the doorway, the phone tumbled from her hand, landing in the sink of dishwater with a plop.

"Cooper!" Davon sped toward him. Their hands slapped together, half handshake, half high five.

"Sorry, my man. I went to the wrong place."

Golden-brown eyes narrowed at her. "Sloane, what are you doing here?" Then realization dawned. "Oh, right. My mom."

"You know Miss Sloane?" Davon asked.

"Yeah, I've been subjecting these kids to my cooking for a few years," Sloane said, trying to dispel the jitters in her stomach with a laugh. "Davon's been here since the very beginning, and he looks okay to me. Even though I fed him *spinach* today."

Cooper drew in a theatrical gasp. "Spinach? No!" He nudged the boy, who pushed him in response.

Sloane took their momentary distraction as an excuse to fish her phone from the murky bubbles. Very disgusting. And very dead.

"Oh, man!" Cooper winced. "Is it toast?"

"Toast. Do you mind if I use your phone to call my driver?"

"Driver? I didn't know internet celebrities needed chauffeurs."

"Perhaps." She matched his fake upper-crust English accent. "I can just borrow one of yours, Mr. *Cooper.*"

He raised his hands in surrender. Good to know the right emphasis on his last name was his checkmate every time.

"C'mon. You didn't know Miss Sloane doesn't

drive?" Davon asked as if it were something Cooper should have learned to pass kindergarten.

Her pulse pounded behind her temples.

"I do now." Cooper furrowed his eyebrows. But to her relief, the question in his eyes never left his lips. *Why?*

Sloane shifted her gaze to Davon and her sputtering attempt to change the subject drew a blank. Of course Cooper would know there was a story when a twenty-eight-year-old woman didn't drive.

But he was going to have to wonder. Maybe forever.

Cooper pulled out his phone.

"Why can't she ride with us?"

Sloane shook her head before Davon even finished his sentence. After being caught in the cross fire of weird male domination that lived in that family dynamic, it was probably best that she limit their encounters to work settings.

But Cooper pursed his lips in agreement. *Why not?* said the shrug of a shoulder.

"Oh, no." She raised a hand. "You don't have to do that. I wouldn't want to interrupt Big Brother time."

"We can at least run you to the store to get a new phone. Seriously, Sloane. There's one on the way." Cooper's tone told her he wasn't going to leave her there.

She gave a relenting nod. "Okay." She couldn't function without a phone. And it was on the way to their destination anyway, he'd said. She followed them to the parking lot across the street, almost choking on a surprised laugh when she saw what clicked at the other end of Cooper's keyless entry.

It was some kind of Land Rover, with the squared-off lines of a model from the '90s maybe and a shiny silver paint job that emphasized the car had had some work done. With its racks and raised grill, it looked more suited for off-roading than navigating the urban sprawl of the Dallas-Fort Worth area.

"What?" Cooper asked when Sloane paused on the curb. "Why are you looking at the Defender like that?"

She snickered. "The Defender?"

Cooper rolled his eyes. "I guess it takes a man to appreciate her awesomeness. Right, Davon?"

Sloane heard the boy laugh in response as he climbed in the backseat. Her seat. "Davon, you can have shotgun," she said.

"His mom doesn't want him to ride in the front. It's all yours."

Sloane glanced at Davon's cheesiest grin, the one that looked so much like Aaron it twisted her insides every time. Cooper already thought she was a freak for not driving. So her last thread of pride left her no choice but to climb into the front seat.

She said nothing on the drive, eyes squeezed closed, listening to bits of their animated conversation about baseball and the Texas Rangers, which she was almost positive was the major league team based in the Dallas area.

"We're here, Sloane." Cooper's voice was uncharacteristically flat, his posture trained straight ahead, the ripple of his jaw knotted with tension. Certainly confused by her death grip on the door handle.

"Cooper?"

He lowered his voice so Davon couldn't hear. "Look, I don't know what you've read, but if you didn't feel comfortable getting in the car with me, you could have just said so."

"No, it's nothing like that. It's nothing about you. It's just…" She sighed. "Personal." What? Was she feeding him breakup clichés now?

Cooper's eyes softened, as if he comprehended the significance in her words, and he nodded.

"Go easy on Coop here." Sloane forced a grin for Davon's sake.

"No way!"

Sloane darted one last apologetic look at Cooper before she faced the storefront, paper-towel-wrapped phone clutched in her hand. But before she reached the walkway, Cooper rolled down his window. "Sloane! Hold up just a sec!"

She turned around, crossing her arms over her chest. Bracing her already aching heart for whatever he was going to say.

Cooper jerked his head to the side, motioning for her to come to his window. "I'm sorry about your phone."

"No big deal. I might have done it on purpose just to get the upgrade." *It had nothing to do with seeing you. Nothing at all.* "See ya."

"Sloane." He stopped her when she started to turn around, but paused as if he'd forgotten what he was going to say. "Was he upset?" His voice was so low she could barely hear it. "That I was late?"

She shook her head. "I haven't seen him this happy about something in a long time." She crossed her arms and squeezed against "The Defender" as a car approached in the distance. "Just show up at the right place next week."

An arresting grin spread across Cooper's face. "I think it's really cool that you work with the kids."

"Hey!" Davon leaned forward. "Are you talking about me?"

Sloane winked at him. "I was just letting Cooper in on a little secret." She pulled her hand sanitizer from her purse and squeezed some between her palms. "You'll find out really soon that you're the lucky one in this whole Big Brother-Little Brother arrangement. Davon's a really good kid."

Cooper nodded and said goodbye.

As Sloane walked into the store, images of their interactions rolling through her mind like rapid-fire snapshots, she was sure of something else. Davon had it pretty good, too.

CHAPTER NINE

Marian Cooper lived in a two-story, Tudor-style home on the edge of Northeast Dallas. Though she could probably fit her entire lot in just one wing of her ex-husband's sprawling mansion, her home had a charming appeal and warmth that Cooper would never feel at his father's monstrosity of a residence.

He climbed porch steps flanked by tall, potted topiaries, Maddie following close behind him, and knocked on the brick-red door. Footsteps approached.

His mother opened the door, wearing an oversize University of Texas hoodie, her long, silver-streaked brown hair swept into a clip. "Graham." Her East Texas voice held a lilt of surprise even though they'd just spoken on the phone not thirty minutes before. "And Maddie came, too!" She bent to rub Maddie's ears.

With her ceremonial sniffs, kisses and tickles out of the way, Maddie disappeared to explore, nails clicking on the floor.

Cooper kissed Marian on the cheek and wrapped his arms around her. The faintest hint of her rose perfume mingled with a buttery scent coming from the kitchen and whisked him back to his childhood. Working dough at her feet while she cooked dinner. Being on the receiving end of her discreet pinches in church. Hurried hugs on his way out the door to basketball practice. "Did somebody order a pizza?"

Marian chuckled at their longtime inside joke. "No pizza, but I did order a tall son to help me reach things and got two."

"That's funny, because I only see one here."

The humor faded from Marian's eyes, and Cooper sucked in a breath.

"I know, Mom. I'll stop. I promise." He knew his mother felt pulled like taffy when he and Owen weren't getting along. And the last thing he wanted to do was stretch her, which was why he wasn't going to think about his shortcomings while he was here. Every time she got that pained look on her face, Cooper braced himself, worried it would be ages before he'd see her smile again. That had been their reality from his late teens through his grad school years.

But some time while he was in Paris, Marian

had become a different person. He'd returned stateside to a full-color version of the woman who'd been living in black-and-white when he left. Now she had her foundation to look after, tennis, social clubs, charity events.

And, well, now she had him back.

"Three bulbs are out in here." His mother led him to her spacious living room by way of the remodeled kitchen that had been her first order of business when she moved in. The buttery scent he'd picked up grew stronger, and her restaurant-grade oven range hummed on the job.

Her home inspection apparently complete, Maddie padded into the kitchen behind them, nosed the handle of a pot on the stove and plopped on the floor next to the oven to keep guard.

From the open kitchen, Cooper saw the three canister lights on the vaulted living room ceiling that had burned out. A ladder was propped just below one of them.

"As you can see, I tried to replace them myself and couldn't quite reach," Marian explained. "But then I thought, *Do I really want to get a taller ladder when I could call in a favor with someone I gave* life *to?*"

Cooper chuckled. So she was pulling that

card. Again. "Next time, don't even try it, Ma. You know you can always call me first." He mounted the ladder and reached for the light-bulb Marian offered him.

His mother waited until he'd reached the top of the ladder before pouncing for the kill. "So, what do you think of the consultant—what's her name again? Is she meeting your expectations?"

Cooper rolled his eyes. "You know her name, *Mom*." He carefully replaced the bulb and began his descent to steady ground. "And, yes, Sloane's been very…helpful."

"Her presentation was spot-on, don't you think? A little rattled…" His mother studied his expression almost hungrily as she whisked something in a metal mixing bowl balanced on her hip. Maddie's nose bobbed in and out of his vision next to her.

"Yes." Cooper moved the ladder toward the fireplace, keeping his tone noncommittal. "She's very good at what she does."

He knew that look, and he wasn't going to give his mother any shred of false hope, especially not when he was almost positive she'd engineered his placement with Davon with dual motives. If she saw some wisp of a possibility, if he faltered the least bit right now, it would be settled. She'd have him and Sloane married with two-point-five kids before he'd even entertained the idea of asking her on a date.

Not that he was entertaining the idea of asking Sloane on a date. No, he needed her for his restaurant and couldn't even think about the inevitable ruin of another relationship.

Please change the subject. Please change the subject.

"What's she like?" Marian squeezed a lemon over her hand, its juice trickling through her fingers into the pot.

Or you can ask what she's like. He climbed the ladder again to buy himself some time. "She's—I don't know."

Haunted. Grieving. Slightly unstable. A puzzle he couldn't solve.

Sort of…gorgeous.

He landed on, "Smart. She's very smart. And good with details."

"I see." Marian raised her eyebrows and pressed her lips together.

Cooper climbed down and snatched the third lightbulb from the counter. This was getting out of hand. His palms were already starting to sweat, which would do him no good when he was balancing twenty feet in the air. "What are you making? Smells lemony." He grunted as he reached to screw in the last bulb.

"Your payment for helping me, of course."

His stomach growled as his sense of smell and the sight of the tray his mother was pulling from the oven collided with happy memories. She had made the cookies he loved when he was a kid—dense, rich butter cookies with a thick lemon glaze.

He hopped off the ladder and pulled his mom into a hug before she could finish taking off her oven mitts. Somehow, through all the years, he could never reproduce the deliciousness of her recipe. That's why he left baking to other people.

Sloane. He ground his heel into the memory of their conversation the last time he'd seen her, smashing it like a bug before it could surface. Maybe the cookies had nothing to do with his baking ability. They just didn't taste right if they didn't come from his mother's oven.

While the glaze on the cookies set, Cooper helped Marian wash the dishes. They laughed, remembering stories that got even funnier and more ridiculous by the minute.

"Well, I have an early flight to meet with a donor tomorrow," Marian said as she layered the cookies in a storage container. "But I'm so glad you came over."

Cooper snatched a cookie before his mom could close the lid, almost getting his fingers pinched in the process.

"Hey!" She swatted him with a kitchen towel.

The cookies had cooled enough to crumble in his mouth, filling his senses with their citrus freshness, rounded out by the creamy flavor of his mother's favorite Irish butter. Exactly as he remembered them. "Mom. These are… Wow."

Her eyes filled with pride. "Aren't they?"

"Invite me over to cook for you soon." Cooper ran his palm along the sleek edge of the stainless steel oven range, picturing all the fun he could have with the high-end model. "I'm serious."

Marian laughed and pulled him into her arms. "Love you, Graham."

"Love you, too." He bent to kiss her cheek. "See you soon." He whistled for Maddie and waited for her to come bounding to the entryway then smiled as he watched his mom bend to give the big dog a proper hug. Laughing without reserve as she nearly got knocked over in the process.

As he let Maddie in the rear of the Defender

and reversed out of the long, landscape-lined driveway, his mother's image, full of life and joy he hadn't associated with her in ages, left a lingering satisfaction.

Simone had been one-hundred-percent right in her advice to him as her health failed and he debated what to do when his culinary externships came to an end.

"Your mother has already suffered the loss of one child. Don't do it to her again."

CHAPTER TEN

"OH, THAT'S PERFECT." Cooper sucked the last bit of sauce from the edge of his thumb. "I think we nailed it this time."

They were sitting in the kitchen at Marlo's Pizza, the Cooper family's second restaurant, polishing off a slice with the perfected lemon-pepper crust they'd spent the last few hours troubleshooting for Sloane's latest assignment. The photos she'd taken of the restaurant were divine. The pizza? Not so much.

First it had been too doughy because Cooper had insisted on adding more yeast. Then it was too garlicky. Then it didn't have enough lemon.

And then it was perfect.

Sloane took another bite and wrinkled her nose. "Yeah, I don't think it can get any better than that."

"It reminds me of these lemon-pepper wings I used to get from a place not too far from here. The best ever."

"Mmm." That sounded so good.

"They melt in your mouth. I don't make wings because I know I'll never be able to do them justice."

"I think I'm going to have to pick some up on the way home." They'd been nibbling on crust samples all evening, but the idea of eating juicy chicken off the bone in front of some *Gilmore Girls* reruns sounded so good to Sloane after a long day. "Where is this place?"

The slightest flinch flitted across Cooper's face. "Oh, it's just a little sports bar around the corner. I..." He hesitated. "I could take you there. If you want."

Sloane's spine curled as if to absorb the cannonball that just hit her in the chest. Cooper's easygoing nature melted her apprehension a little more each time she worked with him. But going somewhere without having a project as a buffer? "I don't know, Coop. I have to get some work done tonight."

"Yeah, of course." He straightened from the island and flexed his hand like it wasn't a big deal. "Maybe some other time."

They stacked the plates and pans then took them to the sink, elbows brushing as Cooper scrubbed the dishes and Sloane dried them. She paused, disrupting their productivity when she spied what looked like the edge of a tattoo on the inside of Cooper's forearm, just visible under the bunched-up sleeve of his Henley shirt.

Warmth rolled in her midsection. She tried to concentrate on drying the last baking sheet, but it was useless. "Hey." The words tumbled from her mouth before she could stop them. "How 'bout those wings?"

"Yeah?" Cooper's eyes lit up.

She nodded. Maybe her body needed some protein after eating all that bread.

"Let's go. I'll drive."

Sloane took a breath as Cooper opened the passenger door of the Defender and blew it out in the secrecy of the car before he got in. Why was she so nervous right now? This wasn't *all that* different than chopping ingredients and washing dishes with the guy, was it?

Eyes open as Cooper turned out of the parking garage, she sat on her hands to keep from picking at the microscopic bits of dryer lint on her linen pants. They were the most comfortable pants in the world, but they attracted spots like flies at a barbecue. Not exactly ideal for someone like her.

By the time they got to the restaurant, seating was completely full.

"Your best bet is the bar," the perky young

hostess told them, motioning to the glossy cherry fixture situated on the back wall.

"No problem," Sloane replied at the same time Cooper asked how long the wait for a table would be. There was uncertainty in his shifting eyes. Maybe after all the publicity, he was one of those people who didn't want to be associated with alcohol at all. Maybe it was an image thing, though he certainly didn't seem to be caught up in the cloud of press he used to be.

"It shouldn't be longer than twenty or thirty minutes." The hostess studied the seating chart on the podium. "But it looks like some space just opened up at the bar."

Cooper glanced at Sloane for direction. *It's up to you*, she told him with a shrug.

"Okay," he said. "But we'll move once a table opens up."

They filed through the crowded space, squeezing past chairs and trying not to knock over the tall frosted glasses. Sloane's mouth watered as the smell of buttermilk breading wafted through the air.

She so needed to do a post about this place.

"What'll it be?" The burly bartender asked in a thick Brooklyn accent before they were even seated. Cooper looked at Sloane expectantly.

"I'll have water," she said. "No, make that a Coke." She normally only ordered water, but there was nothing better than the taste of fried food with something acidic or fizzy to cut the flavors a little.

The bartender's gaze flicked to Cooper and widened as if he recognized him. "Well if it isn't Junior. What's it been? A few years since you've been in here?"

Cooper forced an uneasy laugh. "Yeah, but—"

"Do you want me to start you off with your usual?"

"Just water for me tonight," Cooper said firmly, daring the bartender to push it with the steel in his eyes. "And we'll share an order of your lemon-pepper wings."

"Oh, you'll be ordering a second basket." The bartender smirked, turning to punch their order into his computer.

Sloane tore the edges of her napkin into minuscule shreds, afraid to meet Cooper's eyes. It was clear he wasn't going to let her in on what that was all about. But she couldn't pretend the whole exchange never happened.

The bartender slid their drinks across the

polished cherry bar and mumbled that their wings would be out in a minute. His tone brightened as he turned to tend the rest of his patrons. There were plenty of other fish willing to bite at his easy conversation.

"Oh wow, Sloane." Cooper broke the silence. "I, uh, I think you got it."

What? What was he talking about? "Got what?"

He motioned to her hands and the neat pile of napkin snow she didn't even realize she'd been making.

"Oh." She swept the pile to the edge of the bar. She almost fell off of her barstool when Cooper burst into laughter, something booming and genuine. Something that was contagious.

"What?" She failed to stifle a smile.

"You're funny, Sloane Bradley."

"Funny? Wha— Why?"

"You do this thing when you're nervous about something." He brought both hands up, moving pinched fingers in rapid motion. "Your hands always have to be working. See? You're doing it now."

Sloane stopped fiddling with her straw and wedged her hands beneath her legs. "I'm not nervous." She tried to sound insistent. Confident, even. But her words came out breathy and meek.

The Jedi mind trick wasn't working on herself.

"Good." The flecks of gold in his eyes twinkled in the dim lighting. "You don't have to be nervous with me."

Something about the space and air between them changed. Like pulling apart two magnets, Sloane turned her gaze from his and took a sip of her Coke for something to do since she had no idea what to say to that.

Thanks?

You don't have to be nervous with me, either?

You have really nice eyes?

"So tell me about Davon," Cooper said. "How long have you been working with him again?"

She swiveled her barstool a few degrees in his direction. "Oh, Davon's such a great kid. I've known him for—two years now? And he's just the best. He's my favorite, but don't tell him that."

"He'll tell the other kids."

"Oh, he totally will." She was laughing again. "And it'll be really bad for everyone. Especially you."

One side of Cooper's mouth curved upward. "I believe it."

Their wings arrived in a plastic waffle basket lined with soft newspaper pages. The smell was so glorious that nothing else was worth talking about. The bartender put two appetizer plates in front of them and a folded slip of paper that had to be the bill.

Sloane sanitized her hands and speared a wing from the basket with her fork. While she studied it—glossy golden brown, plump, flecked with lemon zest and bits of black pepper, Cooper dove right in. And she could see why. Once she shredded a bite of the juicy, perfectly seasoned chicken breaded with the ideal amount of lemon and earthy, peppery spices, she didn't even bother with her fork anymore.

First the front seat and now eating with her hands? She was conquering all kinds of milestones because of this man. "I take it all back, Cooper," she said with her mouth full. "These are so good!"

"Yeah? I was beginning to wonder if you liked them." He grinned at the telltale pile of bones picked clean on her plate. "Does our pizza crust do them justice?"

Sloane answered by tearing into another

wing. "You should rename your restaurant after whatever chef came up with these."

Cooper snickered, and they polished off the last few wings in lip-smacking, finger-licking silence.

"You know, Sloane." Cooper wiped his mouth with a crumpled napkin. "It's been really fun tonight. You have a wonderful smile."

A slow pour of heat spread from her hairline to the back of her neck. "Thanks," she mumbled. "And, to think, you got me loosened up without the assistance of alcohol."

Without the assistance of alcohol? Really?

Cooper sat up straighter in his seat. "Is that what it usually takes, then?" There was no judgment or accusation in the question, just a curiosity in his eyes.

"No. I don't know why I said that. I don't drink pretty much ever."

Relief bowed Cooper's shoulders as he blew out a deep breath. "Me, either. I'll tell you a little secret. I—"

Paw-like hands clamped down on his shoulder and Sloane's at once, sending her pulse into a dizzying rhythm. It wasn't an assailant. It was just Cooper's father, alone and looking oddly pedestrian in a ball cap and plain navy polo.

"What are you doing here?" He pulled Cooper to his feet, staggering a little bit. Not acknowledging Sloane's presence as he sized his son up. His face was red and shiny, his speech slurred. Clearly intoxicated. "Have you been drinking again?"

Mr. Cooper's booming voice caught the bartender's attention over the volume of the crowd. He darted ominous glances at the two men.

"No, Dad," Cooper said through his teeth. "I haven't."

"You know what happens if you start drinking, if you take one sip." His father jabbed a thumb into his own chest, swaying with the effort. "You end up like—oh." Sloppy features tightened in distaste when Mr. Cooper registered Sloane. "Oh. What do we have *here*?"

Invisible hands squeezed Sloane's throat at his degrading emphasis on the last word.

The life drained from Cooper's expression. "We're just getting some wings, Dad." He stepped toward his father, reaching back to give her knee the slightest squeeze. A way of apologizing for his father, she understood.

"So you have time to go out with her while your acquisitions are down thirty percent?" He spread shaking palms a foot apart. "While you're missing meetings and have a stack this high in your office to go through?"

"I think we'd better call you a cab." Cooper motioned to the bartender. "He's had enough."

His father slammed a fist onto the wood, rattling the glasses and silverware, drawing every pair of eyes. "Listen to me!" The bartender lumbered toward them, but Mr. Cooper raised his palms in surrender. "It's okay. Call the dogs off." His voice hardened, attention returning to his son. "If you want to learn the hard way—again—have at it. But I want you in at seven-thirty to brief me on the Sanderson pitch, and you'd better be sharp, kid."

The tips of Cooper's ears reddened, his jaw knotted. "That's fine. We were just leaving." The calm chill in his voice sent a shiver down Sloane's spine. Cooper tossed a few bills onto the bar and squeezed her elbow. "You ready?"

The night-and-day contrast of tenderness in his voice for her with the humiliation in his eyes pulled deep in her chest. She pushed off her stool and followed him.

It was like Cooper had been reduced to a little boy after exchanging verbal blows with his father. What on earth was going on behind the closed doors of J. Marian Restaurants? Sloane had always gotten an unsettling vibe from the older Cooper, but no wonder his son was quick to correct anyone who called him Graham.

"You're not doing this because of Jordan, are you?" Mr. Cooper's voice pierced through the hum of the bar.

There was that name again. Jordan.

Cooper's posture went rigid. She could see the outline of his Adam's apple bobbing up and down. "Get home safe, Dad."

"Seven-thirty."

And just like that, their evening was over, the lingering taste of lemon-pepper wings now stale. The friendly banter they'd enjoyed replaced by a rigid silence that made the fall Texas night seem arctic.

CHAPTER ELEVEN

IT WAS NIGHTFALL the next day when Sloane's car dropped her off at *Simone* for another round of recipe development. She had lost track of time answering emails after she'd accidentally written tablespoons instead of teaspoons of baking soda on a recipe.

Working with J. Marian Restaurants was ruining everything—even her readers' cookies.

She'd also had to pick up her running shoes from the dry cleaners after stepping in some unknown sticky substance that refused to leave the cracks and seams despite her best arsenal of cleaning tactics. And after a day of missed running, that errand wasn't negotiable.

Cooper hadn't been far from her mind since last night at the bar. It was a strange tug-of-war, trying to remember they barely knew each other when her empathy kept him closer to her thoughts than should be.

Her phone buzzed in the canvas tote that was doubling as her purse.

Almost here?

A text from Cooper. And another one she hadn't seen in her hurry to clear her inbox.

Dress comfortably.

Sloane looked up as the restaurant door opened, and there he was. Something maniacal flickered in his eyes, a crazy grin taking up half his face. A suspicious grin. What was up with him?

"Let's go."

"What?" Go? Where? That wasn't the plan.

He cocked his head toward the street. "It's a surprise. C'mon."

No way. Sloane didn't do surprises. "What about the recipes we're supposed to be shooting?"

"Listen, Sloane." He rested his hands on her shoulders. "Sometimes you have to relax. We've been working hard."

Sloane heaved an exaggerated sigh, and Cooper's face angled to the ground.

"It's the least I can do after the other night." His voice softened.

So that's why he was so insistent. "Cooper, no. You don't need to—" Her mind went blank as his hands fell from her shoulders. She didn't know what to say. He wasn't apologizing or explaining, so neither of those words fit. But he definitely looked guilty about the whole thing.

"The photos will look better in daylight anyway." Cooper's expression brightened.

The man had a point.

"Fine. Where are we going?"

He wiggled his eyebrows. "Like I said, it's a surprise." His eyes slid down her form and stopped at her patent leather flats. A line creased between his eyebrows. "You didn't see my message."

"No, I just got it." Sloane looked down at her outfit. What was wrong with her ankle-length skinny jeans and black-and-white-striped top? "I have running shoes in my bag, if that helps," she offered.

Of all the days…

She cringed at the idea of bringing her running shoes into whatever mischief Cooper had planned, every mile of their wear logged in a spreadsheet. And they'd just returned from the cleaners. But the adrenaline from the mystery heating up her veins dulled her reservations.

"Where do you live?"

"Kind of in the West End."

His face twisted, calculating. "We can swing

by my apartment and get you a jacket or something to keep you warm." He nudged Sloane out of the doorway and squeezed her elbow. Her brain was racing way too fast to protest.

Cooper seemed unable to sit still on the drive to his place. He was like a little kid, fidgeting in his seat, checking his surroundings, holding back laughter.

"The Defender," as Cooper called it, turned into an alley behind a quiet tree-lined street in Deep Ellum and pulled up to a security gate of a covered parking garage. Cooper pressed a gate opener in his console and parked in a numbered spot.

Something anchored Sloane in her seat at the thought of going in Cooper's home. Wouldn't that be crossing some sort of professional boundary? "I'll just stay here."

"Okay." He paused as he was about to shut his door. "But you can put your camera stuff inside just to make sure it's safe if you want to. I know Maddie would love to meet you, too."

Maddie? Who was Maddie?

Her heart pounded as Cooper led her to a landscaped sidewalk next to a fenced dog walk, it looked like, and up the second path to their right that led to the door of a tall, handsome brownstone.

"Maddie, I'm home!" he called, jiggling his keys loose from the door. But when the keys were stuffed in his pocket, the jingling sound continued, getting louder until a big black dog appeared from the hallway.

Sloane laughed out loud, an uncontrollable product of relief and self-ridicule. "You didn't tell me your... Maddie...was a dog!"

The dog pranced in excitement, shifting her weight back and forth on stiff legs as if trying to fight the urge to jump. She yawned and stretched.

"Oooh, someone was sleepy." Cooper took the dog's face in his hands and scratched her ears. "It's short for Madeleine, because she's one of my favorite sweets." He spoke about Maddie with the pride of a new dad announcing that his newborn baby had arrived.

The dog noticed Sloane for the first time and perked up, resuming her excited little dance.

Sloane took a step back. "Hi, Maddie." She reached a tentative hand out to pat the dog's squared head and was rewarded with a swath of pink tongue across her palm. "Oh, hi!"

Must. Get. Hand sanitizer.

"I'll let you two get acquainted while I find you something to wear."

Sloane had graduated to scratching the dog's

upturned belly by the time Cooper jogged down the stairs, a wad of black fleece clutched to his chest.

"This is too small for me now. I kept it because Simone bought it for me."

"It'll work." Sloane held it up for inspection and breathed it in. Its clean detergent with a drop of Cooper's spicy cologne already made her feel warmer.

"It'll swallow you whole." Cooper grinned. "But it will work."

ONCE THEY WERE back in Cooper's truck, Sloane's excitement manifested in a rogue case of restless legs syndrome. Yet another reason she didn't like to skip her scheduled runs. She kicked her flats off and changed into her running shoes to keep her lower half occupied.

Since she'd never driven in Dallas and didn't venture far past downtown, Sloane had no idea which direction they were going, nor where this particular highway led.

Cooper steered onto an exit ramp and glanced at Sloane. The dance his eyes were doing and the fact that she could see all of his teeth clued her in that they must be getting close. Then she saw it in the darkness, a network of glittering lights crowned by a tall Ferris wheel.

Her jaw dropped. "The Texas state fair?"

"The one and only." Cooper bypassed a long line of cars for a lot near the front, rolling down his window and slipping the attendant a purple pass of some sort. "Please say you haven't been here before."

"It's my first time." Sloane couldn't tear her eyes away from the Ferris wheel. A smile twitched, one she quickly trapped under her teeth. Aaron was scared of heights—terrified. She'd gotten him to ride the Ferris wheel one October only after winning a bet. The way he completely fell apart at the top made his incessant complaints one-hundred-percent worth it.

And this monstrosity made the puny one at the little county fair in Indiana look like a wheel in a hamster cage.

The sound of Cooper's low laughter brought Sloane to the present.

"What?" She tugged his fleece around her, relishing its soft warmth.

"Nothing. I've just never seen someone so enamored with the Texas Star."

"Was I staring?"

"You, um, kind of can't take your eyes off of it."

She laughed then adjusted the strap of her bag, much lighter than usual without her camera equipment, and blew out a breath.

This was an unfamiliar intersection—memories of Aaron that made her laugh? Spending time with someone—in the flesh—who thawed the cold dew of the past that tended to cling to every moment of her present? It felt off-limits, like it shouldn't be allowed.

A gentle breath of wind rustled against the exposed back of her neck. A breath of peace. And permission.

"It's okay." Cooper pressed his lips together. "I'll give you a moment if you need one. Really."

No, she didn't need a moment. She would laugh at the memory of Aaron hyperventilating if she felt like it. She would stop looking through the peephole of her own life and open the door—even if only a crack.

"Okay, I think I'm good."

At the ticket booth, again Cooper produced some kind of magical pass that got them past the long line to the unoccupied second counter.

"Does being in the Cooper family get you a Proceed-to-the-Front-of-the-Line card?"

Cooper's expression darkened. "Something like that." He checked his watch. "C'mon. We have a little less than an hour to do whatever we want."

"Including the Texas Star?"

He cracked a smile. "Especially the Texas Star."

Mission accomplished. With both the smile and the Star.

The first thing Sloane noticed was the unmistakable sweet smell of batter hitting hot oil. It was glorious. They walked past booths and vendors and makeshift buildings until they reached a T in the path where a large pair of painted plastic boots stood. Sloane looked straight up.

And up.

And up some more.

She got the full breadth of the Texas state fair mascot, the giant cowboy Big Tex's height. "I think I'm going to have a seizure."

"You can write your medical bills off as workers' comp." Cooper motioned to their left and started walking. "They can send the invoice to J. Marian Restaurants, care of the CEO."

Sloane laughed at the image of his red-faced father seated in a plush mahogany office somewhere getting that bill.

"So what's the number-one fair tradition you judge the most?"

Sloane fidgeted with the matted cuffs of Cooper's too-long jacket as they walked. "I'm not quite sure what you mean?"

"Is it the abundance of mullets? The exorbitant price you pay to stand in line most of the time? The fried foods?"

She wrinkled her nose at his last suggestion.

"The fair food? C'mon, everybody loves the fair food!" he said.

"I'm just not sure I agree with their mantra that literally *everything* is better fried." They approached a bank of food vendors with bold red marquees listing their offerings. "I mean, a deep-fried bacon cinnamon roll?"

"Eat one thing." Cooper's tone dared her. "Just one. I'm buying."

Did he know how many miles she'd have to run to burn off one of those things? She was pretty sure there wasn't a calorie counting app in existence that could tally the damage of a fried bacon cinnamon roll.

Oooh. Her tune changed when she saw the Fried Cookie Dough emblazoned above one of the vendors. And unfortunately, the words slipped right out of her mouth.

"Okay, it's settled."

"Settled that I'm not eating anything? You're exactly right."

Someone walked by with one of those cardboard boats, wafting the scent straight through her nose to her brain and taste buds. The sight of those twin orbs of dough fried to a golden crisp and sprinkled with powdered sugar drew her closer. The drizzle of chocolate sauce did her in. Perfection.

"You'll share it with me?" Sloane turned to Cooper who was already standing in a mercifully short line.

They devoured the fried cookie dough as they walked. It was sweet then savory. Crunchy then creamy. Like he'd been doing all night—maybe ever since she met him—Cooper had somehow convinced Sloane to ignore the ramifications. To kick her reservations to the curb for a little while.

Cooper tossed the container into a wide plastic bin. "Ready for another one?"

Sloane shook her head. "I'm actually enjoying myself tonight. And I want it to stay that way."

She almost didn't hear Cooper's low voice against the chatter and carnival music around them. "I'm glad you're having fun."

They walked in silence for a while, watching the people who passed them. "You know, I was afraid this was going to be rough. This many people." She scratched her forehead. "I don't know if you've gathered this, but I'm not exactly a big crowds kind of girl."

Cooper dipped his head a little then nodded.

"But it's been fun. Thanks for talking me into blowing off work. I might let you do it more often." Her breath lodged in her throat when her brain caught up with that last bit. "I mean, um, I'm learning to be more flexible. The whole work-fun balance and everything."

Just stop.

He grinned at her the way he'd grin at a baby deer, all spindly legs, bumbling around. "You don't have anything to be afraid about with fair people. They don't bite. Well, at least most of them don't—oh, man."

"What?"

Cooper had stopped in front of a bank of fair games. "The High Striker."

"The what?" He didn't answer her, glazed eyes fixed on the flashing lights that resembled a really tall thermometer. "Oh, the hammer thing?"

He nodded, jaw working. "I used to *love* this. My brother and I always argued over who got to swing first. And then our dad would move us aside and hit it all the way to the top every time. We thought he was the strongest dad in the world."

"You should try it."

"Yeah?"

Sloane planted her hands on his firm back and nudged him in the direction of the game, catching the attention of the balding fair worker who was polishing off a turkey leg. The erratic fiddle of a country song came over the loudspeaker.

"Step on up and take a swing, sir." The carny tossed the turkey bone into the trash and scrubbed his hands down the sides of his blue polo. "Or young lady?"

She took a step away from the dingy plastic handle he offered her and flashed the politest smile she could muster. There was no way she was touching that thing without some kind of hazmat suit.

Cooper paid and unzipped his cotton hoodie, handing it to Sloane. He took the mallet from the man, muscles contracting through his thin T-shirt down his triceps and forearms as he twisted it in his hands and squared up to the High Striker. He balanced on the balls of his feet and tested the motion before swinging it with the explosive force of a lumberjack splitting firewood. In an instant, the gong at the top sounded, and computerized arcade music drowned out the country twang.

Cooper whirled, fists pumping at his sides. A laugh bubbled from Sloane at the triumph in his expression, drowned by the booth worker's booming cry. "Winner!"

He tugged her elbow to the display of stuffed animals and prizes and pointed at one. The booth worker pulled a small stuffed black puppy from the row. And the look in Cooper's eyes obliterated the visions of germs and dust mites squirming in Sloane's mind as he extended the puppy to her.

"From me and Maddie."

She couldn't ruin this gesture. Not when he'd been so kind to her. If the puppy were riddled with contaminates, surely the spicy, apple cider warmth that rushed from Sloane's core up to her earlobes and down to her fingertips would neutralize it. Right?

"Thanks." She tucked the puppy into her purse so its head was barely visible between the straps. "He can, um, hang out in here."

They walked toward the midway, Sloane's grip tight around the handle of her bag. *It's just a puppy.*

But if it was just a puppy, why did looking at

Cooper feel like a risk? The answer was easy and so complicated at the same time.

Because one glance would undoubtedly turn up the burner on the unfamiliar stir-fry sizzling in her middle.

CHAPTER TWELVE

COOPER DEBATED CANCELING his Saturday plans with Davon.

His father had shown up to the restaurant unannounced the day before to "check in" on some outstanding emails—and probably to ensure Cooper hadn't been drinking—effectively ruining his postfair good mood. After working late to catch up, Cooper was snapped like a wishbone between conflicting urges to take some serious tension out in the weight room or settle into his sofa for a shoot-'em-up movie marathon on TV. His third option prickled the back of his neck like the sensation of being watched, unvoiced because the minute those words came to life in his mind, his willpower would be gone.

What would Simone say if she saw him like this, or worse, pouring fifty dollars down the drain and stashing the bottle? She was always good for a dose of tough love. But she'd probably roll her eyes and tell him he was being "ree-dee-cu-LOSS."

It had to stop. Cooper had to figure out some way to stay on top of things at work and still get everything done for the restaurant launch. And there were a lot of things to do.

So instead, he went to the restaurant to check on employee training and get off on the right foot with the people who'd be operating his restaurant. He trusted Janet to run a tight ship with an enjoyable work atmosphere, and the employees she'd hired seemed to have it together already.

Cooper's phone was a permanent fixture in his grip, tethered to his temptation to call in sick with Davon and the itch in his fingers to dial Sloane's number and satisfy his curiosity. He'd been introduced to a whole new dimension of her at the fair. Would she revert to the starched suit when they met later tonight to work on some more recipes?

Focus, Coop. There was no way he was going to set the precedent of bailing on Davon, even if he hadn't exactly signed up for this. Plus, it would mean Davon's mother would have to find other child-care arrangements for her study session.

So Cooper left early and, as the Defender

rolled into the crumbling parking lot of Davon's apartment complex, his attitude completely changed.

Davon answered the door before Cooper could knock. "Cooper! You're here!"

"Yeah! Ready to go have some fun?"

He nodded so fast it would have given anyone else whiplash, his green eyes enormous. "I forgot! I want to show you something." He disappeared down a hallway.

The excitement on the boy's face made Cooper feel at once like a million dollars and an inch small. How could he have even considered not showing up?

Davon's mother, Alicia, stood in the doorway of the apartment's kitchen, drying a plate. "Do you want to come in? Can I get you some water?"

"Oh, I'm all right. But thanks." He stepped onto the chipped yellow kitchen floor, which smelled like lemon cleaner.

They'd met before—twice now—when Cooper dropped off Davon. Each time, Alicia donned a contagious smile, her brown eyes, though tired, still shining bright.

Davon returned with a basketball, smaller than the NBA standard size, striped with the

Dallas Mavericks' blue and green. "Look what I won at school!"

"Cool. Is that an autograph?"

Davon rattled off the name of a player Cooper had met a few times with Owen and explained that the player had visited his school.

Cooper filed away a mental note. If Davon was this excited about meeting a player from the Dallas Mavericks' bench, what would he think about sitting courtside at a game? Meeting the team in the locker room? Maybe getting to keep one of the players' old shoes? Sometimes Owen's shameless desire to tout his connections really did pay off.

"Where are y'all headed today?" Alicia looked between Cooper and Davon.

"Oh, just to the Treasure Center." Cooper wiggled his eyebrows, but was met with a blank stare from Davon. How could he not know what the Treasure Center was? It was one of the most fun places for kids in the Dallas-Fort Worth metro.

Alicia nudged her son. "You've heard of it, Davon. Remember, that commercial you saw? The go-karts?"

Davon's eyes lit up at the last word. "Go-karts? We get to ride go-karts?" He hurried to the door. "See ya, Mom!"

"Oh, uh-uh." Alicia donned a practiced mom attitude that made Cooper grin. "I think you're forgetting something."

Davon checked to see if Cooper was watching. "Yes, ma'am." He trudged to his mother and gave her a hug and a kiss. "I love you, Ma."

"I love you, too. You be good for Mr. Cooper." She turned to Cooper. "If he doesn't act right for you, I want you to bring him home that instant, okay?"

Cooper gave her a two-finger salute. "Yes, ma'am." Somehow he didn't think that was going to be a problem.

Davon could hardly contain himself on the way, shifting in the backseat every few seconds, it seemed. Fortunately, they didn't have far to go before the animated alligator mascot of the Treasure Center appeared in the distance. It had been updated since Cooper had last seen it, but still sported its trademark pirate eye patch.

The last time he'd been to the Treasure Center was during grad school at an after-hours party. The details of that night were all sort of staticky, but he'd had to foot the bill for some serious damages. And he was pretty sure they'd banned alcohol from the premises after that. Surely that manager was long gone, though, right?

"Wow." Davon stopped in the doorway of the main floor arcade.

"Yeah. It's legit."

Cooper's senses were assaulted by sugared-up kids whizzing past him, the tinny sound of arcade games and the smell of cheap pizza—a special kind of heaven that lost its luster for adults. But he was going to find that kid inside of him if it was the last thing he did. For Davon.

"Well?" Cooper snapped the boy out of his sensory overload. "What'll it be first? Video games? Pizza? Putt-putt?"

Davon tilted his head back and measured Cooper up. "*Anything*, Mr. Cooper?"

Cooper nodded. "Anything. And it's just Cooper to you, my man."

"Go-karts!"

Cooper should have predicted that hybrid shout-laugh response. They encountered a long line—apparently the go-karts were the popular attraction. And since the name Cooper was more associated with destruction than charitable donation here, there was no skipping to the front of the line this time.

The wind had picked up, a touch cooler than

it had been at the fair but still a few weeks away from hat-and-gloves weather. A hint of pungent exhaust from the go-kart motors tailed the breeze. Suddenly Cooper was twelve again.

Davon craned his neck past the line, eyes glued to the track as the cars whizzed past them with their chipped, bright paint jobs and grating engines.

Then a thought occurred to Cooper. Could Davon get hurt on one of those things? Should he have asked for Alicia's permission first? Was the kid even tall enough to drive them? The height marker on the post next to a few people in front of them indicated Davon was a few inches taller than the minimum requirement. But Cooper was still wary.

Then his gaze moved to the right of the line. There was a separate corral of sorts, but the line was totally empty. Double Riders, it said in bold lettering with a checkered border. The perfect solution. Though he was pretty much making up the whole Big Brother thing as he went along, at least they had go-karts.

"Hey, what would you think about heading to the front of the line and riding shotgun with me?" He offered a high five, and Davon slapped it eagerly.

"Yeah!"

There were two double-occupancy go-karts and zero demand for them. So Cooper and Davon got to ride their shiny green one around and around again.

Cooper drove extra carefully at first, but once he got a little confidence, he took off with it, passing other drivers—not discriminating whether they were grown men or preteen girls—and narrating every move for Davon over the volume of the motor like a cheesy sports announcer.

After their sixth turn around the track, what Cooper assumed to be a group of fathers and sons was waiting for them at the beginning of the line.

"Want to wait in line and go again?" Cooper shook out his hands, trying to wring out the buzz of the engine's vibration that still reverberated through his fingers.

Davon shook his head, lips pursed as he watched the pairs file past them. "Did your old man bring you here when you were a kid?"

The question sucked the air from Cooper's lungs. "Yeah, he did." Images filled his mind. Fighting with Owen over who got to ride with their dad—a very different version of their dad. Dividing up tokens. Gobbling pizza so they could begin their mad frenzy to spend those tokens.

Davon's wilted posture and glazed expression put a halt to his trip down memory lane.

Cooper felt like the biggest loser to ever walk the earth. He might want to strangle his father sometimes, but at least his was still alive. "What do you want to do next?" He nudged the boy's shoulder to get his attention.

"I think I'm ready to school you in basketball now."

Cooper grinned. "School *me*? Please. Do you even know who you're talking to?"

"Some washed-up white boy?" The tone of Davon's voice deepened, giving him the chops of someone much older. A sly smirk spread across his face, but the message in his eyes was playful, good-natured.

So that was how it was going to be. Okay.

"Let's go." Cooper raised his eyebrows in challenge, biting back his urge to inform the boy that he was starting something with the person who set a Texas state scoring record in high school. He wasn't ready to return the trash talk. At least not today. But when the kid was a little older, it was on.

He put a few bills in the coin machine and retrieved the gold tokens, handing some of them to Davon. The arcade-style basketball game was open, twin hoops corralled by netting. "Ready?"

Davon was already putting his coins in the slot. "That depends. Are you ready to lose, Mr. Coop?"

"Keep talking, Davon. Keep talking." Cooper pushed his own coins through the slot and punched the flashing red button to start the game.

A lever flooded several basketballs through to the holding pin. Cooper picked one up, measuring its smaller grip and size in his palms so he could adjust his muscle memory.

But Davon got right to work. He missed the first one and then drained two in a row.

Forget the fact that he was a kid. Davon's fluid shot was lights-out good.

Okay. Yup. Forget later. It was on *now*.

Cooper tried to concentrate on his own hoop, making good on most of his attempts. But it was hard not to notice Davon swishing shot after shot. The buzzer sounded half a minute later, and the score was lopsided.

He'd been beaten when he was actually trying. By an eight-year-old kid.

Davon's mouth stayed clamped, dimples

trenched in both cheeks. The triumph and gloat in his eyes said everything.

"Do you want to play again?" Cooper asked through his teeth. Could his pride even take another beating?

"Naw. I won't do that to you, son."

After a few different games—Cooper watching and cheering for Davon from a safe distance—they broke for some pizza. Better pizza. At a place Cooper had grown up eating that wasn't too far away.

"So, how long have you known Miss Sloane?" Davon shielded a mouthful of cheese with his hand.

"Oh, a few weeks. You?"

"She's been doing the classes since I was six." Something flickered in Davon's eyes. "Is she your *girlfriend*?"

Cooper almost choked on his water. "We work together." The image of Sloane pulling her sweater up over her bare shoulder hijacked his mind. "We're just friends."

"But you want it to be more, right? I see you."

He felt his face flush. "Has anyone ever told you you're nosy, Davon?" Cooper made sure the tail end of his sentence was light. Because the front end had been a little stilted. Off his game.

Davon grinned and took another bite of pizza. "All the time."

They went to a see a Pixar movie when they were finished eating even though Davon tried to finagle Cooper into a PG-13 one.

Alicia had insisted on picking her son up when she finished her study session at four, and her pale blue sedan was in front of the movie theater as they'd arranged.

"Thanks, Coop." Davon retrieved his things from the Defender and then buried his face in Cooper's side, stretching his arms around his torso. And Cooper could have sworn he heard the muffled words, "It was the best day of my life."

As he drove behind them for a few blocks, the picture of the mother and son in front of him brought back the heart-churning conviction from earlier. The absence of Davon's father.

Cooper made a vow. No matter what happened, Davon and his mother were going to be taken care of. Always.

Cooper replayed the day in his mind, the fun he'd never expected to have. What was Davon telling his mother about their time together?

Schooled by an eight-year-old. Geez.

At a stoplight, he eased off his brake when

the signal turned green and Alicia's bumper started to creep forward. He didn't see it until the last moment, a green pickup truck hurtling through the intersection from the right.

Straight into the sedan's passenger side.

CHAPTER THIRTEEN

THE DOOR WAS locked when Sloane arrived at the restaurant, weighed down by a bag full of notebooks, another containing photography props and her camera. This was new. The lights were off inside, chairs overturned on the tables. Cooper was always there waiting for her.

"Where are you?" She spun around to look for him, but a small crowd of white-haired men and a pair of moms with strollers were the only people in sight.

Fifteen minutes later, the evening had seeped through her thin sweater to her skin. The sun had sunk behind the restaurant, bathing the entire street in shadow. With her shoulder now aching under the weight of the bag, Sloane set everything down and pulled her cell phone from her pocket. Maybe she'd missed another text from him. She scrolled through her contacts for Cooper's number.

"Hey, this is Cooper with J. Marian Restaurants. Please leave your name—"

She scowled and pressed the end button. Where could he be? He was always mindful of their time together.

Could something have happened to him? She felt the blood drain from her face. No. Something didn't always have to be wrong. He was a busy man, working a hectic job and about to open a restaurant, for goodness' sake. He'd probably forgotten or was stuck doing his father's bidding or something.

She drew in a deep breath and let it out slowly, willing her shoulders to release some of their tension.

Another ten minutes later, she'd given up on Cooper and texted him that she'd be at the Starbucks a few blocks away from the restaurant. She set up shop with a latte and her tablet, brainstorming a pressed cranberry and Brie sandwich for the fall.

The door to the coffee shop opened, allowing a gust of wind in. Cooper's voice startled her. "Sloane."

She prepared her sternest expression for him, but her frustration quickly disappeared as he approached and his features sharpened into focus. He was uncharacteristically rumpled, his expression pained.

"It's Davon. We gotta go."

Sloane's body tensed to protect itself from what he was about to say. Somehow it anticipated she was about to find out something terrible.

"Cooper..." She rose, fumbling for words. "What—what happened to him?"

"He's been in a car accident."

She stood paralyzed as Cooper picked up her notebook and tablet from the table and shoved them in her bag. "Oh, my word. Is he..." She swallowed cotton. "Is he *okay*?"

Davon's face flashed into her mind. Whole, grinning, ornery like she liked him to be. She couldn't picture him any other way. If she did, the fragile connections that held her life together would dissolve.

"They've taken him to Children's. I was in the car behind them and saw the whole thing happen. A teenage girl, texting. At least Alicia made it out fine."

Tears blurred Sloane's vision at those words. Fine? *Fine?* She was pretty sure that description couldn't be any further from how Davon's mother was doing at the moment.

Cooper slung her bag across his shoulders.

"Sloane? C'mon." He grabbed her hand and led her across the street where the Defender was still running and crookedly parked, half sticking into the street.

She climbed into the front seat, clinging to the leather upholstery with a white-knuckle grip, distantly aware of the ache in her nail beds.

Shattered glass. Metal crumpled like aluminum foil. The smell of leaking gasoline. Fighting was futile as the images invaded. Cooper's front seat felt like it would swallow her whole. Darkness slid from the periphery of her vision until she was transported to the accident.

To *their* accident.

"You're going to be fine," Aaron kept telling her, fisting blood from his nose. "Just don't look at it."

Both bones in her lower leg had broken multiple times just above the ankle. She was delirious and hysterical from the pain and the way her leg looked like contorted rubber twisted around the mangled undercarriage of her parents' car.

And then there was fire.

"Sloane, are you okay?" Cooper's voice ricocheted her to the present with whiplash intensity. He brought his hand up as if to grip her arm but let it drop to the console. "You're shaking."

She blinked hard—she didn't even realize she'd closed her eyes—and slackened the tension in her muscles until she was no longer wedged against the seat.

"Yeah. Yes." She set her jaw to project some semblance of confidence. Some illusion that she had it together.

Cooper sighed and covered her hand with his, spreading warmth up her arm. "He's gonna be fine, Sloane."

She wanted to believe him. But she'd heard that one before.

To wall off that dark place that threatened to consume her, Sloane turned on autopilot as Cooper navigated the hospital parking lot and leaned against the admitting counter to figure out what was happening to Davon. But her shield of numbness was no match for the piercing reality of the slump in his broad shoulders. The fingers that raked through his hair. The words that couldn't be cushioned no matter how gently Cooper spoke them.

Her favorite kid in the world had been rushed into emergency surgery. And all they could do was wait.

They found Alicia, her chin bandaged, clinging to her sister Tiffany in the waiting room. When she saw them approaching, she rushed to Cooper and collapsed into him. "Oh, thank God you're here."

"We came as soon as we could." Cooper wrapped his arms around the much shorter woman.

Alicia's bloodshot eyes sent pain like an electric shock through Sloane's chest. "Thank you for coming, too, Sloane."

She nodded and studied the speckled tile at her feet. It felt like she'd swallowed rubber cement.

Tiffany nodded from her chair. "Oh, you're all that child talks about." Her full lower lip trembled. "Miss Sloane this. Miss Sloane that. I can't believe you actually got the boy to eat some spinach. He never touches the stuff at home."

Sloane opened her mouth then flashed a look of desperation at Cooper when nothing came out. *A little help?*

"He'll be happy to know she's here when he wakes up," he supplied, rubbing Alicia's shoulder.

"They said they're doing exploratory surgery for internal bleeding," Tiffany told them, the mauve upholstery squeaking under her shifting weight. Her tear-stained face was frozen in a shell-shocked mask.

At this fresh reminder, Alicia pried herself from Cooper and sank into the chair next to her sister, burying a new round of tears into Tiffany's track jacket.

Cooper's eyes were laced with pain. He motioned to the perpendicular row of chairs, and Sloane sat with him, enveloped in tension that was almost palpable. She bent forward, forked her fingers through her hair and then sat up again, forcing everything out of her mind—her thoughts, her worries, her awareness of Cooper next to her and the panicked sisters sitting across from them. Numbness was beginning to overtake her when something breached her force field and poured energy into her bones.

Fingers pressed into her skin, maneuvering and exploring until they were laced with hers. The hand she was now touching was undeniably masculine. Knobby-knuckled, fingernails clean and trimmed. A map of textured scars and old oven burns.

She slid a sidelong glance at Cooper. His eyes were closed, faint whispers escaping from his lips. It was as if he was unaffected by the fact that he'd grabbed her hand, maybe unaware. As if the move was some sort of reflex.

But Sloane was aware. Aware of a strange, comforting feeling that was a night-and-day contrast to the pain. To the numbness. Was this what peace felt like? It'd been so long that it was hard for her to recognize it when it sneaked up on her.

Whatever it was, she wasn't about to stop it.

After what must have been a few hours of dozing and praying and fetching coffee, a gray-haired man in scrubs who she assumed was the surgeon appeared, talking to Davon's family with his back to Cooper and Sloane.

She'd been asleep, her head resting on Cooper's shoulder as the last warm semblances of safety were overcome by the searing reminder of their current reality. She sat up and snatched her hand away from the place it'd been resting near Cooper's knee.

He looked at her, something flickering in his eyes for an instant before it was gone. His focus, like Sloane's, was on the hushed conversation taking place between Davon's mom and the surgeon. From the way their hands were covering their mouths, Sloane couldn't tell if the prognosis was good or bad. Temptation clawed at her to eavesdrop, but she forced herself to stay planted out of respect.

Alicia and her sister disappeared behind the

heavy metal doors without a word to them or glance in their direction.

"Where are they going?" To say goodbye?

No. *Don't fear the worst, Sloane. Don't even go there.*

Cooper stared at the doors as if trying to see through them. "I'm sure he's just waking up and they want to be there when he opens his eyes."

Sloane's head bobbed in agreement, but she was only half-cognizant of what Cooper had said. They stared at the door for a long measure before he snapped into motion. "Let's get you some more tea," he suggested. "They have a great little coffee shop in the basement. C'mon."

They returned five minutes later, a throwaway cup of Earl Grey in Sloane's hands and an order of strong black coffee in his. At the same time, the heavy double doors squealed open and there was Tiffany.

"Oh, good," she said. "You're still here."

"Is he…?" Sloane didn't dare finish her sentence.

"Awake? Kind of. They had to remove his spleen where the seat belt hit it."

Sloane released a breath she didn't know she'd been holding.

"They'll have to keep a close eye on him." She took off her glasses and slipped them into a hard case from her purse. "But it could have been a lot worse, you know?"

"Yes, it could have," Cooper murmured.

Tiffany pulled her cell phone from her purse and tapped the screen with a hot pink acrylic fingernail. "I need to make some phone calls. But Lici told me to tell y'all to come on back when you're ready."

"Oh, no." Sloane held her palm up in surrender at the same time Cooper said, "Yeah, that'd be great."

"We don't need to do that," she said before Cooper could protest.

He furrowed his eyebrows, searching Sloane's eyes, and she saw it. The realization that something wasn't right with her. It was clicking in his mind, if he hadn't already pieced it together.

"She really needs the company," Davon's aunt persisted. "It would be good for Davon to hear your voices, if you can."

Great. How was Sloane supposed to say no to that?

So she allowed Cooper to lead her through the double doors, focusing on her tiptoe steps as she tried not to touch the lines of the square tiles. She must have looked ridiculous, but compulsion paid no mind to appearances.

Cooper tapped a timid cadence on the glass door as they walked in Davon's room.

Darkness clouded the edges of Sloane's vision as she laid eyes on Davon, small and swallowed in the big hospital bed. Surrounded by blankets and machines to the point that his big green eyes were pretty much the only visible part of him.

She gripped Cooper's elbow to steady herself.

Davon looked so little. So scared.

So much like Aaron at that age.

Sitting by his bedside was Alicia with the protective posture of a lioness.

Sloane bit her lip and resisted the urge to double over. It was as if she'd swallowed a bunch of nails and her throat had been glued shut. It was crippling to see Davon like this.

I shouldn't be here.

Cooper inched toward the bed and gently touched the slim lump of Davon's arm under the hospital sheet. "We're here for you, buddy."

Davon's heavy eyes fluttered a fraction wider and then closed completely. Sloane backed into the wall. Any second now, the nurses were going to bust in here and do their thing to try to save his life. But the machines stayed steady, and Davon's chest rose and fell in an easy rhythm.

"We should go," Cooper whispered, crossing the room to Alicia's chair. She stood to hug him and whispered something Sloane couldn't understand.

Cooper nodded and his lips moved in response. But over her shoulder, his golden-brown eyes were trained on Sloane with concern. A concern that didn't soften even as they said goodbye to Davon's family and navigated the maze of the parking garage.

The drive to Sloane's apartment was silent. When it was clear Cooper wasn't ready to ask the questions in his eyes, she stopped fighting to appear composed and normal and allowed the melancholy to wrap its cold, bony, familiar arms around her. To numb the piercing pain that had taken residence in her chest and wash away Aaron's haunting smile that was burned in her memory.

The silence stretched until Cooper walked her from the curb to the door of her building. "Are you going to be all right?" He took a half step toward her.

The unguarded care in his eyes made the muscles in her face slacken for half a second before her measured facade of control fell into place.

No, she was not all right. How could she explain to him that she was skirting the edge of a thousand-foot rock face? Why today, after Davon's accident, after seeing him in that hospital bed, she was hanging on with white knuckles?

Sloane mustered a smile and nodded, adjusting her bag on her shoulder. "I'm fine." *Always fine*. "Just worried about Davon. Call me when you figure out when works best to reschedule."

Her heels scraped against the concrete, unable to take her away from Cooper fast enough. Her mind was a tangle of confusion. How could his presence put her at ease one minute and make her completely unhinged the next? How much longer until he found out the truth? He was too perceptive for his own good.

Then there was the image of Davon in the hospital bed to contend with. The mental picture she wished she could somehow erase or override with something happy. Because any time her mind went there, it inevitably crept to hard places she'd rather not confront at that moment. Or ever.

CHAPTER FOURTEEN

COOPER WATCHED SLOANE disappear into her lobby. Should he say something? Go after her? She clearly wasn't okay.

Yet she clearly wanted to work through it alone. Or not work through it at all.

He drove home. He pretended to watch the news. Took Maddie for a walk. But as he hung Maddie's leash on its hook, he grabbed his keys.

If Sloane didn't want to talk, he could at least take her to the restaurant and make something that would help her feel better.

"C'mon, Maddie. Let's go see Sloane."

The dog ran in excited hops to the car. Cooper dialed Sloane's number, but got voice mail. "Look, I don't care if you're in your pajamas. I want to make us some food." At a stoplight, he sent her a text saying the same.

"I'm here to see Sloane Bradley," he told the lobby attendant, who was watching what appeared to be a courtroom drama on a small black-and-white TV.

The man straightened, lines of recognition creasing on his forehead. "Sir, she hasn't come back in from her run."

A run? In the dark downtown? Did she do this often?

"How long has she been gone?"

"Mmm, no longer than an hour or so."

Cooper squinted at his watch. "I'll wait outside."

He walked to the Defender, wind whipping through his button-down shirt, then moved the vehicle to an empty spot with a full view of the building entrance. At this rate, Sloane had run at least six miles. Was she a hard-core runner? Maybe she'd stopped for water or a coffee somewhere.

Thirty minutes later, a pool of acid had taken residence under Cooper's rib cage. Raindrops plinked against the windshield, each one pumping an urgent energy into his veins until he physically couldn't stay still another second. He had to do something.

He turned the key in the ignition. The streets of downtown Dallas passed in blurred lights and lines of rainwater streaming down his windows. Wet wind cut across his cheeks when he opened his window to make his search a little easier. The area around her apartment was pretty much deserted except for a few hurried corporate drones getting off work late.

No sign of Sloane.

He gripped the steering wheel with jittery hands, adrenaline and panic pumping through his muscles. What if something had happened to her? What if she'd passed through one of the parks where the homeless congregated? He'd seen horror stories on the news about those places.

Maybe she'd taken some odd, zigzagging route. He turned in the direction of her apartment. She could be home taking a warm shower for all he knew. His phone—he'd checked about a hundred times—showed she still hadn't called.

He parked in the same spot, not bothering to pay the meter, and sprinted across the street. Something lurched in his chest as he saw her in the glow of the lobby light, bent at the waist under the canopied entrance. Her body heaved, taking in massive gulps of air.

"Sloane?"

She tensed and bolted upright, scrubbing under her eyes with her palms before she turned in a stiff movement.

"Are you all right? I—I was looking everywhere for you." He shook droplets of water from his hair, giving no care about how creepy he must sound.

"What are you doing here, Cooper?" Her tone was as gray as the washed-out cityscape around them. "Is it Davon?"

"Your doorman told me you went for a run." He let out a shaky breath and brought a hand up to squeeze the back of his neck. "You've been running this whole time?"

"Is. Davon. Okay?" Sloane took a step toward him and pitched forward into Cooper's arms, her nose scrunching before she quickly straightened away from him.

Was she hurt? Cooper's gaze fell to her bare legs, to a scar on the outside of her left leg that peeked from beneath her cropped tights and disappeared into her shoe. The sight of it, angry purple and jagged against her pale skin, electrocuted him.

Sloane pivoted her leg out of his view. "Listen, I really need to go." She took a few steps toward the entrance. Short, stiff, clearly painful movements.

He wanted to help her. But when his gaze swept to her face, the unrelenting Job Interview Sloane was back. The Sloane who had been warming to him was gone.

"I—I just came to make sure you were okay. You seemed a little... I don't know." His eyes darted to her leg again before he could help himself and then settled onto the steely expression that seemed to challenge him, *I dare you to look at it again.*

"As I told you, I'm fine." Sloane smoothed the loose strands from her ponytail behind her ear. "I'm worried about Davon. Aren't you?"

She was a terrible liar.

"You sure about that?" He took a small step in her direction.

"Fine." She swallowed hard and pressed against the door of the building. "You know what? I'll email you to reschedule as soon as I have a minute. I have a pretty big ad campaign to work on this week."

Another deflection.

She pulled something from the pocket of her running jacket—a cloth handkerchief, it looked like—and fumbled the door open.

"Wait." Cooper had an idea. "Just one second. Wait."

He jogged to the Defender, pausing for a few cars to pass.

"C'mon, Maddie." If Sloane wouldn't allow

him to help her, then he would have to send in a backup.

Something that sounded like a cough came from Sloane when she saw Maddie bounding up to her. She bent awkwardly to rub the dog's ears, again favoring that left leg.

"Let Maddie keep you company."

"Coop—"

"No, please. I insist." He crouched next to the dog and looked at Sloane. "I'll pick her up in the morning. She's already eaten and won't be any trouble."

Sloane nodded.

"I don't want you to be alone right now."

Their eyes met over Maddie's head. For a moment, Cooper saw an explanation forming in Sloane's eyes. But she stood and whirled around, focused on Maddie at her feet. "C'mon, girl," she said without looking back.

Cooper's goodbye stuck in his throat, trapped in the sticky confusion of Sloane's mystery and the anguish in her eyes.

Who—or what—had done this to her? And how could he help her fix it?

CHAPTER FIFTEEN

THERE WASN'T ANYTHING she could do to stop it. The moment she lost the battle to her body's heavy exhaustion, she was in the car again, in her dad's Lexus sedan that she'd taken. Only this time, she was locked in a glass-walled prison in the periphery, fully aware she was dreaming.

She watched Aaron running around the rear of the car. Trying to open her door. Slamming on the window in frustration. "Open the sunroof!"

No. She wasn't going to look at him. In this dream, she was going to die with him.

But just like in reality, his long fingers gripped under her arms. She screamed as he lifted her through the opening in the roof, her lower leg folding like an accordion. But no sound came out.

"Don't look at it," Aaron said as he laid her on the side of the road a safe distance away. "Just look at me."

Dream Sloane pressed Override on Real Sloane's wishes, her chest twisting as she met his serious dark eyes. Blood trickled from his nose, dark and thick in the swaths of firelight from the fully engulfed car.

"My parents are going to kill me!"

He flashed his trademark crooked grin. "You think they're going to care about anything but us being okay?"

A faceless firefighter appeared beside Sloane and lifted her, no stretcher or neck stabilizer or anything. Was it worse when her dreams were exact replica flashbacks or when they deviated from what had really happened?

"No!" she screamed. "Take him first. He looks okay, but his brain is bleeding. If you take him first, you'll find it. I promise." But the firefighter continued to carry her toward the ambulance.

She squeezed Aaron's hand as tightly as she could, fighting the firefighter's momentum, until her body was almost parallel with the ground. She looked up for one last glimpse of Aaron's face.

But the smooth, sepia tone of his skin was lighter, his eyes softened to a caramel color. The warmth that had become familiar to her over the last few weeks shone, kneading her insides like dough.

"No!" Not Cooper.

At the sound of her scream, fear took the life out of Cooper's eyes, just as it had Aaron's. He squeezed her hand tighter, stretching her against the firefighter's pull.

"You're going to be okay, Sloane."

She woke up, drenched, in midmotion. Twisted in sweaty sheets, hanging halfway off of the bed.

Maddie's eyes shone in the darkness next to her and then dipped as she burrowed her warm snout under Sloane's hand, digging until her arm was draped around the dog's warm body.

Sloane untangled the sheets, rolled onto her side and curled around Maddie, using her as a warm compress against the place where the grief physically pained her middle. Where it pulled her inside out.

There was something new, something foreign within her. An ache to hear Cooper's voice, to reassure herself that he was all right.

At least the dream was over. At least she was free of that slide show of horrifying visions. When her breathing was finally manageable, Sloane pushed herself to the edge of her bed and waited for her sore legs to stop shaking so they could support her weight.

There was no hope of going back to sleep, she'd learned. So she pulled out another bag of frozen peas for her inflamed lower leg and unwrapped a new toothbrush from the supply she kept under her bathroom sink.

Her apartment was due for a deep clean anyway.

CHAPTER SIXTEEN

IT WAS FINALLY HERE, the moment he'd been dreading for the past four days. After Cooper had told his father's secretary the wrong time for Sloane's presentation, he didn't consider that Sloane would reschedule with his father directly. She and Cooper could have strategized together if she'd been willing to talk to him.

After he'd picked up Maddie from Sloane's apartment, she hadn't returned his calls or texts. Their communication was limited to emails containing only the most pertinent information. Still, Cooper read right through her behavior.

"Good morning."

Cooper turned and stifled a wince when he saw Sloane. She was pale, her eyes puffy and red despite some serious makeup. It looked like she'd fought a hard battle all night—and lost.

Yes, whatever motivated her change, it stemmed from something way deeper than

Davon's accident. She didn't have to do this meeting right now—he didn't want her to—but he suspected he'd be wasting his words if he told her that.

"Morning." He attempted a smile, but it couldn't have looked legitimate.

Sloane's hands jerked as if they had a mind of their own, trying to find something to do until they finally settled around the strap of her bag. "I apologize in advance because I had an energy drink and it seems to be having an adverse effect on me."

"Hey, don't worry. This is going to be a breeze." At least he hoped. "I told my dad's secretary to reserve the auditorium and have him meet us there." Cooper guided Sloane through a hallway on the ground floor of J. Marian Restaurants' high-rise.

"The auditorium?"

"Yeah. You'll see. If you give me your flash drive, I can set up your presentation." He pushed open a pair of metal doors, revealing a large room with rows of white leather chairs arranged in stadium style, sloping toward an asymmetrical stainless steel podium. Behind the stage a glass wall overlooked a manicured green space.

"Don't tell me J. Marian doubles as a college."

Cooper smiled. "Kind of. This room is used for franchisee trainings."

"That's a lot of franchisees."

"Yeah." He started down the steps. He'd stood at the podium hundreds of times addressing a crowded room. He opened the laptop mounted on the inside of the podium and looked up as he pressed the power button.

Sloane was shuffling down the steps one at a time, a grim expression on her face. The memory of the scar on her leg, dark and jagged, prompted him into motion.

"Let me help you. Is it your...leg?"

The desire to know the answers that would fill in the blanks about Sloane surged. But the way she yanked her arm away when he reached to help said he wasn't about to find out.

"That's not necessary. I'm just a little sore from my run the other day."

"I've already seen it, Sloane," he said. "You don't have to keep pretending something didn't happen to you."

She scowled. "Let's cut right to the chase, why don't we?" She pushed past him down the steps, pointedly masking her limp. "I don't want to talk about it, in case I haven't made myself clear."

"You can barely walk. You shouldn't be running—"

"Why does it matter right now? I'll be fine for our meeting that starts in—now."

Cooper massaged his forehead. "You've been kind of...off since Davon's accident."

"I'm always kind of off. It's who I am."

"Why?" His voice rose to meet hers, and he hastily lowered it. "You don't have to pretend with me."

The color faded from Sloane's face, bleak grief and fear exposed in her eyes.

"Whatever it is, you can't do this to yourself."

"No, Cooper." Sloane aimed a razor-sharp glare at him, but her lower lip trembled. "You don't understand. *You* can't even begin to understand."

He closed the distance between them. "So that's what this is about? You won't tell me because you think you know what it's like to be me?"

"What it's like to be a *Cooper*, you mean?" Sloane indicated the room with its uplit floors and rich furnishings. "If you don't like working for your dad, then quit. *You* can change that. I can't—" Her eyes widened for a second. "But apparently you aren't concerned about the way your life is going or else you'd have stood up to him by now."

His mouth fell open while she plugged her thumb drive into the computer as if nothing had happened.

"I need to take a walk." He climbed the steps three at a time then burst through the door so forcefully it slammed against the wall. Which he hated because it was exactly what his father would have done.

He kept his head low, ignoring the people in the hallway, until he took the rear entrance into the greenhouse—a warm, misty sanctuary of glass and fragrant green and bright, jewel-colored vegetables.

Cooper must have had a target painted over the lapels of his blazer. Because Sloane knew exactly where to aim to slice him the deepest.

He filled his lungs and allowed the humid air to replace the anger and lingering frustration.

It was true that Sloane had witnessed an un-edited version of his father running all over him that night at the bar. Real-life footage Cooper never let anyone see. Of course, she didn't know the full story. The leverage his father had on him, the complicated push-pull that ensured he'd work two jobs until the day he died. The pain that drove his father's ruthless tenacity—

Sloane.

Cooper had left her with his father.

He raced out of the greenhouse. A short-cut would get him to the pit through the instructor entrance on the main floor. When he opened the door, he saw his father standing over Sloane, his face purpled, fists balled at his sides.

"I don't know what you're talking about." She was indignant, unafraid as she shrugged past his father. "I think you're getting your facts mixed up, Mr. Cooper. I don't have *designs* on anyone. I'm only here because Marian asked for me, and Cooper needed my help with the restaurant."

"Oh, I'm not delusional. I heard with my own ears that there's something, probably a fat check, in it for you!" His voice rose another decibel. "My son—"

"Your son has more talent and *courage* in his pinky finger than you could ever have. That's what you're delusional about."

Cooper swallowed hard. She was fighting for him. She *believed* in him.

"If you can't see how online marketing can

help I Marian, then don't hire us," Sloane continued. "In the meantime I will do everything I can to make sure Cooper's restaurant is successful."

His father laughed, a low and foreboding sound. "That's sweet and all. But I don't trust a single word coming from you."

"And why's that? Because you think I'm out for money? I have plenty of money."

No. Cooper recognized the sinister triumph in his father's smile. With that first question, Sloane had all but doused herself with gasoline in the face of a lit match. His father definitely had some ammunition. And she'd all but locked and loaded it.

"Maybe I'll ask Aaron Jacobsen's parents how much I can trust you."

"Aaron?" Sloane choked out the name as her posture seemed to deflate.

Sloane's Achilles' heel. This was it. But how on earth did his father know? And why was he using it against her?

"H-how do you know about Aaron?" She sank into a chair in the front row, looking like she was going to lose her breakfast.

"Hey!" Cooper, finally spurred into action, moved to shield her from his father's view.

"Back off. Have you lost your ever-loving mind?"

His father squared his shoulders. "You don't know this girl from Eve." He looked toward Sloane in disgust. "She's like the rest of them—out to get what she wants."

Cooper flexed his hands to restrain himself from physically attacking his father. Two years ago with a little alcohol in him, this situation would've, no doubt, ended a much different way.

"Don't *ever* talk to her like that again," Cooper commanded. "In fact, don't ever talk to her again. If you have something to say, you can say it to me."

Graham Sr. deflated, as if Cooper had actually punched him. He definitely wasn't used to having *someone* stand up to him. Yet he recovered quickly, contempt radiating from him. "Do your research, son."

"I like my chances just fine."

"Suit yourself. Don't say I didn't warn you." His father started up the far aisle and disappeared through the doors. The slam of metal against frame echoed in the room.

Sloane released a shaky breath and buried her face in her hands.

She didn't deserve this. She'd done nothing

but help him. Nothing else mattered. Whatever it was, Cooper didn't want to know. Not after witnessing what it cost her.

"I'm so sorry." He knelt next to Sloane's chair, gripping her elbows. "I don't even know where that came from."

Her lips moved with soundless words, eyes filled with an untold anguish. Then she burst out of her seat, nearly knocking him over, snatched her bag and started up the stairs.

"Sloane!" Cooper caught up to her in long strides. "Please don't go."

"No, Cooper." Her voice echoed against the walls of the empty auditorium. "Your father's right. Not about the money part or whatever he thinks he overheard, but—" Sloane's face contorted. Angry, then defeated.

"You can tell me."

"If I tell you about Aaron, I can never take it back." She maneuvered out of his grip. "It will ruin everything."

She had no idea. If she saw him the way he saw himself, through a tunnel made of destruction and empty bottles, she could never believe that.

"I can guarantee—" he gave her a sad smile "—your worst has nothing on mine."

She shook her head; tears pooled in the corners of her eyes. "He was my best friend." Her words seemed to tumble out by their own free will.

"And I killed him."

CHAPTER SEVENTEEN

"WHAT—" COOPER CLEARED his throat. "What did you say?"

A sob escaped Sloane as she stumbled toward the door.

No. She had finally given him an inch and he wasn't letting it go. He matched her steps until he was looking her square in the face. "I don't believe for a minute you killed anyone."

"It's true." She evaded his gaze. "Now you know."

Cooper searched for the perfect response, but got nothing. He was sure about one thing, though: Sloane was no murderer.

"Let's take a drive. Clear our heads." He held the door as an invitation. "You don't have to say a word, but there are a few things I need to clear up with you."

She remained where she was, her jaw working as she deliberated.

"Please, Sloane. Just hear me out."

She nodded and walked toward him with her

head down. She might be reluctant, but at least she was going with him. At least she tucked her hand into the crook of his arm when he offered it to her.

Cooper sorted the events of his past into messy piles. He decided where to start as he navigated the Defender from the dimly lit garage into the full midmorning sun.

"There's a reason my dad gave me so much trouble that night at the bar, Sloane. The same reason I didn't drink." His voice was gravelly. He reached into his pocket then handed Sloane his wallet. "Look. In the first slot."

She slipped out a large coin, gleaming black and blue. "'To thine own self be true.'" She ran a fingernail over the Roman numeral two. "What is this, Cooper?"

"It's a sobriety coin," he said. "I haven't had a drink in two years."

She shifted, but remained silent.

The right words didn't want to be found. "There's, um, a reason I started drinking. Not that it's a good excuse or anything, but—" *Just spit it out.* "I had a little sister, and she passed away."

Out of the corner of his eye, he saw her turn in his direction, looking at him for the first time since they'd gotten in the car.

"Her name was Jordan Marian Cooper—the *J* in J. Marian." It had been so long since he'd talked about his sister that he'd underestimated how hard it would be, much heavier out loud than in his thoughts. Even after all the years.

Sloane's hand, shaky and tentative, covered his. "What happened to her?" The little squeeze of her grip calmed him.

"She was diagnosed with leukemia when she was twelve—Owen and I were sixteen," he said. "She fought it for about a year, and it went away. But it came back."

"Wow, Cooper. I'm—I—"

Cooper stopped at a light and laced his fingers through Sloane's. *It's going to be okay.* Were the words meant for her or him? He gave her hand a light squeeze, then returned his to the steering wheel.

"You don't need to feel sorry for me."

"I didn't want people to feel sorry for me, either," Sloane said. "I didn't feel like I deserved their pity. But I felt it everywhere I went. In the stares people seemed to think I didn't see. In the cheerfulness they forced when they wanted to pretend everything was normal. That's why I haven't been back home."

"That's why I moved to Paris." He paused. "And I'm about to show you another reason."

"What?"

He turned right at the next intersection and eased between two cars at the curb. He swallowed hard as he gestured past Sloane. "Do you see that building? Where that man is?"

"Mmm-hmm."

Several shops lined the street, and a man leaned against a brick wall under an awning that read Cleaners. He wore an apron and nursed a cigarette between his fingers. "That was Marianelli's—the restaurant my family built before Jordan got sick. It had her last painting in it—this amazing mural that filled an entire wall. And I burned it down."

"You...what?"

"Yep. It was right after she died, and I had so much to drink that I don't remember it. I was angry and ended up passing out with the burners on." He let his head fall to the steering wheel. "The firefighters pulled me out, but the restaurant was a total loss. All those memories with my sister."

Sloane remained silent. He felt her hand find his again, and he lifted his head.

"That's when my father decided I needed to go off the grid for a while and calm down before I could cause any more damage." He straightened and shifted the Defender into gear. "I guess that's one way to find out you like cooking. Maybe not the *easiest*."

Sloane made a face, and Cooper could sense the pretense between them lifting like a curtain.

"So, how did you get past it?"

He checked for traffic and pulled onto the street. "I didn't get past it. But I sure tried everything I could think of. Spoiler alert, nothing works."

Sloane laughed, a short, bitter sound. "Yeah. You've got that right. But how are you so happy? Normal? Unless you have any unhealthy tics, disorders or something else I don't know about."

"I'm not normal." A collection of faces spun through his mind.

His mother telling him he wasn't to blame— although her eyes said something different— then picking him up from the airport and treating him like a king.

Jake and the hurt in his voice when Cooper blew him off for the last time only to welcome him in, no questions asked, when it was too difficult to stay sober.

Simone pushing him from her doorstep causing him to fall backward into the fountain after he'd crashed her dinner party totally wasted. The little nod of relief she gave when he showed up after midnight and, over a cup of her beloved tea, broke down for the first meaningful time since his sister's death.

"I wouldn't have made it without letting really good people in on what I was going through. People who pushed me to take responsibility for my actions, and to try to do right by those I hurt so I could live with no regrets. And grief counseling."

"Grief counseling? Really?"

He nodded. "I started going to a group at a church once I got out of rehab. Talking with them helped me see I'm never going to truly be over it and that it's okay. Knowing that is the first step to healing."

Sloane looked unconvinced. "Hmm."

"It's hard to explain—it took me a long time to get it. Once I realized that it's an active process you have to work through, I started having more good days than bad."

"I see," she said. But her jerky movements made it clear that she didn't.

He pulled into a parking spot in front of *Simone*. "It's like with the alcoholism."

He saw her flinch at the word *alcoholism*.

"I have to guard myself against giving in to it because the desire to drink doesn't go away," he said as they crossed the street. "There are days when I'm more susceptible to it than others. But every day is different, you know?"

"So what happens when you have a bad day?"

Cooper unlocked the front door and let her in ahead of him. "Well, it's a cycle. For me, some kind of stress or memory leads to the craving. I tell myself I can have just one drink—that I can say no anytime I want. But I can't. One drink leads to another and I regret it. Then it's back to some kind of stress or memory because of my regret." He flipped the light switch in the dining room, throwing his keys on a table next to a mound of paperwork that was waiting to be signed and faxed.

"So I try to break that cycle in a healthy way. Talk to someone I can trust. Go play basketball with Owen. Lock myself in the kitchen with some loud music and make a bunch of bread."

"Sounds familiar." Her tone was dull as she sank into a chair. "That must be nice for you. I can run for hours—as you noticed the other night—but it does me about as much good as a Band-Aid on a broken leg. That feeling that I'm half crushed in the car...it never goes away."

Cooper took the chair across from her and leaned forward. "You can't outrun the pain,

Sloane. Recovery isn't a sprint, and it's not even a marathon. It's the movement you make every day." He closed his eyes for a moment. "Even if you only crawl."

When he opened his eyes, Sloane was staring at the picture of Simone. "Do you ever miss her?"

"All the time." He cleared his throat. "I wish she could see all of this. But we had plenty of time to say goodbye. We knew it was coming."

A tear slid down her face, her gaze still on the portrait. "I didn't get that chance."

"If you're ready to tell me about it, I'm all ears."

Sloane swiped at her cheek. "Why don't you ask your father? He seems to know everything."

"My father doesn't know anything." Cooper scowled. "He's just— I don't know what he's doing."

She rested her chin on the table and picked at the wood. "He overheard me tell your mom something on the night of the soft opening— which explains the terrible look he gave me. I'm pretty sure he thinks I have a devious plan to get VisibilityNet a huge contract with you." She blew a stray stand of hair out of her eyes and sat up. "I know they'd love it, but I couldn't care less about that."

"It doesn't take a rocket scientist to know you can't wait to be done with us, but why, Sloane?" He was flirting with the line between persistence and overstepping his boundaries. But he was sure the honesty would set her free. And he so wanted to be that outlet for her, to witness that breakthrough. "Tell me what happened."

Sloane squinted at him, calculating. "Chicken." She stood abruptly and hobbled in the direction of the kitchen. "I'm gonna need some chicken."

"I'M STILL THINKING. Just give me a minute." Sloane kept her voice steady despite the tears spilling down her cheeks as she chopped a sweet onion into tiny, uniform pieces.

Cooper set a bundle wrapped in butcher paper on the cutting board, next to a pile of ingredients waiting to be prepped. "Take your time. Anything I can do to help?" He sank onto a stool opposite her. His focus was so intense she could almost feel it wrapped around her.

"No." She picked a piece of onion skin from the cutting board and flicked it into the stock pot. "Aaron liked his onions chopped really finely, almost like a paste so he couldn't tell they were there."

"Even when they're cooked down?" Cooper asked as she added a few tablespoons of butter to the heated pot with a healthy drizzle of olive oil.

"Even cooked down."

The edges of the butter melted into tiny bubbles against the cast iron. Sloane smashed two garlic cloves with the flat of the knife then peeled off the skin. "His mom always added lots of garlic, too. She made this for us when we got sick."

It was kind of freeing to talk about Aaron with someone, even if it was just about how he liked his food while she was cooking his favorite meal. Even if talking about him in the past tense was still odd and unnatural. Even if it was with a man she'd been working with for weeks but only really knew today.

Sloane worked in silence for a few minutes, stealing glances at Cooper. He leaned forward, chin in his hand. Still studying her. Still waiting patiently for her to say something. But he gave her room to breathe even though she knew he was dying to hear her story.

"It was late. We were out too late. It was dark because it was late," she explained. Her knife dropped from her shaking hand to the cutting board, flinging vegetable bits in the process. "Oh geez, Coop. I haven't told anybody this out loud in forever."

"It's okay. Keep telling it only if you want to."

She stirred the contents in the pan then stopped. But her hands were still in motion, trembling. "Aaron was my best friend since he moved to my street in the sixth grade."

"You were neighbors."

"Four houses down and across the street." She added some chopped carrot slivers to the pot. "We were at a party for one of our friends who was about to ship off to the navy. Aaron was going to run track for a small college in Illinois where his dad went. I was trying to get into Wheaton even though I had no idea what I wanted to do with my life." She started to laugh but bit it back.

Was she supposed to laugh when she was telling Aaron's story?

"There was this back road that cut around town along the river. We used to take it because the speed limit was fifty and the cops avoided it." Sloane fished the cooked chicken from the pot to set it on the cutting board. "I was driving because Aaron didn't want to drive my parents' car. He didn't trust himself late at night anyway—the guy could fall asleep anywhere, I'm telling you."

Cooper smiled. "Yeah?"

"Yeah. He fell asleep on a roller coaster ride after a school dance one time." The muscles around her mouth tightened as she replayed that night in her head.

"That's pretty bad."

"It started raining, and it hadn't rained in a while, so the oils in the road made it extra slick." She thought that was how her dad had explained it to her anyway.

"I tapped the brake to slow down, and all of the sudden, we were spinning."

Her concentration on the chicken she was shredding broke when she noticed Cooper sliding off the stool.

"I blacked out when we hit the tree. When I woke up, my leg was broken and Aaron was holding my hand. Scared for me, but trying to keep me calm."

Cooper crept closer as she added the chicken to the pot and cranked up the heat so everything could simmer together. She wrung her hands, searching for something to occupy them. A rag.

"Then the car caught on fire, and he pulled

me out the sunroof—he was so quick on his feet like that. And when the rescue workers finally got there and put me in the back of the ambulance, I wouldn't let go of him. Somehow I knew. Even though all he had was a headache and a bloody nose, I knew things weren't going to be okay. Things were *never* going to be okay." Her voice broke, and Cooper took the cloth from her hands.

"Aaron's parents adopted him. They *chose* him. What they had was so amazing. And I took it from them."

Cooper wrapped his arms around her, holding her together before her pieces could fall apart.

"It's my fault they don't have a son anymore, Cooper," she whispered into his shirt. "My fault they're alone."

He leaned back, putting space between them. "No, Sloane." He framed her face in his hands, his penetrating gaze holding her. "You didn't kill Aaron. It was an accident. It could have happened to anyone."

For some reason, when Cooper said it, his tenderness and conviction made Sloane want to believe it.

"But I wasn't sixteen yet!" She broke from his grip and stumbled backward as the confession spilled out of her. "I didn't have a driver's license. We took my parents' car when they were out of town. It was so stupid—we never did stuff like that—and the one time we did, Aaron paid for it with his life." Her back hit something solid, and she slid to the floor, her body physically unable to stand anymore.

It was like she was having an out-of-body experience until her senses snapped to the forefront and she felt her tears, felt Cooper's embrace.

"If I had waited until I was sixteen—"

"Your car would have spun if you were sixteen or sixty." Cooper said firmly. "The rain doesn't discriminate."

She nodded, looking past him, because it was what she was supposed to do. And when he stood, she allowed him to help her up and leaned into him. He led her to the table by the door and served up the soup she'd made with some cheddar biscuits.

"Aaron's mom used to make this when he didn't feel well," Sloane repeated, the emotion drained from her. "It was his favorite."

Cooper blew on a spoonful and slurped it up. "I'd imagine it made him feel better every time. It's perfect, Sloane."

"Thanks."

"Do you want to tell me about him? What he was like?"

She'd balked at similar questions from countless trained mental health professionals. But there in the intimacy of *Simone's* dimmed lighting with Aaron's favorite meal warm in her stomach, she told Cooper everything.

And it was like she'd been washed clean.

CHAPTER EIGHTEEN

BY THE TIME Cooper dropped Sloane off at her apartment, he was ready to crash—and not just because of the late nights he'd been pulling at work. He was emotionally spent after hearing Sloane's story and helping her carry the weight of her grief. And once he was rested, he could think about how everything had changed between them.

Now that she wasn't carrying the weight of her past alone, he expected she'd be different with him. He'd been there once and knew what that kind of trauma did to a person. But tonight he'd gotten a glimpse of the real Sloane he'd only seen hints of before—and she was more brilliant and beautiful than he ever could have imagined.

As he steered into the parking spot behind his brownstone, gathered his things and started up the stone path to his back door, he replayed the way Sloane had given him a tentative hug.

"Good night, Cooper," she'd said into his

jacket with a little laugh that echoed his own surprise. Relieved, unapologetic, adorable. He'd underestimated Sloane ever since he met her. But he'd also underestimated himself, what it would do to him when he found his answers.

In the deepest parts of him, he wanted things he couldn't allow himself to want with her. Not when he came with a detonator, wrapped in a shiny glass bottle.

Cooper slipped his key into the lock and it turned with no resistance. Could Jake have come home from his work trip early? No, he'd texted Cooper hours before that he would be gone through the week.

Had Cooper forgotten to lock up? Surely he hadn't. He inched the door open.

No Maddie. Weird. Normally she was bouncing at the door when he came in.

The hair rose on the back of his neck. He held his breath to listen for sounds and heard a muffled voice coming from upstairs. Something was definitely off.

He slipped inside and stepped to his office, tiptoeing over the creaky floorboards. The panel in his right desk drawer slid away easily, revealing a metal surface with a rubber keypad. He punched in the combination and opened the door.

Please let Maddie be safe.

The revolver was cool and light in his hands as he loaded it and double-checked the safety. He'd never used it outside of the gun range, and he didn't plan to now unless it was clearly the only option.

Cooper clutched the grip with his right hand, his left positioned to stabilize. He held the gun tilted toward the ceiling, and glanced up the steps. His pulse pounded in his ears. A thin strip of light glowed from beneath the door to the vacant bedroom.

A crash came from within the room. A heavy shuffle of footsteps sounded. And then a familiar voice.

"Maddie, go away. You don't get any."

Cooper popped the gun's safety into place then raced up the stairs two and three at a time, his blood boiling.

"Owen." He whipped open the door.

His brother was slouched in the desk chair, half-empty Tupperware in his lap, forkful of leftover pork tenderloin halfway to his mouth. The leftover pork tenderloin *Cooper* had planned to eat that night. Maddie sat at his feet in begging position, her head turned in her master's direction, ears flat as if she thought she were the one in trouble.

"Where do you come off breaking into my house? Eating my dinner?"

"Whoa, Cooper. What's your problem? Simmer down or you're going to sprain something." He shoveled the fork into his mouth, and Maddie's head snapped toward him.

Cooper slouched against the bed. "You gotta let me know when you're coming over." He unloaded the cylinder of his gun.

"You were going to shoot me?" Owen swore.

"Don't tempt me." Cooper put the cylinder on the bed with a half grin. "Why don't you tell me what made you finally want to come here?"

Owen retrieved a bottle of beer from the floor next to him and took a swig. The smell of it made Cooper's mouth water. The sound of the liquid sliding down the glass neck of the bottle drove him to bite down on his cheeks hard.

"You start by explaining what that was all about at the office. Why the rest of us have you to thank that Dad's now on the warpath."

Warpath?

"Sales numbers have dropped since you hit the ground running with this restaurant, Coop." Owen shrugged.

"Not anymore. Tell him to check again. I've been working double time to stay on track."

"It wouldn't matter anyway." Owen sat up straighter. "It's not *you* he's after. He has it in his head that blogger is going to bring down our whole family. He thinks she's hiding something."

"No. Absolutely not. He's not going anywhere near Sloane."

"Of course he's not." Owen's lips curled. "Like Dad would actually do his own dirty work. He'll leave that to someone else."

Cooper had never wanted to level the smirk from his brother's face more. With the amount of hot energy coiled in his veins, he could do it in one punch. But that wouldn't help Sloane. "Please, Owen," he said. "Just listen to me. Dad doesn't know what's going on with Sloane. You have to convince him she's harmless."

"Why don't you tell me and let me be the judge?"

Cooper looked away. "I can't do that."

"C'mon, Coop." Owen put the food container on the floor next to Maddie and stood. "You just started working with this girl. She could be anyone."

"And he really thinks she could do worse after all the bad press we've gotten?"

Owen raised an eyebrow. "All the bad press *we've* gotten? He's not worried about us—he's worried about you."

"Just drop it, Owen. Seriously."

"You don't make it easy to be your brother, you know." Owen crossed his arms. "Do you think I like being stuck between you and Dad? It's hard enough working for the man."

"Then don't. You could do your own thing anytime. You should try it. It's nice."

Owen's jaw knotted. He would never leave the company. Not if it meant giving up his luxuries. "So that's how it's going to be, then? You're siding with some girl over your own family."

"What family?" Cooper stood to face his brother. "Ever since Jordan died, we haven't been a—"

"*Don't* bring Jordan into this." Owen's voice wavered. He blinked hard and shouldered past Cooper, stopping at the top of the stairs. "And don't act like going off to Paris really qualifies as doing your own thing. Dad saw what you were doing to yourself then and he sees what you're doing to yourself now."

"What exactly is that supposed to mean?" Cooper flinched. Owen was a practiced marksman with verbal bullets—a trait he'd inherited from their father.

"He made you leave because he thought you were going to get yourself killed. And he'll do whatever it takes to stop you from self-destructing again."

CHAPTER NINETEEN

"WHAT DO YOU think of a Korean barbecue slider?" Grace, dressed in one of her husband's oversize T-shirts, jumped right to the point the minute she appeared on the computer screen.

Sloane snorted. "This is what your nine-one-one text was about? At midnight my time?"

Grace looked up from the slab of beef that was the victim of some intense knife work. "Well, yeah. I saw you were online." Obviously, recipe writer's block classified as an emergency to Sloane's odd duck of a friend. "I'm thinking the usual—soy sauce, sesame oil, garlic, a kiss of brown sugar. What do you think?"

She closed her eyes, allowing herself to visualize the flavors together. But before she could respond, the screen split.

"There you are, Levi," Grace said. "What do you think of a Korean barbecue slider?"

"What about it?" Levi drawled in his heavy Southern accent.

"Is it something a dude would eat?"

"If it has meat in it, the answer is always yes. I don't know why you have to get all fancy calling it a slider, though."

Sloane chuckled. "If it sounds good to Grace, it sounds good to me." Sometimes Levi was a little too argumentative.

"But why can't you just call it a burger?" He clearly wasn't going to back off.

"Because it's smaller than a burger."

"But are they overdone?" Grace asked. "Is everyone doing them right now?"

Sloane shook her head and repositioned to lean into her left leg until she felt a stretch in her hamstring. "Maybe a few years ago, but now I don't think so." *That's it. Right there. Feels good.* "But you should definitely make your own bun."

"Ooh, something steamed like a Vietnamese pork bun."

"Go with it."

"As much as I love listening to you two talk about food all day…"

Grace ignored him. "And I'm feeling some kind of slaw with lime and ginger and carrots." She slid her glasses from the top of her head to the bridge of her nose and scribbled in her notebook.

"Yes. With scallions." Sloane straightened.

The exaggerated boredom in their web designer's features pulled a sharp laugh from her. "You know you love us, Levi."

"That's debatable."

At the sound of her laughter, Grace's head snapped toward her screen. Then she gasped. "Oh, no, Sloane." She clapped a hand to her chest. "I'm the worst friend in the whole world."

"What?"

"Here I am, going on and on about Korean barbecue like an idiot. And I haven't asked about Davon. How's he doing?"

Sloane smiled at the mention of him. "He's doing great. He's recovering really well from his surgery and went home yesterday. Cooper said you wouldn't know anything happened to him except for the broken arm."

"*Cooper*, huh?"

Stupid. Stupid. Change the subject. "Yeah, we're, um, I'm supposed to go see him tomorrow once they're all settled in at home."

"I'm so glad he's okay, Sloane," Grace said. "And I'm glad you're okay. You look really good. Doesn't she look great, Levi?"

He shrugged, looking up from what he'd been otherwise occupied with. "I guess."

"Maybe it's all the time you've been spending with *Cooper.*" Grace looked like a fox ready to pounce through the screen.

"Can we talk about this later, Grace?"

"Ooh! What's there to talk about?"

"Yeah, Sloane," Levi chimed in with artificial enthusiasm. "What's there to talk about?"

They were making a huge deal out of nothing, all talking over each other. But if it was nothing, then she should just say so, right?

"Okay, I told him!" She folded. Relief washed the tension from her shoulders as soon as the words left her mouth.

"What?"

"I told him everything. It just sort of happened."

"Wow." Grace's smile seemed smug.

"I know."

Levi sat in silence, lips pressed together, shaking his head.

"Okay, you can stop with the judgment, Levi."

"I can't believe you'd tell him. Have you not learned anything from what you read?"

"She's not stupid," Grace interjected. "If she thinks she can trust him, she can trust him."

"Whatever, y'all. I'm out. Enjoy your sliders, Grace." His hand made a dramatic arc to the keyboard as he closed the conversation screen. And he was gone.

Grace rolled her eyes. "So he finally got it out of you."

"He did."

"And how did he react?" Grace disappeared behind her island then returned with a spray bottle in hand. Her personal world record for sitting still remained unbroken.

How *did* Cooper react? Sloane sighed. "He was wonderful, Grace. He's been through some stuff in his own life and talked about dealing with grief."

"Yeah?"

"He made me think of things—about grief and guilt and all that—in a new way. And you know how I've gone through the accident a million times from every angle."

Grace paused, slapping her damp kitchen towel on the island. "Right. Good for you, then. I'm proud. Talking this out is good for you."

"I feel...different now that he knows. Now that I've told someone besides you guys and really talked about it. I told Cooper more about Aaron than I've told anyone—maybe even you. I don't know why, but he somehow turned off my overthinking switch or something. It's weird."

"So, what's going to happen between you two?" Grace was back in front of the computer screen. "How is this going to affect things?"

"Oh, it's nothing like that. We—"

Speaking of. Sloane's phone vibrated against the kitchen counter, flashing Cooper's name. She sent the call to voice mail. "We're friends now, I guess."

"Just friends, huh?" Grace beamed a megawatt grin that was impossible not to return.

Sloane's smile faded as the intercom buzzed. It was after midnight. Who could possibly be downstairs right now?

"Hey, I gotta go." She closed the lid to her laptop before Grace could say anything and hurried to the intercom. "Hello?"

"Hi, Sloane. A Mr. Cooper is here to see you." The night doorman's voice was thick with disapproval.

Goose bumps rose on her forearms as she pictured the CEO's red face spewing viciousness in the conference room. She pressed the video surveillance monitor and waited for the image to load.

Please be the son. Please be the son.

It was the younger Cooper. She could see the top of his hair and the curve of his shoulders. His head was propped against the wall like he was sick. Weird.

She cleared her throat. "Let him up." Cooper wouldn't come to her door after midnight unless it was for a good reason.

"Um, Miss Bradley? I can't do that."

"What? Why?" The old man probably thought Cooper's visit had less-than-honorable leanings.

"Because it appears he's been drinking, ma'am. And he needs a lot of help."

A SLIVER OF LIGHT seared through Cooper's skull. He squeezed his eyes shut. Head pounding, palms sweaty, limbs heavy. Had he been mugged or something?

Then he remembered. And the remnant of that warm, numbing, out-of-body experience confirmed it. He was going to slink into a hole in the depths of the earth and stay there forever. That's where he belonged.

It took a little effort, but his last waking moments came to him in blurry fragments. Owen waiting for him in his house. The ugly end to their argument. The responsible text message he'd composed to Jake then deleted. The phone call he'd made to his culinary school friend instead. He'd met Guillermo for dinner, hammering his conversation with Owen and the stress of his work further into the back of his mind with each over-the-top story told in his friend's heavy Spanish accent.

As Cooper had expected, it'd been just like the old days when they first arrived in Paris. One sip had turned into a whole glass. One glass had turned to two or three. Shots were ordered. And, well, he couldn't remember much after that.

He burrowed deeper into his pillowy nest, pulling the softest blanket ever tighter around his body. Of all the strange couches he'd ended up on, this was by far the most comfortable. Maybe he could avoid reality here. Forever.

"How are you feeling?"

The words rolled a wave of nausea through him. Sloane. He recognized that voice. But she couldn't be here. She couldn't be around him when he was like this.

He bolted up, then winced, squeezing the heels of his wrists to his temples.

"Easy, Cooper. Take this." The press of Sloane's fingers in his palm rippled up his arm.

"Thanks." Cooper pried an eye open and took a tall glass of water from her, throwing back the pills in his hand. At least she didn't seem angry like someone who'd had a big mess to clean up. That was promising.

Sloane moved to the opposite couch and tucked a snowflake-pajama-clad leg beneath her. As comfortable as if she'd been settled in that position for quite some time. She studied him with concern-clouded eyes. No judgment. No disappointment. Just compassion.

"Can I get you some tea? Coffee?"

"Coffee." Cooper exhaled in relief. "Strong and black, please." Maybe it was a good thing he'd lost his edge when it came to alcohol. He'd lost some of his immunity to it.

Sloane went to the kitchen. "If there's anything else that will help you get past this, let me know. I'm just gonna put it out there that I don't exactly know what works in situations like this."

Cooper sat up to see her over the couch. "So you're saying you've never inflicted this on yourself, huh? You're a smart one."

"Can't say I have," she said just above a whisper. "Just black, right?"

He nodded and sank into the cushions. The clean white sheeting pulled under his shifted weight, revealing a swath of walnut Italian leather beneath it. Sloane must have covered the couch for his benefit. Or the couch's. A small wastebasket triple-lined with plastic bags waited next to the head of his makeshift bed. Beside that was a neat stack of aubergine towels.

She apparently knew *something* about hangovers.

A machine whirred in the kitchen. "Is that what I think it is?" He strained for a closer look at the sleek machine on Sloane's counter. "That's not supposed to be on the market until next year. I looked into them for the restaurant."

It was part espresso machine, part coffeemaker. But Cooper was pretty sure it could tie his shoes if he asked it to.

"The company sent me one to demo."

He'd forgotten—again—how important Sloane was. How many times had he underestimated her since the moment they met? And now he'd forced her to vomit-proof her apartment. Angry or not angry, who knows what he'd said or done to her last night. He couldn't be trusted.

Guilt tore through him. Of all the doorsteps, why did he have to show up at this one? Why couldn't it have been Jake? Someone whose relationship with Cooper had already been tarnished by this responsibility. If he had any control over his sensibilities, he'd have called Owen. He'd certainly been on the other end of these wild nights more times than he could count. Sloane didn't deserve to clean up after Cooper's mistakes.

"I can't even begin to say how sorry I am, Sloane. If I said or did anything last night, I—"

"You couldn't do or say much of anything." She returned with a mug of coffee that smelled rich. Puffs of steam swirled from its surface. Her lips puckered into a tiny smile. "Don't worry."

"You're the best." Cooper pushed into a sitting position, but his coordination failed him.

"Whoa." Sloane dropped to the couch next to him then cupped a hand under his arm for support.

He blinked against the Tilt-A-Whirl behind his eyes and anchored a leg beneath himself. Success. He took the mug of coffee slowly, angling toward Sloane.

Her eyes searched his like she wanted to say something helpful, even though her body language—legs crossed, leaning away from him—created distance.

The full gravity of what he'd done settled in his stomach like he'd downed an entire tray of Guillermo's stuffed poblano peppers. He reached for his wallet on the end table, wincing as a drop of coffee singed through his jeans. The front slot was empty, the raised circular stretch of the leather the only sign his sobriety coin had ever been there.

"I took it." Sloane brandished the blue-and-black disk between her first two fingers. She faced him, both legs on the couch and crisscrossed. "I'll give it back to you if you make me a promise."

"Sloane…"

"No, you have to promise." She held his gaze. "You're going to keep it with you. You've earned it no matter what happened last night."

Cooper let his head fall against the cushion and closed his eyes. His conviction burned a deeper sear into his chest, behind his temples. "Sloane, those are only for people who've—"

"Look at me, Cooper." Her tone commanded obedience.

For a few breaths, they sat in silence. Sloane looked younger. More innocent. Her features were softened with no makeup. But like the raw, powerful grief he'd seen in her before, there was a deep sincerity in her eyes. An authority behind everything she said.

"Do you *feel* like the person who goes out

every weekend to get trashed for fun? Was this natural for you? Enjoyable?"

Cooper shook his head. This time had been different for him. It hit harder in more ways than one.

"That's because you're not that guy anymore. You're just a recovering person who had a bad day. Recovery is a crawl sometimes, right? Who told me that?"

"Sober people don't crave it like I do, Sloane. You don't—" He sighed. "I don't think I'll ever go a day without having to convince myself I don't want it."

She squeezed his knee. "But the difference is you don't *want* to want it. And you have help."

She snatched her hand from his leg and, in a fraction of a second, she lengthened the gap between them, swinging her feet to the floor and staring straight ahead. "You just have to remember that and believe it." Her voice was shaky.

The warmth from her hand lingered on his leg. Was she talking about him believing in his own strength? Or was she talking about herself?

"Do you believe *you're* strong enough, Sloane?"

She fidgeted with her fingernails. "No."

His heart sunk. He wanted so much for her to believe it. His curiosity itched to see how far this brilliant woman could go at full stride.

"But for the first time, I think… I think I actually *want* to want to."

CHAPTER TWENTY

ON THE NIGHT that September breathed its last sticky breath, Sloane found herself staring at the tall brick walls of Globe Life Park in Arlington. She was supposed to be finishing last-minute details for the conference, readying her apartment for Grace's arrival. But her dread about the conference translated to procrastination. And her favorite eight-year-old had insisted.

Davon—sporting a Texas-Rangers-blue cast—and Cooper wound her through the stadium, past concession lines until they reached their section of seats.

"This is us," Cooper said as Davon squeezed through a row to a spot close to his mom.

Sloane balked when she saw the crowd, retreating until her back hit metal railing. A lot of the same faces from the soft opening.

"No, it's okay." Cooper held up calming palms as if she were a rabid animal.

He'd reserved an entire deck for the staff

involved with his restaurant launch and their families.

"Is your dad here?"

"Not yet. But even if he shows, he's not coming anywhere near you. You hear me?"

Sloane nodded and allowed him to lead her to their seats.

"I should have warned you. I'm sorry. But you've been a huge part of this, Sloane, and I'm glad you're here." He paused at the entrance to the row so she could move toward Davon. "It's important to me that you're here."

"Well, I'll try to be on my best behavior." She gave him a half smile.

"Before you sit down, Miss Sloane…" Davon's voice stopped her midway. "Can I have another hot dog?" He looked at her with a mixture of hope and exaggerated innocence. But it was the mustard stain on his lip that got her.

"I'll get you one." Cooper flashed a glance at Alicia, who was seated next to Marian at the end of their row.

Alicia nodded and continued her conversation with the older woman.

"Do you want anything, Sloane?"

"No, thanks."

"We've been missing you in the kitchen,

Davon." Sloane nudged him with her shoulder. "When are you coming back?"

His posture deflated. "I don't get this dumb cast off for months."

"Months?"

"Try six weeks," Alicia said.

"Six weeks!" His head fell back. "I'm never gonna get to do anything."

"Let's make an agreement."

"What kind of agreement?"

"You come back and be the kitchen supervisor and official taste tester. What do you think about that? Do we have ourselves a deal?"

A grin spread across his face. Goodness. The way his eyes crinkled. He couldn't look more like Aaron if he tried.

"Deal."

"Good. Then I expect you to report for duty this Thursday if it's okay with your mom."

Just as she expected, Alicia turned to them and nodded. Moms and their superpowered ears. How did they do that even in the middle of other conversations?

"So, what's your favorite sport?" She winced. "Probably not the best question to ask a kid with a broken arm, huh?"

Davon looked at his T-shirt then her like she was one crayon short of a box.

"Oh, is that some sort of jersey?"

Again with the look. "You're not that into sports, are you, Miss Sloane?"

"I'm into running."

"Running?" Davon's voice reached a falsetto close to the range only dogs could hear. "You think running is fun?"

"Hey, what's wrong with running?"

"Running is never fun. And it's not a sport. Hey, Coop, is running a sport?"

Cooper put a cardboard box in Sloane's hands. "Running? Like, running by yourself or running with a track team?" He sat and reached for the box.

"Running is a sport *no matter what*."

Davon raised his good arm in surrender. "Okay, okay."

Something on the tray caught her eye. A small cup with a scoop of glossy chocolate gelato and a tiny pink spoon sticking out.

"I got you some gelato." Cooper grinned, handing it to her. "Your own cup."

"How'd you know I like gelato?"

"Because you wrote about it. The chocolate raspberry gelato at Mooney's? That's one of our restaurants."

Wait a minute. Cooper actually *read* her website?

Sloane felt heat spread across her cheeks and took a bite as Cooper distributed drinks and snacks. It was delicious, the perfect cool and creamy consistency that only came from gelato. Heaven. In. A. Bite. "Thank you, Cooper. It tastes even better because you remembered."

"You're welcome." His gaze lingered on her, good-natured humor transforming into something more intense. An echoing response radiated to the tips of her body.

"What's that?" Davon's question broke the spell.

"What, this?" Cooper held up a brochure. "Something for Miss Sloane's website."

"Oh, yeah?" Sloane leaned in for a closer look. "What's that?"

He shook the folds of the brochure open. "Behold the Boomstick. Two feet of all-beef hot dog."

"A two-foot hot dog?" She shuddered. It sounded worse than fair food.

"That's cool!" Davon said.

"That's disgusting!" Sloane said at the same time.

The males on either side of Sloane spent the next inning trying to explain baseball to her. They seemed smart, but everything went over her head. There were way too many rules to keep track of. They were trying to explain a squeeze play to her when Davon's mom announced he'd had enough fun for the night and it was time to go home. The Rangers were winning by seven in the sixth inning, so the game seemed a wash anyway.

They said goodbye, and Cooper walked them through the company box. When he came back a few minutes later, there was a noticeable space between them now that Davon wasn't there as a buffer.

"He's a good kid, huh?" Sloane said. The nervous laugh tacked on the end didn't help matters much.

Cooper nodded, taking a bite of the pretzel he'd gotten earlier.

"How'd you get paired with him anyway?" It had never come up.

He held up a finger as he chewed, and the crowd's cheers grew louder. There was some kind of media time-out or something.

"Oh, you have a little something right here." Dip from his pretzel had smeared in the stubbled groove between his lower lip and chin. She pointed to her chin. *Must. Not. Laugh.*

"Where?" Cooper swiped at his mouth, but he only made it worse.

She rubbed it clean with the knuckle of her thumb. "Got it."

The cheers of the crowd catapulted to a deafening volume. "What'd you say?" Cooper leaned close to her.

Sloane's chest constricted when she saw the camera. The ripple of heads turned in their direction. Their faces plastered on the jumbotron. The swirl of hearts outlining the screen.

Kiss Cam.

Her insides plummeted like some sick Tower of Terror flashback. She stared straight ahead. This couldn't be happening.

Cooper's head swiveled toward her and she turned to meet his eyes, which were bright with amusement. Softened with hope. He raised brows asking a question she answered with a nod.

His gaze swept down Sloane's face, locked in on her lips. He brushed her hair behind her ear, scattering tingles from her core to her every edge.

She closed her eyes and felt the pads of his fingers on her jawline, his lips against her cheekbone, a whisper-soft contraction of flesh. And then nothing but the phantom stamp of his touch against her cheek and the intoxicating warmth coursing through her veins.

A smile formed. She gripped her armrests, grateful to be sitting because her world was now spinning on its side. Was it possible for a kiss on the cheek to cut off the oxygen supply to the brain?

Cooper's gaze met Sloane's, and he burst into laughter like a fifth-grade boy, then trained his attention to the field.

They watched the rest of the game making small talk about the players and things they needed to do at the restaurant. But Sloane replayed their Kiss Cam moment over and over. Too distracted for meaningful, coherent conversation. Too distracted by the tiny, unimportant detail she couldn't deny.

She wanted more.

CHAPTER TWENTY-ONE

SLOANE THOUGHT ABOUT bailing at least once an hour. Posting a proverbial sick note on her social media and burrowing under her bed. She had the restaurant opening to prepare for. It wasn't a good time to get behind on her posting schedule. She could just experience the conference via simulcast like she always did.

But the conference was practically in her backyard, she didn't have to teach any seminars, and several of the power-player brands were going to be in attendance, so Dana had asked her to touch base with them.

Then there was the matter of Grace staying with her. It had simultaneously excited her and terrified her when the animated redhead had brought the idea up a few months before. So Sloane had agreed, though the prospect of exposing her closest friend to her inner sanctum was enough to work her into a clammy-handed cold sweat.

It was just Grace, Sloane had to keep reminding herself. And Grace knew *pretty much* everything.

The intercom buzzed as Sloane was maneuvering her last curl, eyes trained on the step-by-step YouTube video a beauty blogger acquaintance had posted. She switched off the curling iron and padded to the intercom.

"Let her up, please," Grace said before the doorman could get a word out.

Sloane rushed around her apartment, straightening and shuffling and restacking in a frenzy. One last dollop of hand sanitizer, two shoes shoved onto her feet, three steps to the door.

And a knock.

She swung open the door and looked into the freckled face she'd seen so many times before—which was much higher than she'd imagined it would be.

"Hello, Meezy." Grace shouldered past Sloane, rolling a huge vintage floral suitcase behind her. She slid an unapologetic, measuring glance up and down Sloane. "How'd you hide the fact that you were so short?"

"How'd *you* hide the fact that you're part giant?"

The two women regarded each other for a tick before their uncertain tension dissolved into laughter. Grace crossed to her in one huge stride and scooped her into a hug so enthusiastic that Sloane's feet left the floor. "I thought I'd never get to do this. You're so brave."

Sloane snorted. "Brave? I don't know about all that. Let me get through tomorrow and then we'll talk. You know how I am with crowds."

"Don't think of them as strangers." Grace put an arm around her. "Think of them as friends. Readers. Coworkers. Your adoring fans."

"Like that makes things any better."

Grace's big green eyes narrowed. "Levi's going to be there."

"What?"

"He decided to come after all. Drum up some new clientele."

"Right. About that." Sloane and Levi hadn't spoken since he'd dished attitude about her telling Cooper everything.

Maybe he'd anticipated what would happen next. The way Cooper's place in her life would bud into a warm, soft, colorful spring. If Levi caught a glimpse of what that kiss did to her, he'd be so self-satisfied. She'd never hear the end of it.

"Look, he's promised to be on his best behavior." Grace shifted on her feet. "Now, are you going to show me where to put my suitcase or what?"

AFTER GRACE GOT settled in Sloane's seldom-used second bedroom, they were off to the convention center for registration, meetings and mixers.

Also known as that thing where people spout from every cranny of the room in endless droves. Hyped up on lots of caffeine.

The conversations went like this: "You're Sloane from *Mise en Place*, aren't you?"

Cue blank stare.

"We can't believe you actually showed up this time."

"You're even shorter/prettier/blonder in person."

Thank goodness for the conference's huge name tags. Whoever had thought to put real names and blog titles on them was a genius. And thank goodness for hand sanitizer. Though there was no conclusive proof it could ward off everything from this rapidly moving crowd. At least the sanitizer's pungent, clean smell reminded Sloane of home. And home helped her focus through the small talk.

Meanwhile, Grace zipped through the evening, stopping to talk to friends she found—or made—in her path. But to her credit, she kept an eye on Sloane, darting glances at her every once in a while to make sure she was okay.

Sloane had just excused herself from a conversation with some *Paleo* bloggers when she felt a tap on her shoulder and turned to face a woman with striking blue eyes and a tight, dark brown French braid.

"You're Sloane Bradley? Oh, good."

Sloane stretched her sore facial muscles into a polite smile. "Yes, ma'am."

"I was hoping I'd run into you." She pressed a business card into Sloane's hand. "My name is Karen Fox, and I'd love to talk to you about doing a cookbook with Johnson and Fox."

The room swayed a little around Sloane. Johnson and Fox? They'd published some of the cookbooks that had a permanent residence on Sloane's counter. *Focus.* "Yeah, sure. I'd love to talk about that." *Love* was an understatement. She had an entire secret Pinterest folder of cookbook designs she loved and recipes she'd include.

"Get your proposal ready and send it to me." Karen took the card and scrawled a phone number on the back. "This is my direct line if you need me to put you in touch with an agent."

Agent? Direct line? Proposal? Sloane said goodbye to Karen then looked at the card. Did that really just happen?

"There you are." The voice shot energy through Sloane's spine. Levi. She'd been so overwhelmed by the new faces that she'd almost forgotten he'd be there.

She faced him slowly. "Hi." Her vision of him swam before her. No matter how hard she tried, her eyes couldn't focus.

"Whoa, Sloane." Levi gripped her arm just below the shoulder. "You all right?"

"Just a little overstimulated, I think. It's so good to see you."

His image sharpened before her. Shaggy hair that couldn't decide if it was the lightest shade of brown or the darkest shade of blond. Gray eyes fringed in thick lashes. A smattering of pale freckles she'd never noticed over their video chats.

"Why don't I take you home, then? I told Grace—"

"No." The edge in his voice was enough to sharpen her senses. "I'm fine, Levi. Promise."

His face eased. "Why don't you sit down for a bit then? We'll get you something to drink. Juice?"

Sloane nodded and allowed him to lead her to a tall pub table and chair she practically had to hoist herself into. She watched Levi head to the bar for her drink.

This was just like Levi, making sure she was okay. It was in his nature as the bloggers' resident techie geek to serve, even at the conference.

Maybe she'd been too hard on him about Cooper. "Can we call a truce and get back to being friends yet?" she said when he returned.

Levi slapped down a napkin and set a short, squared tumbler filled with pink fizzy liquid and a lime wedge on top of it, settling his wiry frame into the chair across from her. "Is that a nice way of asking if I'll shut up about Cooper?"

"Yep. Pretty much."

"I don't like you working with him, Sloane. This whole thing seems like you're playing with fire."

She sighed.

"But you're here—actually at this conference—and if he was the one who finally got you out of that apartment, then I guess I can't argue."

Sloane would have made some joke about taking a picture or recording those words to memorialize the single time in his life Levi couldn't argue, but his eyes narrowed as if the admission had taken a few years from his life. "Thank you," she said instead, "for trusting me."

"Whatever." Levi scrubbed a hand over his face and stood. "Hey, I have a meeting I need to get to." His tone softened. "Catch up with you later?"

She nodded. They were okay, thank goodness. "Later."

As she watched Levi walk away, the volume of the room pressed in on her. It was as if the hotel existed at a high altitude that messed with her equilibrium. Her consciousness shifted with the realization that she'd been staring at a chair across the bar for longer than was socially acceptable. Her conversation with Levi had short-circuited something in her wiring, and she couldn't tear her eyes away from it.

Her phone buzzed in the little emerald-green clutch she carried.

Why was Cooper's name blinking on her screen?

She accepted the call with a swipe of her thumb and ducked through the lobby, half jogging on her high-heeled boots until she was outside.

"Hello?"

"Oh good, you answered. I know you're at your conference, but do you have a minute?"

She nodded even though he couldn't see her. "Sure. What's going on?"

Play it cool, Sloane.

"I'm leaving for New York tomorrow, and I can't find the flash drive with those photos you took. You know, of the food."

"Oh! The flash drive." Sloane could pinpoint the exact little compartment of her workbag that contained the flash drive. "Yeah, it's at my apartment. Do you need me to go get it? Or I can bring it to you."

Great. Now she sounded overeager.

His chuckle sounded breathy with the line's static. "I don't want you to miss your conference. I can figure out another way to get them. Email, maybe—"

"No, really. It's not a problem."

Please say okay. Please say okay.

"Okay."

Yes!

"I'm driving that way in a few minutes so I can pick you up and swing by your apartment if that's all right."

"Yeah, whatever. It's cool." When had a frat boy overtaken the speech center of her brain?

They hung up, and Sloane immediately fired off a text to Grace explaining that she was going home then another to the car company, asking them to be on call until Grace was ready to leave. She stepped inside the frosted glass doors and watched for Cooper.

The sight of him in the driver's seat brought her senses from dulled to sharp with laser precision.

"Are you doing all right?" he asked as she climbed in. Even toned, stoic. Broad shoulders pinned to the back of his seat.

Sloane angled her head toward him. Despite the robotic delivery of his question, a patch of streetlight illuminated concern in his eyes. That slackened the tension in her chest, flinging her iron-forged trust fortress wide-open. She nodded without hesitation, with a peace that it was safe to be honest with him after all of the information he was already protecting. "It was a bit much in there for me, so I was ready to leave. But I'm okay."

"Good." Cooper checked his mirrors and turned in his seat to look for a break in traffic. "I'm really proud that you went, Sloane. You know it?"

Warmth suffused her face. That was the difference between him and Levi. Both knew what the accident had done to her, but instead of treating her like a fragile flower, Cooper made her believe she could stand strong and healthy like an oak again someday.

That's why, if Levi had given her any kind of our-friendship-or-him ultimatum, her answer would have been easy.

"So, New York." She broke the quiet that had stretched for a few streets. "What are you doing on your trip?" The man beside her made her feel wonderful. And she wasn't letting anything ruin that.

Cooper pulled into a spot across the street from her building. "Oh, you know." They stepped out of the car. "Checking in on a higher-profile franchise opening, meeting with some vendors, a little PR. Trying to avoid World War III with my father. That sort of thing."

She winced as they crossed the street. *Better him than me.* She slowed her pace just long enough to indulge a full look at him. She took in his black, zip pullover, the distressed leather bag slung over his shoulders, the way his muscular legs filled his jeans. A warm, dizzying wave rushed over her.

"Is this a really big deal, then, since your father's coming along?"

"Oh, no. He just doesn't trust that I know how to do my own job right now."

Sloane eased past him as he opened the lobby door. "Well, I'll pray for your survival."

She glanced up with a sympathetic smile, but froze under the intensity in his eyes. The way he studied her.

"I'd appreciate that." The tenderness in his voice melted the knots of anxiety.

So this was what happened when she let her walls down. Sloane could feel every reservation slipping through her fingers like dough that had too much liquid and couldn't be kneaded into submission.

Was it okay not to fight it this time?

"I'll, uh, go get the flash drive if you want to wait down here." Yes. Definitely safer down here.

Cooper nodded and sat on an antique upholstered love seat.

Breathe in. Two...three...four... Sloane willed her heartbeat to slow as she rode the elevator to her apartment and finagled her key into the lock. She pressed her back to the door behind her.

Out...two...three...four...

The thumping drum behind her ears slowed. The pressure of the blood pumping in her veins dulled. She found the flash drive exactly where she'd left it.

When the elevator doors opened downstairs, Cooper was sitting in the same place, back to her, computer opened in his lap. She paused to take in the sight of him. Maybe she wouldn't be such an awkward mess this way.

She saw familiar images flashing across his screen as he scrolled through them.

Were those her images? The ones he'd come all this way for?

At the ding of the elevator closing, Cooper minimized his laptop screen as if he were defusing a ticking bomb and set it on the table in front of him. He turned, a trace of urgency lingering on his face.

Sloane moved forward as if she'd just arrived and hadn't been standing there for a few moments.

Did this mean what she thought it meant?

A grin spread across his face as he stood. "Did you find it?"

Had the images been on his computer the whole time?

"I…um," Sloane stammered, her ability to form a coherent thought disarmed by his closeness—near enough to touch—and by the delicious conclusion her mind was processing. "Here it is."

She held out the flash drive, and he covered it with his palm, wrapping his fingers around her hand. Lingering, lips parted as though to speak words that made her fingertips tingle with anticipation. If she could reach out and grab those words—

"Sloane, you're here."

She took a giant step back from Cooper. "Hi, Grace. Did you have fun?"

Grace's attention zeroed in on the six-foot distraction to Sloane's left. Her gaze zipped between the two of them then landed on Sloane with an expectation. *Well?*

"Oh, sorry. Grace, this is Cooper. Cooper, this is my best friend, Grace. She's staying with me this weekend."

"Well, this is our first time actually meeting," Grace said. "But we've been friends through our blogs for a few years."

Cooper blinked as the pieces visibly clicked together in his mind. "Oh, right. Right. *Grace.* You're here for the conference." He nodded. "Nice."

Sloane flashed a look at Grace in the awkward pause that followed. *We're so leaving. Now.*

"Well, it was nice to meet you, Cooper." Grace's voice boomed across the marble lobby as she shook his hand. "We'd better get some sleep. Busy day tomorrow and everything."

Cooper's head swiveled to Sloane, eyebrows pulled together.

"You can just keep the flash drive, Coop," she said before her insides could do that droopy puddle thing again.

"Are you sure?"

"Yeah, I have everything I need." She took a step toward the elevator. "Good luck in New York."

"See you when I get back?"

Most definitely. Sloane nodded.

"Nice to meet you," Grace called again. The lilt in her voice hinted that she was dying for him to leave so she could pounce on Sloane.

"Man alive. He's even dreamier in person." Grace fanned herself with a conference brochure when they were inside the elevator. "Why are his biceps so big? Bee sting? Does he need some Benadryl?"

"Stop!" But Grace was kind of right.

"So *that's* why you left. No wonder." Grace huffed an indignant breath, finger-combing her red curls. "I thought you said you guys were just friends."

Heat bloomed across Sloane's cheeks. "We are." At least, in all scenarios that weren't her imagination, they were.

"Right. Uh-huh."

The disbelief in Grace's tone made Sloane smile in a slow, satisfied way. Maybe Cooper had been fudging the truth when he asked for the flash drive. Or maybe he'd found the images that moment in the lobby.

But, no shadow of a doubt, he would have found a reason to come see her before he left on his trip. She just knew it.

CHAPTER TWENTY-TWO

THEY DIDN'T TALK for four days.

Four whole days of meetings and promotional appearances, Cooper had told her. Interviews with big-name magazines and TV spots with Food Network celebrity chefs. Certainly not thinking about her back in Dallas. Certainly not allowing an innocent kiss on the cheek to drive him crazy like Sloane was doing.

Sloane and Cooper hadn't gone on a date. There was no logical reason she should be checking her phone this much. He was minding his own business. Promoting his restaurant. Rubbing elbows with the bigwigs.

After Grace left, Sloane recategorized her cookbook and magazine collection, arranged it on her floor-to-ceiling bookcase accordingly and catalogued it in an Excel spreadsheet. All of the pieces she was responsible for on the J. Marian account were ahead of schedule or awaiting little things like restaurant openings before she could finish them. Thanks to the cookbook organization project, the content calendar for her website was full of enough recipe ideas to last until the end of the year. Two full weeks of posts were photographed, edited and scheduled for publication. And she was starting to conceptualize the cookbook proposal that had come from nowhere.

"These are divine, Meezy," Grace said around a mouthful of roasted grape and almond crumble bars Sloane had packed for her to take. Crumbs spilled onto the only empty space of countertop that was visible on the webcam. The rest was cluttered by stacked pans, cutting boards, scraps of what looked like some sort of crust and various cooking utensils. "You should send some of these to Levi."

"I think I will." Not as a peace offering, but as a symbol of solidarity for their don't-ask-don't-tell agreement.

"So, is your cooking spree over yet?"

Sloane angled her laptop and opened the door to the refrigerator, which was lined from top to bottom with neatly stacked glass storage containers. "The homeless shelter actually told me I'd given them too much. And my fridge is *still* full."

Grace stopped chopping herbs and looked at Sloane warily. "That bad, huh?"

Caught. Sloane should have downplayed her anxiety about Cooper. Even through the stretch of cyberspace, her friend could still see right through her. She closed the refrigerator door. "I wish you were here to help me eat it."

"Yeah, me, too."

Strangely, Sloane's apartment felt emptier without Grace even though Sloane had lived alone for years. The idea of having a roommate had never even crossed her mind. She wasn't sure she could subject someone to her special brand of chaos. Her hands worked deftly to rearrange the Honeycrisp apples in the fruit bowl, the glossiest reds to the ones that were predominantly yellow.

And in the same way her apartment felt emptier now that its walls had known Grace, so did her time since she'd known Cooper. There was an ingredient missing from the life she'd been desperate to get back that made it decidedly bland—and he was about six feet tall and handsome.

"You could donate some to your crazy rich neighbor." Grace's words broke through her thoughts.

"Oh, I'm way ahead of you. I ran into her on

the elevator and told her I was testing frittata recipes. And, wouldn't you know, she ordered some fruit-and-cheese trays from a specialty store and made a fancy brunch out of it for her Bunco friends."

"She would."

Sloane's phone buzzed on the counter. When she saw who it was, she dropped the phone and it clattered into the composite sink.

Fortunately, there was no water in it this time.

"I gotta go, Grace." She crossed to the computer.

"Is that Cooper? Enjoy."

Sloane soaked in Grace's teasing, big-sisterly grin long enough before she closed the lid of her laptop and answered her phone.

"Hello?" She heard the connection click and tried again. "Hello."

"Hi, Sloane." The smile in his voice tugged her into her chair as his golden-brown eyes flashed through her mind again. "It's good to hear your voice."

A grin stretched across her face. "How's New York?"

"It was busy, but I'm back now, a little earlier than planned." Cooper breathed a little nervous laugh. "Hey, um, listen, Sloane. This might be totally inappropriate for me to ask, and I'd completely understand if you don't want to go." The last part of his sentence stretched into a hesitant sound.

Sloane leaned her elbows on the table in anticipation. "Uh-huh?"

"My grief support group is meeting tonight, and I wanted to know if you'd go with me."

"Yes."

Did she really just say that?

"Okay, awesome."

If Cooper hadn't responded, she might have imagined that word coming out of her mouth. No questions asked. No overanalyzing it. Just yes.

"Pick you up at five-thirty," he said.

Sloane stared at her phone for a full minute after the call had disconnected. Did that really happen? Did she just agree to what could equate to getting her soul scrubbed raw with a metal sponge—in front of Cooper? Again?

What were these people even like? For all she knew, they were barbarians who'd tie her up with flames licking at her feet until she spilled her guts.

"I'm pretty sure that's how they break people in some cultures," she told Grace an hour later, computer perched on her bed as she dismantled her closet.

Grace made the sputtering sound that let Sloane know she was rolling her eyes. "Sloane Bradley. That's not going to happen. Do you wanna know how I know? Pick the green one."

Sloane held the dress up to her body and peered at it, smoothing the soft cotton blend. "How?"

"Because there's no way on earth Cooper would *ever* let that happen to you."

COOPER THOUGHT NEW YORK would be good for him. Time to insert distance between him and Sloane. But, as much as he tried to distract himself, he'd thought of her every time he saw a blond ponytail. Black yoga pants. Pretty much every time he ate. Every time a server brought him a drink menu and he refused it.

The truth was he couldn't keep looking in the rearview mirror, waiting to get hit. Not when he was trying to help Sloane believe she could move on.

Besides, Sloane had already proven she could handle everything that came with him. But hopefully she wouldn't have to.

He hadn't bothered with the formalities this time. No recipes to develop. No food to taste.

No ideas to hash out. No proposals to review. Just an admission he wanted to see Sloane as soon as possible when he got off the plane. Just a guy picking up a girl to expose the most protected part of his life. No big deal, right?

He was a few minutes early but knew Sloane would be watching for him from her apartment window. Sure enough, a minute later, she appeared through the lobby double doors. Blond braid draped across her shoulder. Green cotton dress. Gray sweater. And that lip-nibbling smile she wore when she was shy.

Basically, it was all over for him.

"Hi." Cooper walked around the front of the Defender, unable to control the goofy grin. While he hadn't gauged how much he'd miss Sloane, he also didn't expect this almost magnetic reaction to seeing her—like he couldn't get to her fast enough.

"Hi." She stopped at the curb.

He closed the distance, unwilling to allow any space between them.

Were they doing this?

Commit, Coop. He swung an arm behind Sloane and drew her close to his side.

He guessed they were.

She slid her hand across his back.

"It was weird not seeing you," he said into

her hair, which smelled a little like a strawberry milk shake. He stepped forward to open the passenger door.

"Yeah. You, too."

There, on the seat, he'd left a slim brown box with orange script. Jacques Torres. She picked it up, scanned it from every angle and handed it to him.

"These are for you, actually."

"For me?" She sat to untie the orange ribbon, and tried to pry open the lid. She adjusted her grip three times, careful and methodical the way she always was.

Finally, after he'd gotten in and started the vehicle, the lid wiggled free, revealing twelve assorted chocolate confections complete with elaborate designs. They'd had Sloane's name all over them.

"Chocolates!"

"I stopped by his shop while I was in New York. It was like Willy Wonka opening a shop in Paris. Best hot cocoa ever, too."

Sloane studied the chocolates. Some had been poured into perfect fruit shapes. Others were squared or circular with patterns so precise they looked printed. "They're almost too pretty to eat."

He idled at a stoplight, looking at Sloane for

a moment before he laughed. "Well, in that case, hand 'em over."

"No way. You'll be lucky if I share."

They somehow avoided eating the chocolates as they caught up with each other. Sloane told Cooper about the conference and cookbook proposal she'd started putting together, a new knife set she'd been sent to demo and a little girl in Davon's cooking class who'd been placed with a permanent family for adoption. "Enough about me. What did you do?"

"Oh, you know. Shook a lot of hands. Saw some sights. Got a lot of work done in my hotel room." He cleared his throat. "I didn't get an in with Johnson and Fox, though. That's awesome, Sloane."

"Thanks." She shifted in her seat.

"We're getting pretty close to the church." The houses were starting to get bigger, the buildings more ornate.

Sloane nodded and took a deep breath.

"Southern Methodist University is in this neighborhood." Cooper said as Sloane leaned over to get her purse. "It's a beautiful campus."

"Yeah, I'll bet if it's around here."

Cooper pointed at the biggest house yet with ornate Georgian columns. "I wonder who lives in this house. Probably someone famous."

"I bet three of my apartment could fit on that lawn." Sloane let out a nervous laugh.

Cooper made a left turn, and the church appeared in the middle of the neighborhood—gleaming in the evening sun, majestic. "This is us."

Sloane took a tin of breath mints from her purse, the chalky white tablets clattering against the metal in her shaky hands. As he parked, he saw her trembling hands pop a few in her mouth then extend the tin across the console.

His gaze met Sloane's. Was she going along with this to placate him? "Sloane, you don't have to do this."

"No, I want to." She trapped the mints between her teeth and swallowed hard, putting the tin away. "I want to. I promise."

As they walked up the steps to the carved wooden doors of the church, Cooper pressed his hand lightly against the small of her back. Just enough to let her know he was there.

Cooper peeked through the window of the sanctuary as they passed it, swaths of color slicing through the darkness courtesy of its stained glass window.

The hallways were dim and empty except for

one room that was lit and filled with chatter. Sloane paused when they reached the room.

Cooper slipped his hand into hers, intertwining their fingers, and gave a gentle squeeze. Before his own first meeting, he had envisioned it would be something out of a courtroom drama with the whole spotlight interrogation thing going on. But this was a warm and cheerful classroom with colorful bulletin boards lining the walls, several round tables in the middle and a longer one at the front that held a coffeemaker, a few homemade pies and plastic plates and cutlery.

"Well, if it isn't our long-lost friend, Cooper," an older woman with almost magenta hair said.

Sloane's grip tightened on his hand. He rifled through his mental files for the older woman's name—Maggie. A few people walked over to them, hugging Cooper in a line like he was a prodigal son making his grand return. He should have made the effort to be there more often. It was good for his soul.

He tried to engage with the people who were greeting him, but he was focused on Sloane as she released his hand and sidestepped the crowd. She produced her hand sanitizer from her purse and rubbed a drop into her palms.

Great. She was uncomfortable. He needed to get to her. To let her know she didn't have to feel alone or scared here.

"And who d'you have with you?" The old cowboy wearing the teal checked button-down noticed Sloane. She looked up like she'd been caught with a purse full of butterscotch at a candy store.

"This is Sloane." Cooper raised his hand halfway in her direction. He wedged himself through the little crowd as the people around him turned to see her.

And as he knew they would, the chorus of warmth his friends gave Sloane visibly eased the tension in her face and shoulders.

No questions asked. Just welcome.

The magenta-haired Maggie guided them to her table. Two men pulled chairs behind Cooper and Sloane even though it was a squeeze for them both to sit there. Someone put plates of warm blueberry pie, sparkling with Turbinado sugar atop a more brown than golden crust, in front of them.

They were a lively bunch, this group. Most of them were smiling and happily chatting between bites of gooey desserts.

Had Sloane expected something different? Before his first visit he remembered imagining they'd all be wearing black. But they weren't, and none of them were today except for one lady. But he didn't think that counted since a huge picture of Michael Bublé adorned the front of her shirt.

"Sorry I'm late, everybody." Kevin, the counselor on staff at the church, walked through the room, heavy-soled boots clomping against the thin carpeting. His lumbering stature and proportional personality almost overshadowed the small young woman trailing him. Her arms hugged her rib cage; her eyes were round and terrified.

"This is Amy. She's going to be joining us today."

There were no open spots at either of the two tables, so Cooper stood and squeezed Sloane's shoulder to join him at one of the empty ones. A few others shuffled around, too, so Amy didn't have to sit by herself. He watched as Sloane sneaked glances at Amy, working to discern information about her, he knew. It was a horrible thing to admit, but he was glad there was another new person here who looked as uncomfortable in her skin as Sloane seemed— as he'd felt before he'd gotten the hang of it.

Sloane made eye contact with the girl and gave a tiny smile. Even when she was uncomfortable, Sloane's instinct was to help. She'd come a long way from the version of her he'd met that first day.

And sure enough, the terror in the girl's face softened at Sloane's gesture.

"Okay, everyone," Kevin said. "Let's get started. For those of you who are new, Amy and..." He paused and the attention whipped in Sloane's direction.

"Roan," the old cowboy supplied.

"Actually, it's Sloane," Cooper corrected.

The counselor grinned. "Sloane. My name is Kevin, and I'm on staff here. We typically open the floor for anyone who wants it before we get started." He rubbed his hands together. "So, does anyone have anything they want to share with the group?"

CHAPTER TWENTY-THREE

SLOANE MENTALLY REARRANGED a pile of crumbs on the table and nibbled at her thumbnail. This was it. They were totally going to make her share her sob story. She could feel their eyes, their silent pressure.

"No one today?" Kevin broke the silence, and Sloane let out a breath she didn't know she'd been holding. "That's all right. Because you know I'm always good for a few words."

A low rumble of laughter rippled through the room. She stole another glance at Amy. Sunken cheeks, shadowy eyes, slumped posture. She knew she should be listening to Kevin, but it seemed surreal that she could pinpoint the spot in Amy's body that was pierced by the pain, the spot that radiated ache. It was an ache Sloane knew too well.

She turned and met Cooper's gaze. The look he gave her filled her with peace and the certainty that, no matter what, she wasn't alone.

"But the place where we're most broken, the

most empty of ourselves," Kevin continued, "is the place where we can be filled in a way that's harder for people who haven't experienced a loss."

Sloane tried to process Kevin's words. How could anything be harder for someone who hadn't lost, who hadn't had parts of themselves ripped away?

The people could choose to surrender, Kevin said. Or they could choose to let their pain define them. Sloane just couldn't imagine a world where guilt didn't come out of nowhere to sucker punch her. Where she deserved life and happiness when she'd taken those very things away from Aaron—and let his parents bury their only son believing a lie.

Her vision blurred as the image of what might have been the Jacobsens' last family photo filled her mind. She'd chuckled when she saw it framed in their living room, Aaron's much shorter parents carrying him between them. The love for each other written all over the laughter on their faces. It saw no differences in blood or DNA.

Her thoughts were interrupted by the clatter. Amy had stood so fast her chair was on its side. But the girl didn't look back as she rushed from the room. Without a thought,

Sloane quickly followed. She turned down a hallway toward the scraping sound of a door and saw it closing. The women's restroom.

"Amy," she called through the laminate wooden door. "Are you in here?"

A sniffle echoed against the tiled walls.

Sloane pushed the door open and stepped in. "I'm here if you need to talk. It's my first time, too. It's a little overwhelming."

Hand sanitizer. Her bottle was still at the table with her purse. She settled for washing them in the sink the old-fashioned way, grateful for something to do. As she blotted her hands with a paper towel, the stall door opened. Amy's face was splotched and tearstained.

She looked Sloane up and down then stepped out of the stall. "I can't believe I lost it like that," she said, leaning heavily against the wall.

Sloane sat on the sink, cold water seeping through her dress. "No, I understand completely. You just had to get out of there."

"Yeah, that's exactly how I felt." Amy sniffed. "So, who are you here for? Who did you lose?"

"Aaron. He was my best friend."

Amy sighed. "I lost my mom. She's—was—my last family left."

Sloane's heart wrenched inside her chest. The girl couldn't have been much older than her. And to have survived her whole family? She couldn't imagine. Suddenly it felt like way too long since she'd seen her own parents.

A knock sounded. The bathroom door cracked. "Sloane, are you all right?" Cooper's deep voice was full of concern.

"We're all right. I'll be out in a minute."

She pushed herself off of the counter to give Amy more room as the girl scrubbed her face under a stream of water.

Amy turned off the faucet and gripped the counter, water dripping from her face into the sink. "So, does it get better?"

"I think so." Sloane handed Amy a paper towel. "I hope so." *I'm probably not the best person to ask.*

"Good." The girl dabbed at her face. "Because I don't think I could take it if the rest of my life is going to be like the past two months."

Two months.

"Thanks for coming in here and talking to me." She threw out the paper towel then grasped the door handle. "I think I'm going to leave and try again next time."

Sloane nodded and tried to smile, incapable of words. Two months. She was going on thirteen years. There was a huge difference in the time lapse, but not a stark contrast in what their grief looked like. Maybe she should be more like everyone else in that room—smiling and social and moving on with their lives.

"You're quiet," Cooper said as they walked to the car.

"Just thinking." She wasn't ready to process this realization out loud.

Sloane reached for the door handle, but Cooper's hand curved around her elbow and pulled gently until she was nestled in that place at his side, wrapped in his arms. "Thanks for coming with me." His chin brushed against her head with every word.

"It was—it was good. Really good."

On the drive home, Cooper talked about a new Asian fusion restaurant that opened in Deep Ellum, and she told him about some of Grace's more far-fetched recipes that could go on their menu.

He stopped in front of Sloane's building and climbed out to walk her to the door.

"Do you want to come in?"

Cooper searched her eyes, his forehead wrinkled in curiosity.

"I have a ton of leftover recipes I did for the website," she told him—just in case he was questioning her motives. "It's practically an all-you-can-eat buffet in my refrigerator right now."

"Yeah, that sounds good."

Sloane's spine prickled as they walked across the street and through the lobby.

The elevator took forever. When the door finally opened, there was Mrs. Melone.

Perfect.

The older woman stopped in her tracks, as her gaze shifted between Cooper and Sloane.

No, friendly neighbor. Your eyes aren't deceiving you. The Bunco ladies would get an earful. Mrs. Melone would probably call an emergency meeting the minute she left the lobby—if she had the decency to wait that long.

"Good evening, Mrs. Melone." Sloane dipped her head in greeting.

The older woman slid an appraising glance over Cooper's form before she straightened to her full height and walked past them. "Good evening." She looked over her shoulder at Sloane and winked.

Ha! Mrs. Melone had totally broken character. Finally.

Sloane nudged Cooper into the elevator doors before he could see more of this unlocked sass—those penciled eyebrows all wiggly and suggestive.

When they got to her apartment, Cooper hesitated in the doorway.

"What? I'm not going to bite."

"Don't you need to clean up a little first?"

Sloane crossed her arms. "For what?"

"Well, women usually—" He stopped himself, and hung his head in surrender.

"What are you saying, Coop? Out of all of the dozens of women you know, I'm the only tidy one?"

"Try hundreds."

She tried to push him into the hallway, but the solid mass of him didn't budge.

"Okay, okay. I won't assume anything about you ever again." He slid past her, raising his arms in victory that he'd made it past her. They fell to his side as he surveyed the apartment. "Wow, you really weren't joking. Were you that sure I'd agree to come up?"

"No, it's always like this. It was this clean when you were here the other day."

"I guess I wasn't in any condition to be observant." He crossed to Sloane's black Crate&Barrel entertainment stand and ran a fingertip along the top. No dust to speak of.

"What, were you a housekeeper in a different life or something?"

"No. Can we just eat?" He was making her self-conscious. She opened her refrigerator and closed it immediately. Spotless surfaces were one thing, but she strongly suspected Cooper would take issue with the state of her refrigerator.

But the tilt of his head and his sly half smile said he knew exactly what she was hiding. "Let's see it."

She sighed and slowly opened the door. Her perishables were arranged symmetrically, each item stored in a sealed glass container and labeled with the exception of the milk. Despite her insistence that they'd get their glass bottles back in better condition than before, the dairy that supplied her milk didn't allow her to label their bottles.

"So, what are we having?" The humor was gone from Cooper's voice, his ornery grin replaced with understanding and something so much worse.

Pity.

Sloane turned away from him—she couldn't take that look in his eyes anymore—and started pulling out containers and arranging them on the counter.

"What? Sloane, are you mad?"

"You must think I'm some kind of freak."

"No, I—"

"I don't drive. You could eat off my stupid toilet seat. I don't have any friends here…"

"Whoa. I didn't say any of that. That's… it's…"

"It's true, Cooper." She clenched her fist against the counter. "All of those people in your group. You're all happy and moving on with your lives. When is that going to happen for me? When am I going to be the one who's free?"

"Sloane." Cooper's voice was even, calm. "How can you be free if you won't forgive yourself?"

She opened her mouth, hoping something coherent and smart and right would come out. But she had nothing. She opened the lids on the containers and began to inspect them.

"Sloane, I'm sorry," he said quietly.

"No, you're right. You're totally right."

He sighed and gripped the granite counter. Probably regretting his moment of straightforwardness. But maybe that was exactly what Sloane needed. Someone to confront her with the difficult questions.

"I need to figure out what I'm going to do

about that. I really do. But let's eat first." She
upended a container labeled Harvest Lasagna
into a casserole dish, smoothed it with a spatula and put it in the oven. Cooper chopped
some greens for a salad to go with the vinaigrette from the fridge. Sloane set the table.

If they talked to each other at all, it was only
about the food. But she could practically feel
his concern hovering over her as they worked.
Finally, there was nothing left for them to do
but wait for the timer to wind down before the
lasagna would be ready to pull from the oven.

Sloane ripped off her cardigan, suddenly
suffocated by the long sleeves with the heat
radiating from the oven. "I'm going to go
change. Be right back." She slammed the door
to her bedroom behind her.

A seam popped at the waist of her dress as
she yanked it over her head. She kicked off her
ballet flats so violently that one sailed over the
bed almost into the bathroom. She fell face-
first onto the down comforter, willing the draft
from the window to cool her—her body and
her mood.

How did one go about forgiving herself
when she was ready? Say it out loud?

The oven timer beeped. Sloane pulled on a
clean V-neck and yoga pants, harnessing the

sweaty strands of her hair into a bun. Much better. Much better on all fronts.

"That sage smells amazing," Cooper said from behind the kitchen island. "Are you good?" There was a double meaning in his words. She could see him restraining his questions, stifling his urge to fix things for her because she wasn't ready. Because he respected her.

"I'm not okay." Sloane gave a pathetic, lopsided smile. "But I feel like I'm going to be." Admitting that out loud had a better effect than she expected. So freeing that an ironic laugh burst from her.

Cooper snickered, breaking the lines of concentration on his face. "That's good, Sloane." He'd already portioned the lasagna next to their salads and filled two glasses with ice and water. They bypassed the kitchen table for the living room and sat next to each other on the couch.

"This is so good it should probably be illegal," Cooper said, after his second bite of lasagna. "Let me see if I can name these flavors."

"You can try." Sloane took a sip of water.

He savored another forkful, square jaw working as he rolled the flavors around his taste buds. "Butternut squash, for sure."

Those lips are luscious enough to kiss. Sloane's hand wandered to her cheek as the baseball game replayed in her mind for the millionth time. "Yes. Continue."

"Sage. Butter—"

"*Browned* butter."

He raised his eyebrows. "Okay, *browned* butter. Ricotta." He smacked his lips. "A bit of dried cranberry?"

Sloane nodded. "Can you taste the other fruit? Butternut squash's sweet wife?"

He cut off another corner of his piece and lifted the top layer to inspect it. "Is that apple?"

"Only the best combination fall has to offer. They're a match made in heaven." She took a bite and closed her eyes to pick out the apple flavor and let it melt across her palate.

They finished their dinner and sank into the couch with matching full and satisfied sighs. A few moments later, Cooper sat up and leaned toward her. "Sloane, something you said has been bothering me."

She straightened. So they'd arrived at the part in the evening where he confronted her about her...oddities. "Mmm-hmm?"

"I don't want you to think anyone in that support group today has everything together," he said. "Nobody has it together. Everyone has good days and bad days."

Interesting. "What do you mean?"

"I mean that, if you had come with me the last time I went, you would have seen me break down and cry like a baby because it was Jordan's birthday."

"My mom calls me every year on Aaron's birthday." Of course, the past few years, she'd let the call go to voice mail. But that was beside the point. "I guess the meeting just made me feel like I should be having way more good days than bad days at this point. Like I'm destined to be—I don't know—frozen in those memories forever."

"You don't have to be." Cooper slipped his fingers through hers.

"I know." Their knees touched as she leaned toward him, spreading sparks of heat through Sloane's whole body. "I know my grief manifests itself in pretty weird ways. That I've spent the last twelve years marinating in it and letting it turn me into *this*." She swept a hand to indicate her color-coded shelves and spotless surfaces.

"Sloane—"

"But I can't grasp what freedom and forgiveness look like. I don't think I've even figured out how to cope."

Cooper took a sip of water. "Life should be so much more than just coping." He traced the outline of Sloane's hand with his fingers, soft like the strokes of a delicate paintbrush. "You have to decide to really live. You have your work, you have the kids. You have your friends and family."

She bit her lip in anticipation when he hesitated.

You have me.

But the words never left his mouth.

"Where do I begin? How do I retrain myself not to focus so much on perfect? Orderly. Predictable."

"It's been better lately, hasn't it?"

She shrugged. "I guess. Yeah."

"The best thing Simone ever taught me was when you look at something, don't look for the imperfections. Try to see the beauty."

She swallowed hard, their locked gaze too heavy for her to hold and process his words at the same time.

Don't look for the imperfections. Try to see the beauty.

Is that how he looked at her?

They sat in silence for a few moments. "So you haven't driven since…?"

"I haven't been behind the wheel since the accident," she admitted. "That was one of Dallas's biggest selling points in the first place."

"Mass transit?"

Sloane nodded, and the confessions kept rolling out. "But I don't leave my apartment very much or at least I didn't before the Coopers came into my life."

He grinned, squeezing her hand. "And the whole organization thing?"

"I wasn't always like this." Visions of her collaged bedroom walls and overflowing jewelry boxes at her parents' house flashed through her mind. "They said it's OCD triggered by the PTSD after the accident."

She watched Cooper's face for signs of discomfort, but he nodded in acknowledgement. "So that's why you need those contracts with VisibilityNet. So you can work from home." His grip remained steady on her hand.

Sloane nodded. "The therapist my parents made me see said it was my brain's natural defense mechanism to make me want to control things since I couldn't control what happened to Aaron."

"Exactly. It wasn't your fault." Cooper released her hand and reached for her leg, gently sliding it onto his lap. "And this is where—"

"My leg broke." She guided his pointer finger along the bones. "Three places here and four places there. And this is where they put in the rods."

Cooper's fingers slid up and down the length of Sloane's scar, sending prickling goose bumps across her arms and legs. The tenderness in his touch...

"What are you thinking about?" she asked him.

"The baseball game."

Her pulse thudded in her ears. "I know." Any doubts about Cooper's feelings for her were gone as her gaze slid over his face.

The truth was written boldly across his features. Hungry. Expectant. Inching closer to her. "I wanted more."

She nodded and felt her lips part, heavy and tingling with anticipation. Begging for the gap to be closed.

Cooper paused, close enough she could feel his breath. He framed her face in his knife-scarred hands. His eyes asked a question she answered by giving in to the pull. By pressing into the distance until her lips met his, gentle and sweet and tentative at first.

But then his mouth parted, and a rush washed over her—a rush at once warmer and clearer than she'd felt in ages. She allowed herself to be bathed in it, not just dipping a toe in the water but sinking until it stretched well above her head. Only it wasn't like being underwater at all. Because, for the first time in ages, she didn't have to fight to breathe.

Their lips untangled, but her momentum went rogue. Sloane swayed toward him, fighting to remain upright. When their eyes met, her exhilaration was mirrored in Cooper's eyes.

He wrapped his arms around her shoulders and pulled her so close she could smell smoky hints of the bacon he'd cooked earlier that day and his rich cologne. "Are you glad that happened?"

"Really glad."

"Crazy family and all?"

Sloane nodded. "Crazy OCD and all?"

He tilted his head a few inches, revealing an intensity in his eyes that made Sloane's toes curl. "All of you," he whispered, brushing his lips against her forehead and returning her to her rightful place.

Against the cadence of his quickened heartbeat, Sloane absorbed what had happened. Did she really kiss Graham Cooper? She would have howled in disbelief if someone had told her that a few months ago.

"I'm going to need you to be patient with me, Sloane."

At the gravity in his voice, she squeezed his arm in support and to encourage him to continue.

"I've destroyed pretty much everything I've ever touched because of my drinking—every…relationship." He kissed the top of her head. "But when my plane touched down today, I knew I had to try."

"Don't see the imperfections, right? See the beauty."

"That's right." Relief softened the tension in Cooper's face. "Can we work on that? Together?"

She pressed her lips to his cheek.

A glint flashed in Cooper's eyes before he kissed her again.

"I need to get home, to take Maddie out. I don't want to, but—" He kissed her again. "This could be dangerous."

This could be very dangerous, indeed.

Sloane walked him to the elevator, their hands woven together. Savoring the last moments of nearness to him. "Tell Maddie hi."

They'd definitely crossed a line they could never take back. When they kissed again to say goodbye, she didn't mind that fact one bit.

Not when it gave her no doubt there was still a pulse ticking under her skin.

CHAPTER TWENTY-FOUR

COOPER HADN'T EXPECTED it to happen this fast.

One minute, he'd been determined to keep Sloane at arm's length, away from the wide surface area of debris his errant addiction tended to create, and the next, he was kissing her. Waking up early on a Saturday to get his work done so he'd have time to see her.

After careful research on her website, Cooper had ordered a brilliant arrangement of Stargazer lilies from his mother's florist to butter up Sloane for his next plan. But the flowers weren't even the icing on the cake compared to where they were going next.

He paused at Sloane's door, rearranging an errant flower he knew she would notice and fix if left askew. The door opened before he could knock. A flash of blond and cream appeared before her arms were around his neck and her full weight slammed into him. He wrapped his free arm around her waist as her lips covered his.

Oh.

He hadn't expected this.

This was nice.

"Hey." Sloane touched her forehead to his. There was no trace of the morose chill, just a warm playfulness as her feet touched the floor. She swept a strand of hair behind her ear, leaving a streak of flour across her cheek. "What are you doing here? With flowers."

Perfect. She was in a great mood. Almost giddy, though trying to tone it down, he could tell.

What had he done to deserve this girl who'd witnessed him at his sloppy worst and still opened her door happy to see him? He would do whatever it took to keep her.

She took the flowers and gift bag then pulled Cooper through the doorway.

And suddenly he felt at home. "Wow, it smells like Paris in here." The warm, yeasty aroma of bread baking washed over him like melted butter.

"Is that a good thing?"

"Yeah, considering I lived next to a boulangerie. Wow." He wanted to bottle the smell and spray it everywhere he went. He wanted to bottle the way Sloane felt in his arms, the sight of her with no makeup, flour smudged on her face. Relaxed, softened, gorgeous.

"I'm making an apple galette." She shook a pan of glossy caramel sauce on the stove. Perfect consistency. Made his mouth water.

She dipped a spoon in it and took a little taste, smacking her lips together to judge the flavor, and then shifted the pan to a different burner and turned off the stove.

What was she trying to do to him?

She stood on tiptoes to retrieve something from the cabinet—a vase. He stepped toward her and took the flowers, resisting the craving to run his hands down the curve of her waist to her hip, to lean her against the counter and taste the caramel on her lips.

"That's sort of perfect," he told her as he put the vase under the tap.

"That I'm making a galette? Why?"

He grinned and set the flowers on the counter. "You'll see." He held the gift bag out to her.

Her eyes stayed glued to the bag as she wiped her hands on a towel then took it from him. She pulled out a small wooden box with ornate designs carved into its surface. "What is this?"

"Open it."

Cooper watched Sloane's face as the hinges

crcakcd open. Λn adorable groove formed between her eyebrows as she slid a card from the box. "Were these…?"

"Simone's? Yes."

"Wow." She removed the cards, sifting through the stained recipes written in Simone's tiny script. *"Cooper."*

Mission accomplished. "I know how much you love to bake and, well, Simone did, too."

"Thank you, Cooper. Having this part of her, it just—it means a lot."

"Yeah, well, *you* mcan a lot to me."

Had he really admitted that to her? Out loud? Her expression confirmed he had. Her enthusiastic embrace and kiss told him she returned the sentiment.

Cooper pressed a kiss to her hairline and took a step back, unable to stop the grin. "As much as I enjoyed that, it's not the reason I came."

"Oh, really?"

"No." He rubbed his hands together. "I'm here to kidnap you."

"And take me where?" Sloane's gaze flicked to the oven clock, to her flour-covered clothes then to the open notebook, stack of boxes and laptop on the table.

Maybe he shouldn't have sprung this on her.

"Well, I had a pretty long day scheduled.

But after *this*—" she gestured to the recipe box "—there's no way I can say no. Can you give me ten minutes?"

"Yeah. Of course. Take your time."

"Okay. I'll be right back." She headed down the hallway to her bedroom.

Strong curiosity shuffled his feet toward Sloane's modern dining room table. It was her work space, clearly. In one corner, her camera tripod was raised high and angled over an aged, end grain cutting board. On the other side of the table was a stack of three medium-size boxes and two smaller ones open next to her laptop. One was a parcel of cooking utensils from a big online kitchen supplier. A handwritten note signed by the CEO of the company rested on Sloane's keyboard. It was apparently awaiting entry into the spreadsheet open on the screen, the next on a long list.

Cooper couldn't resist lifting the flap on a box from Amazon, which was filled with toothbrushes, bottles of hand sanitizer and packets of disposable cutlery.

"Old habits die hard." The velvety sound of Sloane's voice startled him.

Cooper slid the box away from the edge of the table and faced her. "Sorry, I was just—"

"Curious?" Sloane grinned and planted a

kiss on his cheek on her way to the kitchen. "I know, Cooper. By now, I'm fully aware." Her face was wet, hair pushed back with a black headband. "So, what am I supposed to wear on our adventure anyway?"

The oven timer dinged as Sloane was pulling the galette out. Perfect timing.

"Something warm." He swallowed the guilt that was lodged in his throat, like a bear that couldn't resist the taste of honey and got caught in a trap. "Sorry. I shouldn't have been snooping."

"No, you're welcome to look through those boxes. The guy from the post office just came. I have a PO box for mail from readers and sponsors and other people I don't really want knowing where I live."

"Smart girl." He crossed to the kitchen and watched as Sloane expertly poured the caramel sauce over the galette, coaxing it with a rubber spatula. "That looks delicious."

"Very French, huh? Okay, I'll let that set and finish up really fast after I get ready."

He watched her walk to the bedroom, licking caramel sauce from her fingers, and then took her up on her offer. It wasn't snooping if he had her permission, right?

The other boxes, still sealed, were from a

major kitchen appliance corporation—his preferred retailer, actually—and another company that was renowned for its gourmet prepared foods. His favorite store-bought jams, in fact.

So Sloane was essentially a rock star. There was even a rubber-band-wrapped stack of letters probably written by adoring fans. And he and his little restaurant that may or may not even survive had been stealing all of her time and energy.

She reappeared a few minutes later with tall, tan leather boots tucked under her arm, blond hair in a ponytail with a feminine braid framing her forehead, dressed in a long-sleeved plaid shirt and jeans that were tucked into knee-length socks.

Cooper watched in amazement as she sliced into the galette, placed it on a white plate and staged it on a brick-red placemat on the opposite end of the dining table next to the window. An arrangement of Honeycrisp apples was the final piece to her puzzle before she began taking photos in the natural light, twisting and maneuvering her body to capture it from every angle.

"Okay," she said, replacing the lens cap on her camera. "We can go."

"You might want to bring that with you." He indicated the camera.

She slipped it into the black bag, zipped it then turned to the boots next to her.

Cooper knelt in front of her and took one boot, helped guide her foot into it then zipped it up the side.

A peachy blush spread across Sloane's cheeks. "Thanks."

He smiled at her and shifted to the other boot, sliding his hand down her calf to grip her ankle. When her boot was zipped, he straightened.

Sloane draped her arms around his shoulders, her eyelids heavy, her lips the perfect magnet for his. He slid his thumbs along her jawbone and rested his hands in the curve of her neck before he kissed her again. Slowly, lazily, savoring the give of her lips against his and the taste of her strawberry lip gloss.

"I don't deserve you," he whispered.

She rested her forehead against his. "Yes, you do. Whoever or whatever gave you that impression, don't listen. Listen to me."

And she and her strawberry lip gloss convinced him again.

THINGS WERE SILENT and warm between them on the short drive to their destination, fingers mingled together on the console.

As he pulled up to the Dallas Farmers Market, she turned to him, eyes wide.

"How did you know I've always wanted to come here?"

It took someone with a special kind of appreciation for food to experience this place the way Cooper did. Somehow he knew he'd met his match.

"I can't believe this is your first time." He laughed as he got out of the car.

"Well, I always get my produce delivered, so…" Sloane trailed off as they approached the huge first stand—a towering display of pumpkins. "Yeah, I think that's going to have to change." She slipped a hand in the crook of his arm.

Cooper paused in front of the pumpkin stand and faced Sloane. "I think a lot of things are going to have to change."

A look of uncertainty fleeted through her eyes.

"Wait. That didn't come out right. I didn't mean—"

Sloane stifled the rest of his thought with a kiss. And when she pulled away, the warmth in her eyes had returned, coupled with a smile that filled her whole face. "Is it something along the lines of that? Was that what you meant?"

Cooper nodded and brushed his lips against her forehead. "That's exactly what I meant."

They wandered hand in hand through the market, passing huge displays of just-picked, Texas-grown apples. Bags of kale and leafy greens. Ears of corn flanked by spindly gourds. Broccoli and Brussels sprouts. Jars of fresh, local honey.

"What's that *smell*?" Sloane asked just before he caught the spicy scent of sausage.

"A food truck." The marigold-colored truck was parked behind two small displays. Breakfast Burritos was painted in a chubby cursive on the truck's chalkboard sign. "I think we need one."

Sloane nodded. "Let's share. I'm still full from taste testing, but I have to have a bite."

They walked up to the order window.

"Sausage or vegetarian?" asked an aproned girl with jet-black hair.

Cooper flicked a questioning glance at Sloane.

"Definitely sausage."

That's my girl. He exchanged a few bills for a thick, foil-wrapped burrito and a few plastic cups of chunky *pico de gallo*—his favorite *accoutrement* to any kind of Latin-inspired food. As he peeled the top of the foil, he heard the rustle of plastic behind him.

Sloane with her disposable cutlery. Was she planning to share his burrito with a fork?

He watched as she tossed the plastic wrapper in the trash can then froze, oblivious to him. She looked between the fork and spoon in either hand, bit her lip then splayed her fingers, allowing the utensils to fall into the trash.

"Wow."

"I just had a moment, Coop." She wrapped an arm around his waist and snuggled close to his side.

"I know. I'm very impressed with you."

"Good." She pulled the burrito to her mouth. "Now give me a bite."

Sloane let out a groan as she chewed. "This is so good!"

Cooper nodded as he savored his own bite of spinach-flour tortilla, earthy sausage, fluffy eggs and a tangy medley of peppers, onions, and mushrooms. "Reminds me of Paris—eating like this. There was a man who used to sell the best crepes you've ever tasted out of the back of his truck on our street. He'd set up shop, and these huge crowds would come to him."

"Who thought of food trucks anyway?"

Sloane took another bite as they walked along the covered market. "Who came up with the idea to drive around and take the food to the people?"

"Some genius, that's who." Cooper picked out some apples and handed the farmer exact change. "My mom bought a truck and did this whole experiment, but that got shot down by the Suits really fast."

"Lame."

The chicken farmer they passed prickled Cooper's chest with panic. He checked his watch. Whew. Two minutes to spare.

"Sloane, I forgot to tell you I have a quick meeting with the man who might be supplying the eggs and butter for the restaurant. Do you mind coming with me?"

She shrugged and took another bite, apparently more concerned with the burrito than him. "Do what you have to do," she said around the food in her mouth. "I'm having another moment over here."

"You do that, then."

Cooper had only talked by phone with the farmer who had come highly recommended to him, Wilbur Younts. But he was every bit the good ol' boy Cooper expected him to be: head-to-toe coveralls, firm handshake, sun-leathered skin. Their meeting was brief and to the point. Polite. While many details of the restaurant gave Cooper heartburn, this decision was easy. Prices were fair, quality guaranteed and the supply reliable. Wilbur Younts ran his farm with the efficiency of a Fortune 500 CEO and the comfortable manner of a worn pair of Carhartts.

After they exchanged documents and said goodbye, Sloane shot him a pointed look.

"What?"

"Why does your agreement only cover a month? He would probably give you a better deal if you commit to a longer period of time."

Cooper shrugged. "A lot could happen in a month."

"You don't think your restaurant's going to last a month?" Sloane's grin disappeared at his silence. "You don't think *you* are going to last a month." She sighed. "Cooper, why don't you just—"

"I can't quit my job."

Her eyebrows arched. "That's not what I was going to say, but—"

"I don't want to quit my job," he corrected himself.

"You're sure?"

"Positive. Hey, where'd the burrito go?" Maybe changing the subject would keep their adventure from becoming a wash.

Sloane gave an exaggerated shrug.

"I thought we were going to share." Cooper grinned. "We could have gotten you your own, but *no*. You said you weren't hungry."

"I'm not. I wasn't." A sheepish smile crossed her face. "It just tasted so good."

"Well, that's okay." Cooper draped an arm around her and pulled her to his side. "In this relationship, you can take as much as you need."

Relationship. Cooper's pulse escalated as the word left his mouth.

As Sloane stayed silent.

But out of the corners of his eyes, he saw her features light up as they walked to the parking lot, past the food truck where they'd ordered the breakfast burrito. Past the huge display of pumpkins where they'd stopped and—

Sloane yanked on his arm, halting him, and wrapped her arms around his neck. Any doubts he'd had about their relationship status were squashed by her kiss.

"Cooper, Cooper. You're going to be glad you chose a relationship with me," she said.

That was already a given. "Why?"

"Because I think I just figured out how to make sure your restaurant lasts much longer than a month."

CHAPTER TWENTY-FIVE

A FOOD TRUCK was a long shot. It really was. Sloane had seen a glimmer of hope and excitement in Cooper's eyes. An almost childlike idealism that disappeared as quickly as it had come, followed by a laundry list of excuses and ways it could fail.

J. Marian Restaurants had a truck, but their permits were probably expired.

He'd have to look at the budget logistics.

There wasn't time between his responsibilities at corporate and the restaurant launch now days away.

It would take him very little time, Sloane assured. She'd do all the legwork. It was the ultimate promotional strategy to drive traffic to the restaurant, a way she could remove some of the pressure from Cooper's shoulders. And when the most obvious plan appeared in her mind and tumbled out of her mouth, he agreed to try.

Crepes. He'd said it himself. How could they go wrong with crepes?

She'd called the first person she could think of the next morning—Marian. The Cooper who knew how to get things done. Fortunately, she thought the idea was brilliant.

"Let me run some numbers and take care of some red tape," Marian had said. "I think we can make this happen."

Sloane had a lot of work to do. But she couldn't think of someone more worth it. She could tell their little agreement was killing him. That he was desperate to know the details he'd promised to let her take care of.

But his obvious restraint was pretty endearing.

"Today we're going to have a special guest in our class," Sloane told her kids the next Thursday. "And I want you to be extra nice to Mr. Cooper. He's a real-life chef."

Sloane expected the kids to be impressed by that tidbit. But with the exception of Davon, the other kids seemed confused—if they showed any reaction at all. Her glance at Cooper was probably more uneasy than assuring, but he just hiked an eyebrow at her, as steady and confident as ever.

"Thanks, Sloane." He turned to the kids. "I

need a show of hands. Who here likes pancakes?"

Everyone in the room raised a hand.

"What abouuuuut...tacos?"

Another unanimous *yes*.

"Okay, last question." Cooper scratched the stubble on his jawline. "Who has heard of Paris, France?"

Chloe raised her hand. "Isn't that in Europe?"

"That's exactly right. Well, in France, we like to make crepes." He turned on one of the burners on the electric stove. "Crepes are like pancakes that are filled with all kinds of yummy things—kind of like a taco."

Miles's nose wrinkled. "Ew! Like tacos covered in syrup?"

Cooper flashed a smile at Sloane. "Not exactly. More like strawberries and chocolate rolled up in a pancake—except thinner."

"*That* sounds better." Chloe's sweet, matter-of-fact statement warmed Sloane's heart. So very Chloe.

"What do you think?" Cooper arranged the bowls of ingredients Sloane had prepared for him. "Do you guys want to make some?"

The kids responded with shouts of excitement. Now *that* was the enthusiasm she knew and loved.

Sloane watched as Cooper unbuttoned the cuffs of his long-sleeve shirt and rolled them up one at a time, baring tan, muscular fore-arms. Her fingers tingled with the urge to slide up and down the ridges of his shoulders and arms. Fresh awareness of the power behind his clean-cut sophistication flushed her cheeks.

Sloane's gaze was glued to him as he made crepes to order for the kids, muscles rippling between his wrists and elbows as he ladled batter from a metal bowl onto the crepe pans she'd brought along. She was aware of the sound of his voice as he narrated his actions to the kids and filled their crepes based on their preferences—macerated berries, fresh whipped cream, chocolate-hazelnut sauce or a savory pesto chicken option.

Just below the folded cuff of Cooper's shirt, Sloane saw the trace of faded ink, the tail end of the tattoo she'd noticed before. It looked like letters but she couldn't make out what they said. How had she not asked him about it be-fore?

"Miss Sloane?"

A tug on her elbow yanked her from her contemplation.

"I spilled." Juan David. Chocolate and berries smeared down the front of his shirt.

"No problem." Her voice came out breathy and low—proof of where her mind had been. "Let's get you to the sink." She stole a glance at Cooper and met an amused flash of white teeth that might as well have been a cattle prod sizzling every nerve ending in her body.

Get it together, Sloane. But what if she didn't want to?

"Hey, Miss Sloane?" Juan David swiped at his perpetual runny nose with the back of his rounded wrist as she blotted his shirt with a wet kitchen towel. "Is Mr. Cooper your boyfriend or something?"

The towel fell from her hand. Was she so obvious that an eight-year-old kid had seen it? Did that mean Davon knew he was her boyfriend, too?

Boyfriend. It was mind-boggling. A few weeks ago, she had been convinced she was destined to stay single forever. That she didn't have the capacity to feel this way for someone. That she wasn't worthy.

But Cooper—he'd helped her see differently.

She picked up the towel from the floor, unable to control the curve of her lips. "Just wash your hands, Juan David."

"Yes, ma'am." A sly grin appeared.

The moment they rejoined the group, the subject of Cooper and Sloane was no more interesting than dough scraps once Juan David saw the second crepe that was waiting for him.

Cooper multitasked the cooking with helping Davon cut his food. There was a familiarity between them. A trust. A mutual respect between the Big and Little Brother. Nothing even remotely resembling the tension between Cooper and his blood family.

"Can Mr. Cooper come back?" Miles's cheeks dimpled in a smile that was half ornery, half angelic.

"Please?" Chloe folded her hands in a theatrical begging gesture. "That was the best thing I've ever eaten."

Sloane quirked her lips at Cooper. *Told you.* "Of course he can come back. Anytime he wants." She started to tell the kids about *Simone*, and an idea fleeted through her mind for the food truck. Promo cards. Anyone who enjoyed a swipe of frosting at the food truck could taste the entire cake at the restaurant.

"Everyone's going to love them," she told Cooper as they walked to his car with the last of the supplies. He took her canvas bag of leftovers from her and put it in the back of the Defender. "I told you. We can't go wrong with—"

The word *crepes* never left her lips, smothered as it was by Cooper's kiss. Warmth plunged from the nape of Sloane's neck to her toes as he pushed against her and tipped her into his solid arms. She surrendered to the urge that had been building for hours, tucking her hands into his open jacket for a closer exploration of his back and chest.

And, oh, did it ever feel right.

Cooper brought Sloane to her normal vertical position, and she watched the thirst dim in his eyes.

"I've been dying to do that all day." He sounded as if he'd just sprinted a good distance.

When they were settled in the Defender, Sloane leaned across the seat and pulled Cooper's left arm to her. "I've been dying to do *this* all day." She burrowed her hands between the sleeve of his jacket and his warm, solid forearm, pushing the cloth up until it was in plain sight, the words *Sans Dieu Rien* permanently etched into his skin in a clean script font. She traced it with her thumb. "*Dieu* means God, right?"

Cooper nodded then brushed his lips against

her palm before he released it. "It means Nothing Without God." He grinned as he turned the key. "Keeps me humble."

On the drive to her apartment, Cooper's words replayed in Sloane's mind. *Keeps me humble.* He was trying to be funny, she knew. But the more she learned about his past, the more she admired who he was. How much he'd grown.

They took their sweet time saying goodbye parked outside her building. With as much as they had on their plates to keep them busy, who knew when their next opportunity might be? Seize the day and everything, right?

As they finally ended their embrace, she wondered if it were possible to get addicted to this, the best kind of substance-free intoxication.

Watching him walk to his car from where she stood at her bedroom window, her forehead pressed to the cool glass, she got her answer.

THE TRUCK WAS DONE. Sloane hadn't gotten a full night's sleep in days; her eyes were dry from staring at her computer screen and her website content calendar was a week behind. She was still traumatized by her experience getting her food handler's permit at the health department.

But the truck was ready and she was on her way to see Cooper, so nothing could be wrong in her world. He'd insisted on working the first service himself, eager for the chance to forget about everything for a few hours and just cook.

Sloane was grateful he'd have this opportunity to relax, mostly because it meant she could spend time with him. They hadn't seen each other in a week. They'd sustained their connection with nightly marathon phone calls, during which it was perfectly normal—and maybe even expected—that one or both of them would fall asleep. They were that exhausted.

The sight of Cooper leaning against his SUV when her driver pulled into the parking lot made up for the absence. She'd spend a few more days apart from him if it meant he'd look at her that way again.

As she opened the car door a gust of frosty wind that stung her cheeks swept inside. But this weather was normal for Texas football, after all. It would actually work in their favor.

"Hi, beautiful."

A dizzying sensation swept over Sloane at the sound of his voice, low and smooth. Forget a jacket. All the warmth she needed was right there.

"Hi." She tucked a strand of hair behind her ear, blushing as his gaze seemed to drink her in.

If Aaron were here, he'd tell her she was acting crazy. She was an almost thirty-year-old woman acting exactly like the girls they'd made fun of in high school.

But he'd probably be smiling through his ridicule. Happy for her.

"Come here." Cooper pulled her into his arms and pressed a kiss into her hairline. And she allowed herself to get reacquainted with her little nook at his side, memorizing the way this place-she-was-supposed-to-be felt. The groove of muscles in the middle of his chest where her head fit just right, the way his arms gripped her like he wanted to protect every inch of her, the familiar cadence of his heartbeat.

"Maybe we should just forget this whole food truck idea and spend our time doing more *productive* things."

Sloane chuckled. "As tempting as that is—"

"Wow." Cooper let out a low whistle as the ruby-red truck turned into the parking lot.

"Impressive, huh?" She slipped her hand in his. "And all ours—all yours."

He gave her an extra squeeze. "Thank you for doing this, Sloane."

"We have two hours to prep," she said. "I gave us plenty of time."

A man, short and balding with an easy smile, stepped down from the driver's seat of the truck.

"Trent." Cooper released Sloane to greet the man with a handshake-hug hybrid.

"You're Trent?" She could finally put a face with the cook Cooper had handpicked from his restaurant's staff to oversee the truck's operations. The voice of the person who'd slaved over the details on the phone with her. "I'm Sloane."

She pulled a thick manila folder from her bag and gave Cooper a tour of the truck. The inside was a cook's playground of gleaming stainless steel. The burners had been replaced, and the truck had passed its inspection with flying colors.

"What?" Sloane asked Cooper, who was grinning. "So I like a clean work space before I begin a big project."

She briefed the two men on how the evening would unfold—at least if everything went according to plan. Cooper and Trent bore matching glazed expressions of stunned disbelief as she went over her ingredient lists and showed them where the preportioned food containers were waiting.

"Wow, Sloane." Cooper crouched, rifling through the clear storage tubs in the refrigerators. "This is a lot of food."

"We're going to need it." She squeezed his hand instinctively, then dropped it. Trent was standing right there. "I promise." She drew in a deep breath. "Okay. So this is how it's going to go…"

"Authoritative." Cooper winked. "I like it."

Sloane rolled her eyes. "We'll open at nine, but traffic shouldn't be too bad until ten when we send out another status update and the football game ends. They'll be chilly and hungry and want something that will stick to their bones."

She demonstrated how the burners worked and the ideal temperature, ladle size and filling proportions she'd researched and tested then recorded in her notebooks.

"Well, it looks like you've really thought this thing through." Trent cleared his throat. His forehead had been creased with stunned disbelief the entire time she'd talked.

Sloane flashed a glance at Cooper, and the approval in his eyes reassured her.

Most of the time, her oddities were inconvenient. But for once, they made her extra useful. Just the way she was.

"I NEED MORE whipped cream, STAT."

Cooper reached under his station for the chilled tub of fresh whipped cream then heaved it onto the counter next to Sloane. Droplets of ice water from the container sopped through his pants as he turned to the griddle. One false move and he'd have to redo six crepes. Nobody had time for that.

Lines had formed before they'd even opened their doors. Forget the extra social media coverage. Sloane's pregame social media tactics had been enough. And as disgruntled football fans poured out of the stadium just before Southern Methodist University's loss was made official, the steady stream of traffic to the food truck became like rush hour on a Dallas freeway. With multiple lanes of construction.

But thanks to Sloane's hard work, they were staying afloat. He flipped the outer edge of the crepes and readied their respective fillings. She'd been like a conductor, directing their symphony of synchronized movements as they rehearsed their workflow and various duties.

Cooper stole a glance at her, hair curling around her face in the humidity of the cramped kitchen, gray T-shirt clinging to her trim waist as she bent to arrange a sprig of mint on a finished plate.

And then he felt it, the sear of a blade slicing through his pointer finger, somewhere in the vicinity of the top knuckle. He swore in French and scrambled for the kitchen towel he'd just used to clean his knife before the blood could spill, applying pressure like he'd done so many times before.

"This is perfect." Cutting himself like a total rookie. At the worst possible time.

"What?" Sloane paused on her way to the serving window, hands full of finished dishes. "Oh my goodness. Hold on." She thrust the bowls through the window and hurried to him.

"It's not bad," he told her as she guided him by the wrists to the sink. He could feel through the towel that it was at least still intact, which was more than he could say for his worst knife incident in the early days of culinary school.

Sloane held his hand over the sink and bent, rummaging through the cabinets below before she produced a first aid kit. "Cooper." She paled as she saw blots of bright red blooming on the towel.

"No, it's okay. I'll take care of this. You go back to the window."

She bit her lip, but nodded.

Criticisms in his father's voice played through his mind as he bandaged his wound and cleaned up the damage. Having only two on the job had made a frenzy of their well-orchestrated concerto. And that was much more painful than his finger.

"Okay, I'm good," he announced. But his movements were slow and clumsy, and he could barely control the chicken with the packed wound in the absolute worst place. "Scratch that. Sloane, I'm going to need you to switch me spots."

She slid to his side. "*Oui,* chef."

Cooper took orders, put the finishing touches on the dishes as best as he could and ran the register, a tablet with a credit card attachment and a checkout app. Out of the corner of his eye he watched Sloane pick up seamlessly where he'd left off.

"You're doing a great job, beautiful."

"Thanks," Trent deadpanned.

Sloane snorted. And kept chopping. She was

the perfect partner in this venture. And she'd come into his life at the right time.

They ran out of food a few minutes before they were scheduled to close. All three cooks deflated as soon as the chalkboard menus were brought inside and the window was closed and locked.

"We survived," Sloane said. "Or at least Trent and I did. How bad is it?" She crossed to Cooper, taking his bandaged hand in hers.

"How 'bout we get this place cleaned up so we can get out of here?" Cooper lowered his voice, thick and quiet for only her ears. "Then you can make sure I'm okay."

Sloane grinned. "I like that idea."

Peace washed over Cooper as he ran the numbers on the tablet's credit card app. No matter what happened with his restaurant, it was worth it all if it had brought Sloane into his life.

A knock sounded on the window.

"We're closed," Cooper said without looking up.

"Open up, Coop." The familiar voice wrung out a sigh from him.

He felt Sloane tense behind him. "Is that…?"

"My father. I'll go talk to him." He squeezed

her hand with his good one as he scooted past her out the back door.

"You're a little late, Dad. You missed service."

His father's head angled past him to Sloane, who was watching from the doorway. "An invitation would have been nice."

"This was a trial run to see how more…organic methods would work for us."

But his father didn't seem interested in hearing about organic methods. He seemed focused on Sloane. "Hi, Sloane. Looks like you've been working hard." There was a forced, sickening brightness to his tone.

"Yup."

"I don't suppose they have food trucks like this in little old Witherton, Indiana, do they?"

"You're right. They don't."

Cooper closed the gap between him and Sloane. The exchange between those two made him queasy. "Well, better luck next time, Dad." They needed to put an end to this conversation now. "See ya."

Fortunately his father seemed willing to go easily. "Next time," was his flat reply.

Sloane's breaths quickened as she stepped down from the truck. "How does he know where I lived?" Her skin seemed blanched in the fluorescent interior lighting, her face expressionless.

"I don't know." He tried to downplay it. "I'm sure he's just trying to rattle you." But Cooper could see it was working.

They'd told each other everything, right? Or did his father really have something on her? "I mean, is there something else he could know?"

Her eyes rounded with fear.

"Don't answer that. Seriously, I shouldn't have even asked." He framed her face in his hands and kissed the top of her head, inhaling a layered scent of her strawberry shampoo and the crepe batter. "It doesn't matter. You were brilliant tonight."

Silence. Her expression remained unmoving, vacant.

"Sloane." He took her shoulders. "Please just pretend I never said anything. I trust you completely."

She nodded and seemed to snap out of it. "Now let me take a look at that hand."

His finger was swollen, throbbing, but nothing he hadn't seen before. Blood had soaked through the gauze, but when he unpeeled the bandage, the wound no longer bled and had sealed nicely.

"No trip to urgent care for us tonight," he pronounced.

Sloane let go of his hand and smiled. But the sentiment didn't reach her eyes.

"Hey. Look at me."

She met his eyes.

"He does this kind of strong-arming stuff all the time, and it's nothing. He can't touch you."

As Sloane leaned into him, Cooper had a sudden memory of the conversation with Owen about their father's interest in Sloane. Cooper tightened his grip around her. If he held her close enough, maybe he could make it all go away.

The accident was tragic, it was terrible, it was a mistake. But it was just that—an accident. Cooper's attempts to change the past with hundreds of bottles had all failed, so what could his father possibly do to change it?

CHAPTER TWENTY-SIX

SLOANE'S WARM COCOON of sleep was broken by the jazzy ringtone on her phone.

Cooper. What if something had happened to him? Or what if it was one of her parents?

The hair rose on her arms as she picked up her phone and pressed the answer button. But it was too late. The call had already gone to voice mail.

Mom. Why was her mother calling her this early? No, she couldn't even entertain the possibility that something had happened to them.

Sloane dropped heavily into her computer chair and opened the lid of her laptop as she called her mom back.

"Sloanie." The warning in her mother's tone robbed the nickname of all endearment.

"What, Mom?" Sloane's own voice rose in panic. "What is it? Is it Dad?"

"No, Dad's okay. We're all okay."

Sloane sighed. "Then why are you calling me at six-seventeen in the morning?"

"This is going to be hard for you to hear, Sloanie, but some investigator came by here yesterday sniffing around for information about you."

Cooper's father. This reeked of him. "Investigator?"

"I sent him away and didn't think much of it until I got a call from—from Mrs. Jacobsen last night."

Sloane's heart pounded in her chest. "Last night? Why are you just now calling me?"

If Mr. Cooper had brought Aaron's parents into this...

"I don't know. I didn't want to worry you."

Her mother was afraid of setting her off, that's what it was. "It's okay, Mom. Thanks for—"

She was interrupted by the ringing of her video chat. Now Grace was calling when she knew Sloane would be asleep.

"I've gotta go." She pressed the button on her cell phone, then answered the video call.

"Oh, thank goodness you're awake." Grace wore flannel pajamas, hair a wild tangle as if she'd been awakened herself. "I have good news and bad news. Levi intercepted some comments on your website. Bad ones."

"What kind of comments?"

Her best friend ran her hands through her hair. "I don't know. It looks like they're scanned images. I'm forwarding what Levi sent to me now."

Images? What could that man have possibly done? Doctored photos of her or something? Like Cooper said, he was probably just trying to scare her.

Her email notification sounded. With one click, one glimpse of the tiny image thumbnails, nausea enveloped her. "These records were supposed to be sealed."

How could Mr. Cooper have gotten his hands on them? Why?

She scrolled through them. A photo of her parents' car, smashed beyond recognition. The tree with its wounded, charred trunk. The curve of the road, slick with rain. A picture of her next to her attorney, leg propped up in a cast, her face sunken and lifeless.

Had Cooper seen these?

"Levi deleted them and blocked the IP address." By the dull tone in Grace's voice, she had seen them, the piles and piles of scanned court documents that exposed what Sloane had done in fear. That exposed her as a fraud. It was all there, every detail of the court proceedings. Who knew if Grace would stick around once her obvious shock wore off?

"I'm so sorry. I don't even—"

"Don't worry about that right now." Grace shook her head. "Anyway, Levi's positive he deleted them before any of your readers could see, so that's good." Her optimistic words were undermined by the monotone in her voice.

No, it wasn't good. Who cared what Sloane's readers thought? Who cared that her ad network—who set their entire stock on appearances—would likely terminate her contract when they found out?

What mattered was what Grace and Levi thought. What Cooper thought.

Did he even know yet?

Sloane thanked Grace and closed her computer then stumbled to the bathroom just in time before she retched. Unable to handle the thought of Cooper finding out her lies from his father. Again.

And again. This was the ultimate, sickest irony. The man who'd placed so much importance on taking responsibility for his actions— he would never be able to look at her in the face again after he found out.

Sloane curled on her bathroom floor, shredded and empty, all the strength she'd gained over the last few months drained from her. Anger and shame and grief assaulted her until nothing remained but an image of Cooper. She pushed herself up on shaking arms, washed her face and went to get dressed.

Her past may have once again proven it would always keep up with her. But if there was any chance Cooper didn't know yet and she could be the one to tell him—to make things even a sliver easier than his father blindsiding him—she had to try.

SHE WAITED ON the back doorstep of Cooper's house until sunrise when she knew he'd take Maddie out.

"Sloane. Oh my gosh." Cooper clutched his chest. "You should've knocked. I've been up working." The light disappeared from his eyes when he peered at her. "What's wrong?"

He reached for her, but Sloane moved. No, she couldn't let him touch her.

"I have to tell you something."

"Come in. I'll make us some—"

"No, Cooper." Sloane's voice wavered. "I can't. Your father, he—"

"What did my father do?" The anger in his tone bolstered her for a moment until she remembered this was her fault, not Mr. Cooper's.

"It's not what he did. It's what I did." Where was she supposed to begin? "I went to court after the accident, and he found those documents somehow. Posted them on my website. They were supposed to be sealed because I'm a minor—I *was* a minor." Her chest constricted. "And because of my father. I never told you, but he's a judge."

Cooper took a step toward her, clearly confused by her seminonsensical rambling. "But you were just driving without a license. It's not that big of a deal."

"No. That's not it."

"So what happened?"

"I begged Aaron to tell them he was driving because I was afraid of what would happen when my parents found out. Afraid that I wouldn't be allowed to get my license because I was only fifteen." That fear seemed so stupid, so immature and selfish now. "I didn't know he was going to die!"

Cooper stared at her for a long, uncomfortable moment, before he looked away. "So you lied to the police?"

Sloane nodded miserably. "And Aaron went to sleep with his parents angry at him. He died with them thinking he was a joyriding thief. I told my mom and dad the truth as soon as I was coherent because I wanted to pay. I wanted to *rot* in jail forever for killing him and doing that to his parents. But they were my dad's coworkers in that courtroom—family friends my entire life—so they ruled the accident was caused by hazardous conditions and gave me community service only because I begged for some kind of punishment."

There. It was out. The worst was over.

"Your father knows now—he hired an investigator or something. So I wanted you to hear it from me first."

Cooper reached for the doorknob, seeming more disconnected than angry. "Is this the first Aaron's parents are finding out?"

"My dad told them when it happened. I couldn't do it."

He said nothing. Minutes ticked by. Finally, he raked his fingers through his hair. "Gosh, Sloane. Why didn't you tell me?"

"Why do you think? You've owned up to your past. You're moving forward. Working yourself sick at the office even though your heart's at the restaurant because you think you owe your family some kind of debt, for goodness' sake. How could I tell you that I was essentially handed a get-out-of-jail-free card because of my father—and I took it?" Her self-loathing tasted bitter and acidic.

Cooper said her name, but Sloane didn't let him say more.

"I thought that things were getting better being with you. But this just helped me see that Aaron's death is never going to leave me alone." Sloane felt the tsunami approaching and took a step backward and another, away from Cooper before it could drown him, too. "I can't move forward with you because I'm always going to be stuck in the past." The emotions threatened to overwhelm her. She ran to where her driver was waiting while she still had the ability.

And Cooper didn't follow her.

CHAPTER TWENTY-SEVEN

IT WAS TIMES like these that Cooper wished he'd kept one of the muscle cars he'd sold when he moved to Paris. That he could blow off steam as the needle of his speedometer climbed and his engine roared with every shift of the gears.

Instead, he headed in the direction of his father's house in a state of numb disbelief. His numbers were back up, inbox empty, everything up to task at the expense of his sleep and sanity. Yet it seemed his father possessed the ability to dismantle all the good in Cooper's life. What more did the man want from him?

Was this a control issue? Payback? A flex of his father's ego? Because it sure wasn't about Sloane. Cooper still hadn't worked out the details, his hasty text to Owen unanswered since his brother was undoubtedly still asleep.

But he was going to find out.

Cooper had watched her leave, more broken than he'd ever seen her as guilt anchored him in place—*This is your fault. You did this to her.*

And worst of all, she'd pretty much agreed that she could never move forward with him holding her back. All the progress they'd made together was gone.

He twitched as the gate to his father's residence crawled forward. His mind filled the seconds with questions. How could he have been so stupid to believe that Sloane would be safe with him? What consequences would she have to pay for her association with him?

How could he possibly make things right for her if he couldn't make things right *with* her?

Cooper had the door open before he threw the gear into Park and stormed up the ridiculous, imposing steps to the stained glass door. It opened before he could knock. After the quickest nod of thanks to the housekeeper who'd let him in, he hurried down the hallway toward his father's suite of rooms.

"Dad!" His roar echoed through the rich, wood-paneled walls.

No response.

As he neared the suites, he heard voices—a muffled argument—and the door to a living area at the end of the hall opened.

Ivy. His father's wife paused when she saw Cooper, recognition softening the sadness in her eyes. The corners of her mouth lifted for a tick before she skirted past him so fast that he couldn't help turning to watch her.

"What are you doing here, Coop?" The usual bluster and force was absent.

Cooper turned, and the sight of his father leaning against the doorframe at once filled him with anger and sadness. "I just want to know. Why did you do it?"

"Do what? What on earth are you talking about?"

"Don't play stupid with me, Dad. You know exactly what I'm talking about. Nobody else but you would hire a private investigator to go to her hometown."

A fleeting expression crossed his father's face—something that might have been fear. "Frank Maldonado."

"Who?"

"He's an old detective buddy from the bar who does some PI work now." His voice rose. "What did he do?"

"He went to her town trying to mess with things that happened years ago." Cooper took a step toward his father, the energy building in his body with every word. "But it wasn't Frank's fault. It was yours. You knew she had no ulterior motives and kept pushing anyway."

The older man's lined face hardened. "She

was making you sloppy. You were at a *bar* with her."

"It was none of your business, Dad."

"That's garbage. You're my son!"

Cooper couldn't form another sentence. His father sunk his head into his hands, much as he'd done at Cooper's side in the back of an ambulance while Marianelli's burned.

How long would Cooper have to pay? And why did Sloane have to be collateral damage?

The slam of a door interrupted his thoughts, and Owen appeared shortly thereafter. Their eyes met as his brother approached them, and as he had since they were kids, Owen all at once seemed to understand.

"C'mon, Coop." His brother pulled him away, shaking his head in disapproval at their father. "Let's go before one of you does something stupid."

THE STACCATO RHYTHM of the basketball pounding against the polished wooden planks soothed Cooper's chaotic thoughts as he waited for Owen to get his shoes on. Didn't do much for his anger, though.

"I tried—"

"I don't want to talk about what you tried, Owen. C'mon, first to twenty." He dribbled the ball to the top of the three-point arc. "I get ball first. Naturally."

Owen didn't object. He peeled off his fleece pullover and tossed it to the ground, flexing his neck as he took his place between Cooper and the goal. "Let's do this."

"Check."

The ball thwacked against Owen's chest. His lips curved into a wicked grin, and he passed it back with so much force that Cooper's wounded finger twinged.

Cooper zipped past him for a reverse layup. The shot sliced through the net. His anger edged into pride at his brother's indignant expression. "Two-oh."

His jaw working, Owen took the ball at the top of the key. After that display of domination, Cooper was beating him by much more than two points.

The game heated up from there, brothers volleying points in a classic duel. Well-aimed jabs were flying—the kind that bruised and broke skin along with the verbal lashings of a whip that struck the surface but hit so much deeper.

"Get off of me!" Owen shouted at Cooper, who was guarding him like a second skin.

"Sixteen-all." Cooper moved a fraction closer.

Owen shielded the ball against his opposite hip, eyes searching for his next move. Avoiding Cooper's hands as they swiped at the ball. He dribbled, trying to skirt around him, but Cooper anticipated the movement and adjusted his feet to block Owen's path.

"Nowhere to go, little brother?" he taunted. "Whatcha gonna do? Go cry to Daddy?"

In a split second, Cooper read Owen's pivot toward the goal and took the bait. But instead, Owen's shoulder crushed into his jaw with a force that careened him to the floor. He watched from his back as Owen swished an easy jump shot.

Cooper scrambled to his feet, fisting blood from his lip. "What's your problem?"

"What's *my* problem? Every time something like this happens, everyone looks at me like, *What a waste. I wish it was* you *who'd gone off the deep end instead!*" Owen launched into his brother, sending them both crashing to the floor. Like two lions struggling for territory, they swung and shoved and swiveled each other until at last, Owen's swipe at Cooper's collarbone slipped, and Cooper pinned him down.

Owen gave a sharp cry and tensed beneath him. "My shoulder! Get off!"

Cooper relaxed his grip on Owen's shoulder in a panic. Had he hurt him? Aggravated his old wakeboarding injury?

Thud. Gray mesh flashed through his vision before the back of his head hit the court hard. He was trapped, forced to take in a full view of his brother's victorious grin, no trace of pain to be found. And Cooper didn't have the strength left to free himself from beneath Owen's knees.

He'd been fooled. Again. Owen had done it enough in their lifetime to know Cooper would lay off every time if he thought he was hurt. He looked away from Owen to the bleachers where Sloane and Davon had watched last time he'd played. And the ache coursed through his blood again.

"Why didn't you stop him?" he panted. "I get that you guys want me to stop playing restaurant. But tell me, how could you let him do that to Sloane? You don't even know her."

Owen sighed, his weight crushing into Cooper as he rolled off him. They sprawled next to each other, their lumbering breaths clashing in the air.

"I didn't know this thing with Sloane was real until I heard your voice mail." Owen sounded like he was eight again, whispering to him in the dark of their shared bedroom in the suburbs. "I thought Dad had gotten bored with it like he always does, but he had one of his old buddies on it, I guess."

Cooper said nothing. He could still see Sloane—the desolation in her bare blue-gray eyes. He could hear the humiliation and defeat in her voice. It was real, all right.

"And I don't want you to stop with the restaurant, either. You really know what you're doing."

"Dad doesn't see that."

"He's just worried because he sees how worn out you've been lately. He'll snap out of it eventually and see how great this has been for you." Owen let out a low whistle. "Man, if I were half as good at anything…"

Cooper heaved a sigh. "You can be, though. Maybe you should have a breakdown and find out what that is."

"Well, I hope that's not what it takes—no offense." Owen stood and reached to help Cooper up. "But I do hope that, once I get my life together, maybe I'll have what you do with Sloane."

Cooper's lips formed a correction—*had*. What he'd *had* with Sloane—but the words died in his throat. It had only taken a few moments together, spread across the span of a few months, but he knew with aching clarity that he loved her.

And despite every warning sign that told him otherwise, it couldn't end this way. No, if he had it his way, it couldn't end at all.

CHAPTER TWENTY-EIGHT

JUST A FEW more hours and Sloane would be finished with the Cooper family forever after Simone's grand opening, free to leave the exposed brick walls and the crowd that now closed in on her.

She sat, pinned to her chair by the expressionless golden-brown eyes that were missing the usual vitality that did things to her. The eyes she avoided, knowing that looking into them would cost a price she was too bankrupt to pay.

Eight, twelve, sixteen chair legs at this table.

A few more hours until she'd fulfill her obligations for VisibilityNet and terminate her contract with them by her own volition. Her mother had always told her not to make a major decision without giving it time, perspective. But after the way this assignment had gone, Sloane knew with absolute certainty that she was done with them.

The revenue would stop streaming in without those accounts, and it would be hard to find brands with the budget for her since the biggest players were included in her non-compete agreement. Sloane's savings would go fast. She'd have to find a cheaper apartment, to start substitute teaching in some grimy public school or something.

Marian Cooper slipped her hand into Sloane's and squeezed with a compassion that almost brought tears to her eyes. "He won't be here tonight. Graham asked him not to come."

Sloane didn't have the chance to respond because the server arrived at that moment with a tray full of steaming ceramic crocks.

"What is this?" She asked the waiter, not quite believing what she saw. She scanned the crowd for Cooper.

"Last minute menu addition. Aaron's Favorite Soup. Enjoy." And he whisked away with the empty tray.

There was Cooper behind him, studying Sloane's reaction. Giving her a sort of hopeful half smile. The sight of him filled Sloane's hands with rogue energy. She tugged her hand free from Marian's grip and somehow upended the soup in front of her. Sloane shot up to avoid a lapful of chicken broth, shaking the hot excess from her hand.

You do this thing when you're nervous, she could hear him saying.

"Sloane, are you all right?"

No, she wasn't. But she couldn't answer the older woman. The air caught in her throat like it was squeezed in a vise, and she escaped to the restroom.

She scrubbed her hands. If only she could scrub her mind clean of everything that had happened over the past few days.

This was Aaron's soup, and Cooper had added it to the menu for her after everything. To surprise her? Torment her? Try to make some kind of amends?

What was she supposed to do with that?

Sloane jumped as the door creaked open behind her.

"No," she shouted at Cooper, scrubbing harder. "Why does it always have to be you?"

He ignored her and crossed the distance between them in two long strides. "Sloane, you need to stop. Your hands are bleeding."

She hunched her shoulders and pushed back against him as he tried to reach around her. But her efforts were no match for Cooper's strong grip.

His hands closed around hers under the scalding water. She turned to face him, twisting and pulling with all of her strength to wrench her wrist free.

"Sloane," he whispered into her hair. "Stop. Fighting."

At the unexpected calm in his voice, her breath caught in her throat. She angled her gaze to his, ignoring the warning voice inside that told her to run.

But when she heard the door open then the surprised apology of an unsuspecting diner, she used the chance to escape, out of the restroom, through the kitchen door, around the workers preparing food and washing dishes, past the office where Cooper had created a space for her.

In the alley behind the restaurant the night air wrapped around Sloane, thick with coming rain and remnant cigarette smoke. She barely had time to crouch against the brick before the door opened behind her. There was no doubt in her mind who had followed her.

And one look into his eyes, one glimpse of the tenderness he regarded her with undid the tension in her muscles. It wrecked her. She sunk into his chest and felt his hands at the small of her back. White-hot tears stung while the iron grip of pain around her middle slackened a notch. "You should have left me alone."

Cooper sighed. "You think I don't know that?"

He was doing it again. Blaming himself. Carrying the weight of something that wasn't his fault. Is that what he thought she was doing with Aaron?

"Is that what you really want? To be alone?" She tilted her head and searched his eyes. "I…"

Her pulse quickened as his gaze flickered between her eyes and her lips.

"I don't…"

She wished she could hate him. It would make being alone easier if she did.

He drifted closer to her.

"You…"

She had every reason to hate him. For being the one who'd shattered the illusion that she was okay with just getting by.

But she didn't want to be without him.

Sloane covered his lips with her own, weaving her fingers through his thick curls. So urgent for his nearness that she couldn't get close enough to him until his back thudded against the brick wall of the restaurant. Nowhere left to go.

He eased away from her, forehead creasing. But she threw her arms around him, her lips covering the question she knew he was going to ask.

No thinking. For one moment, there would be no overthinking.

Cooper's lips parted, stealing her breath away. All-in and intoxicating now that he had her permission.

Forget about the court documents. Forget about the muddy footprints he had tracked all over her immaculate life. There was nothing in the world except for this man. This kiss.

Sloane's lungs finally felt ready to burst. She pushed away from him, gasping for air. "I know...that we are better with each other. But I don't think... I just can't—"

"You can, though. That's the thing. You were doing it, Sloane."

She looked at him. At the brown eyes that seemed to see right through her and never let her off easily. She dropped her gaze, then saw his black dress shirt soiled with her tears.

On this, the most important night of his life, he was in the alley dealing with her instead of enjoying the fruit of all his hard work.

This was the impact she had on him. What she did to his life—made him mix up his priorities.

"I—I have to go." She had to release him so

he could be with his diners, in his restaurant—the one he'd fought for. The one he deserved.

She retraced her steps through the kitchen, keeping her face averted, then grabbed her purse and camera bag. Without a word to anyone she stepped out of the restaurant onto the sidewalk.

"Sloane."

She tensed at the sound of Cooper's voice.

Why couldn't he just let her go? She turned, waiting for him to say something. But he didn't need to. The message was written all over his face.

"I know," she breathed. Sloane knew he wanted to be the one who was worth it. The one she allowed to see everything and love her anyway.

Her heart was resigned to Graham Cooper Jr. She had no choice in the matter. And yet, her brain commanded she turn her back on him.

She wasn't ready yet. And she couldn't give him hope if she might never be.

CHAPTER TWENTY-NINE

TWO DAYS HAD passed since Sloane had left her apartment. Two days to sleep, pray, cook, sanitize and mourn. Two days to search for new jobs and new futures she couldn't get excited about.

Two days of keeping track of the *Simone* food truck's wild popularity, wondering who was working it. Half wishing it was her who smelled like butter and batter.

Two days of missing him so much she could barely breathe at times.

But as she'd dined on a late dinner of noodles delivered from the pho place on the corner, she promised herself one more night of wallowing. Then it would be time to get on with her life.

So today after her morning oatmeal, she dressed for a run.

Sloane was locking her apartment when she heard a familiar tinkling of jewelry and keys behind her.

"Good. You're dressed."

She turned to face Mrs. Melone, who was clothed in black Lululemon from head to toe, a bright headband holding her silver hairstyle in place.

"Hi, Mrs. Melone. I was just—"

"I don't care. Whatever you were about to do doesn't matter anymore because you're coming with me."

Sloane looked at Mrs. Melone sideways.

"I'm not going to let you waste away in that apartment in the fetal position like some emo hipster—or whatever you kids call it these days. Mick says it's been two days since you've come out."

Sloane felt her jaw unhinge. Of course her gossipy neighbor had talked to their doorman.

"Okay, Mrs. Melone." Sloane blew out a breath and pasted on a smile. She'd promised herself life would resume today. Why *not* begin with an adventure? "Where are we going?"

"Where does it look like we're going? Yoga."

New resolve or not, she definitely wasn't in any position to get her *namaste* on.

"Don't give me that look. It's not a hippy kind of class."

Sloane opened her mouth to say something, but the knowledge that she lived in a world where trendy, Old-Hollywood Mrs. Melone would take such a class still dumbfounded her for some reason.

Nevertheless, twenty minutes later, she was sitting on a bright blue yoga mat—which she'd personally watched the studio employee clean—surrounded by blond wood and bamboo and walls made of mirrors.

"You'll love the instructor of this class," Mrs. Melone said as she arranged a stack of bright-hued foam blocks next to her mat.

Before Sloane could respond, the door opened, and a short, fiftyish woman walked to the center of the room. She was trim and toned with smooth, clear skin and a dazzling smile that changed the entire energy of the room.

Sloane gritted her teeth. People like that always made her uncomfortable in her own skin. But there wasn't anything wrong with them. Nope. That was all on her.

"Welcome to Living Well Yoga. I'm Jana." She spoke with a heavy accent—Eastern European, perhaps—as she unrolled her mat. "You ready to get practice on? Ready to get centered, yes?"

A hum of voices answered her. Out of the corner of her eye, Sloane noticed a man diagonal in the row behind her. Judging by the way he was slightly angled toward the girl next to him, they were probably together.

Cooper would never be caught dead in a yoga class, even if she begged.

Don't think about him. She swallowed a lump in her throat. Thinking about Cooper wouldn't help her be *centered.*

"Now, any new people here today?"

Sloane kept her hands tightly tucked under her thighs.

"We begin our practice with breathing to really get the blood warm."

The class mirrored Jana as she straightened and faced the front of the room, narrating her actions as she guided them through breathing and light stretching and then transitioned into balancing poses. Sloane covertly watched what Mrs. Melone did before making any movements.

"You look like Mr. Roboto," her neighbor whispered. "You have to relax and own what you're doing or it defeats the whole purpose."

Sloane nodded and allowed her muscles to deflate with her lungs. It actually felt sort of good, a slow, stretching burn that also somehow relaxed her.

By the end of the standing series, as Jana called it, Sloane's legs were shaking under her with every deep, balancing stretch. She had a strong lower body from all the running she did, but this class only illuminated her need to add some hip and leg flexibility work into her daily routine.

Routine.

The reminder pulled in Sloane's chest, casting a gray shadow over her as she lowered to the mat. She didn't have a routine anymore. Everything in her life had changed.

Numbness spread throughout her body as she stretched her legs to the front of her mat. She fought tight hamstrings to reach her toes, but her fingers didn't even get close to them. And all she could focus on was the ugly, jagged scar that marred her left lower leg. Purplish and raised and hideous against her pale skin.

It was always going to be there. As long as that leg was a part of her, she'd have the reminder of how she'd gotten that scar. And her emotional wounds were no better, held together with such fragile stitching that she'd been tiptoeing not to rip them open.

Now there was a new dimension to it all that took her pain from dull ache to fresh and stinging. How could she have let this happen?

The strength she felt with the memory of

Cooper's smile, the phantom twinge of his presence next to her was the only answer she needed. He'd been good for her. Sure, she'd have been safe in her predictable routine if she'd never met him. But she'd also be a wreck right now—more of a wreck, anyway.

"Now we move to our final meditation." Jana's heavy accent brought Sloane to the present.

She followed the instructions and lay on her back.

"We are going to take deep breath, and when you exhale, you are going to no longer be anything in your past. You are new slate. Ready? Inhale."

Sloane took a deep breath.

"And exhale."

She pictured herself at the edge of a mountain. And as the steady stream of air passed through her lips, images flashed through her mind and rolled off the cliff.

"Slow and steady."

The car accident. The memory of her hospital room. Her mom's face crumpled in grief.

"One breath at a time."

The seething expression Graham Cooper Sr. gave her in the restaurant. The court documents in an accusing row on her computer screen. Down the cliff.

"Yoga is an amazing thing." Jana's voice was serene. "We bend and we stretch and we feel discomfort. But it sends blood, oxygen, life to your body to heal. Make stronger."

Sloane felt a tear slide into her hairline as the words sank in, leaving a tingly sensation with their truths. And she allowed her mind to conjure the image of Cooper—everything he'd been to her, all lined up in a row.

Disruptor of her perfect, controlled world.

The first to break through her armor.

The one who'd convinced her how strong she was, how happy she could be.

"Just like the pain you have lived, the imperfections make something new. Something beautiful."

A version of Cooper's own words. And something snapped together inside Sloane.

What if she'd been the one to lose her life in the accident? What if Aaron had traded the vibrant goof of a person he was for this…half life? The idea raised goose bumps across her arms.

If Aaron knew what she'd become since his death, that she'd let part of herself die with him, he'd be furious. He'd do that thing where he puffed out his cheeks and shook his head. He'd have no words for her. She knew because she'd have done the same if he missed out on even a second of happiness because of her.

If he had the opportunity for love and didn't reach out and knock everything out of the way to snatch it up.

A strange, distantly familiar sensation washed over Sloane at that mental image. The tingling in her limbs rose to a rolling boil that consumed her entire body and bubbled out of her mouth in chest-heaving, shoulder-shaking, uncontrollable laughter. And the only possible solution was to let it happen.

Awkward glances from her classmates notwithstanding, she was free to breathe. Even though she didn't quite know how, she was ready to start stirring the waters of her grief instead of leaving them stagnant.

The laughter subsided, leaving an almost absurd realization in its wake. There, surrounded by ten or so strangers, she'd zeroed in on the one thing standing in her way. Everyone who mattered had forgiven her. But Sloane had finally forgiven herself. Cooper had been right.

For years, she'd been convinced that it should have been her who died, but now she decided she wanted to live.

CHAPTER THIRTY

IT WAS ONE of his weaknesses, Cooper knew, but he couldn't be certain the restaurant had done well its first week until he saw the report himself.

"Thanks for everything," he told Janet as he walked her out, the revelatory stack of papers tucked under his arm.

"We did good." Janet awarded him a rare smile as she ducked into her car. "And, yes, I ran the numbers twice."

Cooper made a face, grinning as he shut her car door, watched as she drove away and then hurried into the restaurant, locking the door behind him.

He settled into his favorite leather chair in front of the fireplace and scanned the first page. The numbers looked…better than good. Between the food truck and the café, they'd done remarkably well.

His employees had celebrated the end of their first week with a sparkling cider toast, but the only person he wanted to share the good news with wasn't here. Months before, he'd scheduled opening week as paid time off from J. Marian Restaurants, so he worked in the kitchen to keep himself relaxed and occupied. But there were reminders of Sloane everywhere, her squeaky-clean fingerprints all over the place.

His wrist rotated involuntarily as if craving to swirl a glass in his hand. He pictured the amber glow of scotch lit by a fireplace. But Sloane's voice overrode his imagination.

You're not that guy anymore. You're just a recovering person who had a bad day.

Some days he might fail, but today wasn't going to be one of them.

Cooper's thoughts were interrupted by a pounding on the front door. Who on earth was trying to get in almost two hours past closing when this area of downtown was shutting down for the night? As he approached the entrance, he recognized the silhouette of the person peering into the café. What his father wanted at an hour like this—or what condition he'd be in—Cooper didn't know, but it couldn't be good.

He unlocked the door, and a gust of icy wind wrapped around him. He backed away and crossed his arms as his father took his time unwinding his scarf and unfastening the toggles on his coat. Taking an inventory of the space, uncharacteristically rumpled as if searching the walls for the pieces of an explanation.

"Did you, uh, need something, Dad?" Cooper forced an edge of pleasantry in his tone. For Owen's sake.

His father ignored him. "I heard the opening went well." Still looking around.

"We did okay." *What on earth with this chitchat?*

"I wanted to talk to you about Frank Maldonado."

Cooper forced himself to remain still. "What about him?"

"I never asked him to do anything that would hurt the girl." The way he said it, it sounded like an apology. At least the Graham Cooper version of an apology. "You haven't been yourself since you started spending time with her, and I didn't want…" His father capped his sentence with a cringe Cooper didn't need a translator to interpret.

He didn't want Cooper to destruct again.

"If anything, Sloane's the one who's kept me balanced. She—"

"Are you balanced, though?" Peppery gray eyebrows rose.

"Oh, save it, Dad. I've been busting my butt opening a restaurant and making sure nothing slides at work—which you've kept a very close eye on, might I add. What do you want from me?"

"You don't have to work at the company, Coop. There are several people who would give their right hand for that job—and be all in."

Cooper crossed his arms. "You *know* I can't just leave the company. Not after everything this family's been through."

"Enough with Marianelli's." His father released a heavy, wounded sigh. "I'm done."

"What?"

"I'm done letting you hold on to that stupid fire, because you know what?" His fingers jabbed into Cooper's chest. "You're not going to turn out like me."

"Dad—"

His father raised his hands. "No more. Do you know getting that call and seeing you in the back of an ambulance was the most terrifying moment in my life?"

Cooper stepped backward, as if that could prevent him from reliving that night.

"It was never about the restaurant—it was about you. About seeing myself in you and knowing that's what I create. But this—" He waved his hands around the restaurant. "This is what you create, son."

Cooper shook his head. The man standing in front of him seemed different—shirt wrinkled, face lined, unable to cope any other way but muscling and drinking. And if it weren't for the void Sloane had left in his life, a void his father had helped create, Cooper might almost feel sorry for his father. When it came down to it, the man might have had riches and power and success, but he was alone except for his sons. Since Jordan's death, he'd alternated between unhealthy cycles of work, drink, women. Nothing seemed to stick.

While Cooper had given up drinking, he'd done the same thing. In the back of his mind, he'd known for a long time that staying at J. Marian Restaurants wasn't really about the fire. He'd replaced the bottle with work— the high stakes of hitting quotas, of boarding planes to do damage control, of collecting and maneuvering contacts to meet his goals. He'd been trying so hard to lead Sloane to a breakthrough, to show her what life could be like.

But he wasn't there yet himself. As long as he threw himself into his work, he couldn't be.

"I'm done, Dad." Cooper took a deep breath, and the words tumbled out of his mouth. "I can't work for the company anymore."

The decision was easy: there was no decision.

"Fine." His father blinked a few times and then nodded. "Take the weekend and hand in your formal resignation on Monday if you're sure."

"I'm sure." He and his father exchanged brisk nods, nothing and everything left to be said.

"So." His father broke the silence. "Do you have anything to eat around here?"

Cooper raised his eyebrows, and after a few seconds of stunned disbelief, chuckled. "Of course, Dad." He led the way to the kitchen and whipped together a quick ham and Gruyère omelet with a chocolate croissant from the pastry case. He set the plate in front of his father and watched him eat.

"It's good, son." He wiped his mouth with a napkin when he finished. "Really good."

Cooper had waited for this moment, the first step in what felt like a shift in their relationship, from employer and employee to father and son—and, if he was honest, for the debt he'd long perceived between them to be absolved. But now that it had arrived, it sat differently than he'd imagined. His father's approval didn't change anything. The restaurant was something Cooper had done for himself, a pivotal next step in his recovery nobody could take for him and nobody could take from him as a result.

Someone had reminded him that, to move forward, a person had to choose—one day at a time—to step outside that unhealthy hollow of pain and grief. Cooper would forgive his father eventually. He would keep going. But he wasn't going to do it alone if she would have him.

CHAPTER THIRTY-ONE

LIVING AGAIN FOR Sloane meant taking small steps—making a counseling appointment, enrolling in a driving course, baking a cake without a recipe, finding the crumpled business card from the cookbook acquisitions editor and scheduling a meeting with her—and a few very big ones.

It involved summoning a little bravery and lot of support from Grace to buy an early-morning plane ticket. It meant baking some of Levi's favorite chocolate bars and asking him to remove all ties to VisibilityNet from her website before calling Aaron's parents to tell them she was finally taking them up on their offer. More than twelve years later.

After her plane landed she took her parents to breakfast to tell them everything, how she'd essentially existed in isolation except for her City on a Hill kids. How she'd fallen in love and fallen in loss, only to decide she wanted to live again.

And then she asked them to drive her to Aaron's parents' house. Somehow, her heart didn't hammer its way out of her body on the way, even though she felt it was a distinct possibility. Somehow they welcomed her, as if they'd been mourning her absence as much as Aaron's. After she left, she took a long walk, reveling in the memories they'd shared.

It was unseasonably mild for early winter in Indiana, the sky calm and clear. The road, once flanked by woods and fields, was paved now and lined with a gas station, a church, a shopping center, the heart of the city now stretched all around it. And the tree—their tree—stood like an indignant matriarch, tall and regal with a broad girth despite its scorched trunk.

Children played on equipment that had been built near the tree. Aaron Jacobsen Memorial Park. The sign took her breath away.

She sat on a bench that was situated in almost the exact place where she and Aaron had watched the car burn. Her attention alternated between the playground, full of children enjoying the sun, and rewriting the area in her memory. The town had built a guardrail by the tree and installed a stop sign just before that severe curve in the road. How many lives had those simple constructions saved?

The screams and laughter of the children were punctuated by the sound of a car door, and the prickle of every cell in Sloane's body told her who it was before she could turn her head.

Cooper. Not an ounce of her was surprised to see him. It was the most natural thing in the world that he had come for her.

Sloane stood when he was close, opening her arms to his warmth and leaning into that place that was hers. "Cooper. How did you find me here?"

"Grace told me." He eased away from her but kept his hands wrapped around her waist. "I've made a lot of mistakes in my life, but I think I would have regretted not following you again the most."

She kissed him. "I'm so glad you did." When she rocked back on her heels, the glimmer of tears in his eyes constricted her throat and blurred her own vision.

"You were right, Sloane. I may have quit drinking, but I just switched to drowning out the emptiness with work. I hated that you weren't the first to know that—"

"Did you quit your job?"

"Yes, finally," Cooper replied with a laugh, sliding a piece of hair behind her ear. "From the moment I met you, you've surprised me. And not just because you're the strongest... *loveliest* person I've ever met, but because I never imagined in a million years that I could have this with someone."

She nodded, shaking loose the first pair of tears.

"You've helped me remember that I can be someone regardless of who I've been or..." His head dipped for a breath before his gaze was back on hers. "Or what I've done. I love you, Sloane Bradley."

"Say it again."

"Oh, do you like the sound of that?"

She grinned. "*Oui*, chef."

Cooper's eyes crinkled with a wide, knowing smile. His lips pressed against her right cheekbone and then her jaw before his low, husky voice whispered in her ear. "I love you."

"I love you, too." Sloane looped her arms around his neck, and he rested his forehead against hers. "All of you."

She took his hand and led him to the tree.

So this was what full circle felt like, standing where her life had been totaled. Simultaneously filled with the old ache and bursting to tell Cooper about the new developments in her life. To make up for all the kisses they'd missed.

That sacred juncture between past and present was a powerful departure from the vicious cycle her life had been. The hand in hers was the love that had taught her to breathe again.

* * * * *

If you enjoyed this debut
Heartwarming book by Laurie Tomlinson,
you'll also love these romantic stories
that feature culinary delights and foodies!

RECIPE FOR REDEMPTION
by Anna J. Stewart,
FOR LOVE OR MONEY,
HER SOLDIER'S BABY and
THE COWBOY'S TWINS
by Tara Taylor Quinn,
and UNDER THE BOARDWALK
by Amie Denman.

All available at Harlequin.com.

Get 2 Free Books,

Plus 2 Free Gifts—

just for trying the Reader Service!

Love Inspired®

LI17R

Get 2 Free Books,
Plus 2 Free Gifts—
just for trying the Reader Service!

Get 2 Free Books,
Plus 2 Free Gifts—
just for trying the Reader Service!